DAYS *of* FUTURE PAST

DAYS *of* FUTURE PAST

SALLY SMITH O'ROURKE

Victorian Essence Press
Los Angeles, California

For Michael

and Susan
for her unstinting encouragement
and wisdom

Acknowledgements

With grateful appreciation, I thank Victoria Lucas whose
invaluable help with developing the story was a godsend.
And editor Julie Luongo, who helped me make this not simply
a nice book, but a splendid book and me a much better writer.
And last but not least, Janet B. Taylor of *Pride and Prejudice*
paintings fame
who created the astonishing cover, tweaking away as my
continuous changes and desires were met at every level.
Thank you all, ladies.

With much gratitude, I thank the **City of Hope Cancer
Research Hospital** for use of the image of the gate nestled in the
rose garden on the Duarte Campus. It represents what I hoped
to express in this story... that there is far more to us than the
physical body, that our souls encompass the past, present, and
future.

And a special thank you to the **American Red Cross** for their
generosity in allowing me to turn their beautiful San Gabriel
Pomona Valley Chapter headquarters, The Cravens, into my
disaster center.

It is by no means an irrational fancy that, in a future existence,
we shall look upon what we think of as our present existence,
as a dream.

Edgar Allan Poe

Sally Smith O'Rourke is the author of
The Man Who Loved Jane Austen,
Yours Affectionately, Jane Austen,
The Maidenstone Lighthouse
and *Christmas at Sea Pines Cottage.*
Her masterful fiction resonates with modern readers who
long for fulfilling stories, multilayered characters, and
evocative romances that reach through time.

Prologue

Scotland, 1805

Watching her image in the mirror, Catherine turned to the side and smoothed the fabric of her dress over her growing belly.

Her radiant smile, reflected in the mirror as he entered the room, sent a shiver through his body. Joy filled his very being. He slipped his arms around her. She leaned her head back against him and closed her eyes. She heaved a deep, contented sigh.

"Are you ready, my love?"

"I am."

"Hickson has taken the trunks to the ship. We need to leave soon."

Catherine raised her head suddenly.

"What is it, dearest? Are you hurt?"

She grabbed his hand and laid it on her belly. "Do you feel that? He moved."

He smiled and turned her in his arms. "Yes, I felt it, but why are you certain it is a boy?"

She stood on tiptoe and kissed him. "Because I promised I would give you a son, and I always keep my promises."

"Indeed you do." He smiled. The only other promise she ever made him was to make him happy, and she had done that and more. He had never known such bliss. Since the day they married, he could not imagine life without her.

Dirt and gravel settled under the iron rims of the wooden wheels as the coach and four came to a stop at the dock. A liveried footman, his buttons glittering in the late-afternoon sun, opened the door and dropped the steps. The young man in tan britches and a green coat stepped down. At the bottom of the steps, he turned and offered his hand to someone inside the coach. The lovely young woman accepted his outstretched hand and gracefully descended the steps to join him, her blue cloak protecting her from the cool sea air.

Arm in arm, the young couple looked up into the springtime sky at the mast of the ship. She squeezed his arm as they approached the gangway.

"I am so excited and anxious to get home."

"As am I, my dear, as am I."

The trepidation he felt because of his wife's condition was pushed aside by her exuberance and love. His only thought was how much he loved her.

Chapter One

Sunday, March 9, Now

Night fell over the arroyo, and the lights in the garden twinkled to life. The moon, glowing with a halo portending the possibility of rain, rose in the western sky. A light breeze stirred the ferns and mosses that framed the thatched-roof cottage, casting shadows on the walls, making it appear as though someone was home.

Ann smiled at the memory of Alex, her husband of four years, rushing into the house with the charming miniature bungalow. He'd been like a small child bringing in a stray puppy he'd found on his way home from school. He insisted it had called out to him from the display window of a shop in Silver Lake, and he simply had to stop and take a look at it. Carrying it carefully into the house, he said it was the final piece for their woodland backyard, a fairy house. The woman in the shop had told him a story about a young groom captured by an ogre only a few days before his wedding. His bride-to-be begged for help from the garden fairies who did, in fact, bring him home in time for their nuptials. Ever after, the newlyweds set out food and gifts for the fairies in gratitude. "So," the woman continued, "if the garden sprites feel welcome at your home, they will always protect you."

As Ann turned away, something caught her eye. She peered into the dim evening light, almost putting her face on the glass. She was sure she'd seen a figure move inside the fairy house, not a shadow but an actual figure. She laughed at herself. Amazing what your mind could imagine, thinking she actually saw a fairy.

The garden *was* beautiful, everything they had hoped, especially at night. The moonflower vines with their white morning glory-like blossoms now wove their way through the tree branches. The moonbeams caught by the flowers created an almost iridescent glow. It was magical. She gritted her teeth, still angry that Alex never got to see it like this.

It was well past lunchtime when Ann and Alex stood on the patio to look at their handiwork. The overcast had yet to clear, but the cloud cover kept the January morning cool and mild, making the physical labor of creating the woodland landscape fairly comfortable.

Alex slipped his arm around her waist. "Well, we did it."

"It looks so magical. Imagine how it'll look at night with the lights."

Alex leaned over and kissed her. "You're the magical one, my witchy little witch."

All her life, Ann had had the weird ability to know when things were going to happen, not hunches or feelings, but knowledge. Somehow she just knew things. It wasn't controlled, and it only happened occasionally. The first time Alex witnessed it was when they started a day trip to Oak Glen for the apple harvest. Ann told him that he was going to get a traffic ticket. He laughed, saying he hadn't gotten a ticket since he was a teenager. When he got pulled over that day, he decided she was a witch. After he'd seen the "gift," as her mother called it, in action a few more times, he bought her a heather witch's broom that still held a place of honor at the fireplace.

"So, does that make you my warlock?"

"No way. I don't do anything magical."

Ann gave him a very wicked grin. "Depends on your definition of magic."

"Really? Nice to know I've still got it."

"Oh, you've definitely got it." She kissed him.

"I think we should christen the garden with champagne," Alex suggested.

"You don't mean smash a bottle over it, do you?"

"Well, we could, but I'm thinking that it might be more fun to drink it."

He turned her in his arms and kissed her nose. "I love doing this everyday stuff with you." Then he kissed her more thoroughly. "I love doing everything with you," he whispered.

Leaning her head on his chest she sighed. "Me too."

"You too? You like to do things with you too?" he teased. Feigning exasperation, she pretended to try to push away from him. But he held firm and wiped a dirty-gloved hand down her cheek. "Boy, you sure could use a shower."

"Are you insinuating that I'm a dirty girl?"

"I certainly hope so," he said with a leering grin.

"Sir," she said, pretending to be shocked, "what kind of girl do you take me for? I'm a good girl, I am."

"Yes," he said with a raised eyebrow, "and I know just how good."

He picked her up and whirled her around, then set her down gently. Just as he bent to kiss her, the piercing sound of the phone threatened to end their romantic moment.

"Let's ignore it," Ann whispered.

Alex glanced at the phone, then kissed her. But as soon as the voice of Bill Wyman called out Alex's name from the answering machine, the mood was broken completely.

"Hey, guy, we have a plane down in the Sierra foothills. I'll pick you up on the way to the airport if you're there." There was a pause. "Alex?"

Alex looked at Ann, silently asking how she felt about his leaving at that moment in time.

One of his passions was flying, and they'd had the plane, a Grumman Tiger, for three years. Bill Wyman was Alex's flight commander in the Civil Air Patrol, and a downed plane meant search and rescue.

The question was still in his eyes. So, pushing the disappointment down as far as she could, Ann reminded herself that she was married to an amazingly generous man who wanted to help people. How could she say "don't go?"

She smiled and shook her head. "Go... I'll take a bath and put on my sexiest nightgown."

"Never mind the nightgown," he said, winking as he picked up the phone.

"Put the champagne on ice. I'll be back early," Alex said before he left. "And you might hold up on the bath too. We can take one together later. You know, to conserve water."

"Yeah, to conserve water," Ann said with a playful wink. "Good idea." She couldn't help but giggle. Sometimes it felt like they were teenagers, and after four years of marriage, he could still make her giddy.

Then he held her in a passionate embrace, making the long, lingering kiss the last time he ever touched her and the last time she saw him. The fairies had failed them.

Staring out at her fairy garden, Ann rubbed her eyes dry before tears could fall onto her cheeks. She leaned her forehead against the cold glass of the window. He'd been gone more than six years. Why did she keep doing this to herself? Why couldn't she get past it? She knew the clinical term was denial, but it was too hard to accept. They never found Alex or the plane. Her hope from the beginning was that he might be living in some mountain village with no memory of himself. Was it really so awful that she wanted to believe he was still alive? Any psychiatrist worth his salt would say yes. As a psychiatrist herself, she had to admit that this was definitely denial and not hope. Hope had been important in the beginning. The hope that he'd landed in some out-of-the-way place and wasn't able to call, the hope that some Good Samaritan had taken care of him, the hope that he was fine. But eventually, hope had to turn to reality.

She wasn't sure why she still harbored the fantasy when she knew it was a fantasy. When they didn't find the plane after the spring thaw, after all the snow was gone, hope started to dwindle, but she wasn't prepared to give up. So that first summer, she spent weeks driving from town to town all over the Sierra Nevada mountains. On the western slopes, the eastern slopes, in the valleys. She'd even found a few towns that weren't on any of the maps she was using, but no one anywhere had seen him. No one had seen the plane. She knew then that he was gone, but not having his body made it hard to accept. No casket to say good-bye to, no grave to visit. Not that she would visit a grave. She couldn't stand the thought of seeing proof of his death carved in stone.

She took a step back from the window and blew out a deep breath.

Chapter Two

Ann's slippers whispered on the hardwood floor as she carefully balanced the hot tea while juggling a bottle of water and a book. She'd actually thought about using a tray to simplify things but decided against it and was now struggling.

She grinned at the lump on the bed as she shuffled into the room. She set the tea and water on the bedside table, then tossed the book onto the bed which garnered a glare from Gigi. A streetlight dispelled the nighttime darkness outside her bedroom window and turned the leaves in the gutter gold. She closed the drapes and climbed into bed.

It was impossible not to smile when Gigi nestled her head against Ann's shoulder. She wrapped her arm around the massive neck and kissed the top of the big white dog's head.

"You're just a big ol' cuddle bear, aren't you?" She really was a big bear of a dog. A Great Pyrenees, she was more than a hundred pounds of soft white cuddly friend.

"But it's too warm," Ann explained as she gently pushed the animal away.

A dejected Gigi repositioned herself at the foot of the bed.

The unseasonably hot and humid March weather felt more like August in New York than early spring in Southern California. It had been so warm in the afternoon that she had turned on the air conditioner. Although it was cooler this evening, it was still too warm to cuddle with a big furry dog.

Ann stretched and fell back onto the pile of down pillows propped against the headboard. Brushing the hair off of her forehead, she made a mental note to call Chrissy in the morning to make an appointment for a desperately needed haircut.

What was it about a cup of tea that made it so comforting? Perhaps it was the civility of it, like visiting with cherished loved ones over a fresh pot of the fragrant brew.

Gently she set her grandmother's delicate porcelain teacup on its saucer and picked up her book. The restful quiet surrounded her as she flipped the pages. Out of the corner of her eye she saw Gigi raise her head and quickly look around the room.

"What is it girl?" Suddenly the giant animal leapt off the bed and pushed herself under it. Before Ann could say or do anything else, the shaking started.

As the bed began to shudder, she scooted down and pulled the comforter over her head. Squeezing her eyes closed, she waited for the temblor to stop. The basso profundo rumble of the quake was an undercurrent to the sound of glass and pottery breaking throughout the house. She could hear the furniture scratching the mahogany as it shifted on the hundred-year-old floor, and Gigi continued to whimper under the bed. Suddenly, the bed jarred and the dog yelped. The six-foot-tall double bookcase that held the television and stereo had fallen onto the foot of the bed. The shaking seemed to go on forever. She found out later that the 6.8 earthquake was really only twenty-two seconds, but it was a very long twenty-two seconds.

The trembling earth finally stilled. Slowly, Ann opened her eyes and stared at the faint image of lilacs on the flannel sheet covering her face. Her heart was racing, and her mouth was dry. She had been holding her breath and now forced the air from her lungs. Although the shaking had stopped, the terror had yet to subside.

Ann took several very deep breaths and slowly emerged from under the covers, realizing that the sudden flash of light she'd seen fill the room must have been the transformer box across the street blowing out. Since she had no power, she squinted into the darkness. As expected, the bookcase now leaned on the footboard of the bed. She couldn't see the television, but it had to be on the floor along with her stereo and books. The dresser and bedside table were still upright, but everything on the tops had been swept to the floor by the tremor except the clock radio, which was dark for lack of power. The silence was broken by her own nervous laughter. She'd bought the clock because it had battery backup in case of power outages. Of course, it only worked if you remembered to change the batteries, and she hadn't.

Gigi was still whimpering but tentatively inched her way out of her hiding place when she heard her name. She jumped onto the bed, lying down as close to her owner as she could get. The behemoth animal was quivering. Ann wrapped her arms around the dog's neck. "That was pretty scary, wasn't it? But we're okay now."

Adjusting to the dimness, she was able to see her ever-faithful flashlight on the floor next to the remains of a shattered crystal table lamp. Thankfully, she had changed those batteries, so if it wasn't broken she would have light.

Keeping her fingers in the ruff at Gigi's neck, she leaned over the side of the bed and picked it up.

The flashlight's beam fanned out over the destruction in her bedroom. The mirror hanging over the dresser was intact. The triple dresser, however, was no longer centered under it. The telephone was within reach, so once again she leaned over the edge of the bed and picked it up. She hit the talk button. Nothing. No power, no phone. This was one of the few times a hard landline would have been helpful. Her cell phone was in her purse by the front door. That meant she had to get up. It was the only way to talk with her mother and father. That, of course, was if the cell towers hadn't been destroyed in the quake. Still quivering, Ann slowly swung her legs out of the bed and slipped on the hard-soled slippers she kept next to it, a habit instilled by her mother when she was a kid, in case there was an earthquake.

She slipped down the side of the bed and stood up, her knees jellylike. Leaning back against the bed to get her bearings, she took a deep breath and stood up, again panning the flashlight around the room. Stepping gingerly over the broken reading lamp and the smashed porcelain of her grandmother's treasured bone china cup and saucer, she made her way out of the room using her feet to push broken items out of the way as she went.

At the bedroom door, the flashlight revealed framed photographs that had fallen from the wall and now lay on the floor in the hallway. The beam of light landed on one of Alex and his plane. She moved the light up the wall where other photos hung askew.

The kitchen wasn't as bad as it might have been. The previous owner of the house had installed child-proof closures on all the cupboard doors, even the ones above the counter. Ann couldn't count the number of times she'd fought with the little plastic hooks and swore to remove them. She never did get around to it and now was glad of it. Everything on the counter had shifted or fallen over but remained on the counter. Baskets and cookbooks from the baker's rack were the only things on the floor.

For the moment, the kitchen was a minor concern. She needed to get to her cell phone. An abundance of broken glass greeted her as she stepped into the living room. She reached down and picked up a large piece. It had been a beautiful collection of vintage cut crystal. She dropped the shard of glass and picked up an antique sterling-silver cigar lighter. It appeared to be unhurt. The silver curling iron and cocktail shaker were also undamaged. She and Ted, her ex-fiancé, had purchased the three unusual silver pieces during their relationship, surmising that silver was a good investment and wouldn't be destroyed in an earthquake. She set the unbroken pieces on the shelf and shook her head. The silver was intact, unlike the faceted lead crystal she and Alex had collected that now lay in ruins on the hardwood floor.

Along with almost everything else in the house, her purse was on the floor. Bypassing the shattered art glass bowl that used to sit on the small library table in the entryway, Ann retrieved her phone. *Yay, bars!* Quickly she dialed her parents' phone number. Her mother picked up on the first ring.

"Are you ok?" her mother asked immediately.

"I'm fine. Looks like anything breakable is broken, but the house is still standing and I'm shaken but okay. How about you guys?"

"We're okay, lots of broken stuff, but nothing major."

"Have you heard from Tommy?"

"Your brother is fine, but the tree house fell into the pool." The tree house had been a family project when her brother and sister-in-law first bought the house. Her nephews loved it. She loved it.

"Have you heard from Jamie?" Jamie was her mother's older brother and Ann's favorite uncle.

"He thinks they have a gas leak, so they got out of the house and will call when they get wherever they're going."

"Wow."

"The big thing is that everyone is fine."

"Yeah. Thank God."

"I need to get this stuff swept up or the dogs are going to get glass slivers in their paws."

"Me too."

"Be careful, sweetie."

"I will, Mom. You too."

Ann waded through the rubble that had been her living room. To her great relief, the furniture in the dining room was intact. Unfortunately, most of the china and crystal had been destroyed when it came through the glass fronts on the built-in cabinets.

Stepping around the downed books and baskets, she sat at the kitchen table, still a bit shaky, her heart pounding. Thinking back to the series of earthquakes during the late eighties and early nineties (and there had been a lot of them), this one was much larger, stronger, even worse than Northridge. When you grow up with them, you can tell how bad they are. When Northridge hit, Ann knew it had been a big quake but also knew that in Monrovia they weren't at the epicenter. Her brother Tommy was away at college and none too happy with her five-in-the-morning phone call until he found out why she was calling. She knew that once news of the quake hit the television networks getting through by phone would be virtually impossible.

The battery-powered kitchen clock with glow-in-the-dark numbers let Ann know it was almost eleven o'clock at night. It was so dark outside that she couldn't see the condition of the backyard. In large quakes like this, swimming pools often had a lot of water slosh out, and she suspected their pond-like pool had a low water level. The fairy house very likely had been unseated from its foundation. It occurred to her, as she squinted into the darkness, that the giant oak shading the woodland scene may very well have been uprooted.

She'd never been alone during a big earthquake. She was still living at home in 1987 when the Whittier Narrows quake hit. She and Ellie were living in Monrovia when the '91 Sierra Madre quake shook up the San Gabriel Valley, even knocking the seismographs at Cal Tech off of their stands. The strength of the 5.9 earthquake had to be triangulated from Boulder, Colorado. The biggie, the Northridge quake in 1994, happened while she and Ted were planning their aborted wedding.

The beam of her flashlight was the only illumination Ann had as she picked up the baskets and cookbooks and piled them on the baker's rack. She turned away as the first of many aftershocks hit. She leaned heavily on the butcher-block shelf of the rack.

After a few minutes, Ann's legs stopped quivering, and she reminded herself that if she didn't clean up Gigi wouldn't be able to leave the bedroom. *Do they make hard-soled slippers for dogs?* She should look into that.

The half shelf of the broom closet was cleared of the cleaning supplies she kept there, but swinging from a cup hook under it was the emergency lantern Alex bought. Unlike her flashlight, she hadn't changed the batteries in it for some time, so could only hope it worked. Holding the slightly swaying lamp, Ann flipped the switch and the kitchen was filled with a bright light. She turned off the flashlight and left it on the kitchen counter. Then she took the broom, dustpan, and dust mop along with the wastepaper basket from the kitchen into the bedroom. At least if she got that much done, Gigi could get out to the backyard.

Still on the bed, Gigi peered into the white light that suddenly filled the room. The big dog watched her mistress put the largest pieces of broken glass and pottery into the wastebasket and sweep up the debris, finally using the dust mop to pick up the smallest shards and fine dust from the hardwood floor.

Ann went to the bed and kissed the top of the dog's head. "It's okay now. It's safe." Gigi looked over the edge of the bed and then at Ann, who pulled gently on the animal's collar. "Come on, let's go outside."

The dog trusted Ann completely but was still a bit hesitant as she jumped down, sniffing the ground and looking around the room. Ann could see in the dog's eyes a combination of fear and concern. The Great Pyrenees are bred to be guardians, and it was clear she knew something was wrong, but she couldn't figure out what to do about it. How do you explain an earthquake to a dog?

They made their way slowly to the kitchen. All the while, Gigi was checking everything out. Ann opened the back door and watched her pet walk carefully out into the yard. The guardian DNA kicked in, and she slowly made her way around the perimeter of the property, making sure they were safe from predators.

From the patio, the light of the lantern illuminated the yard enough for her to see that the ancient oak was still standing, and the fairy house seemed not to have been affected at all. Maybe the fairies had protected them this time.

Remembering the destruction in the wake of the Northridge earthquake, she cringed at the thought of the condition of the outside world. This was definitely the biggest earthquake she had ever experienced.

A few days after the Northridge quake, she and Ted drove down Ventura Boulevard in the San Fernando Valley and were stunned at the number of buildings and businesses destroyed or severely damaged. Several months later they drove through Sherman Oaks and found many of the small shops and restaurants they'd frequented were gone. The Sherman Oaks Galleria was a ghost town.

Leaving the dog to continue her guardianship, Ann made her way through the living room once again to the front door. The air outside had an eerie stillness. Her eyes, now accustomed to the darkness, could see that not a single leaf moved on the plants or trees. The flag on the flagpole hung limply. She looked up and down the street but appeared to be the only person out. She didn't even see a cat or dog. Over the tops of the houses across the street, several blocks away, she saw fire leaping into the night sky but heard no sirens.

In the middle of the yard, Ann looked up. The stars were extremely bright, the widespread power outage making the darkness deeper than usual. The moon was particularly bright as well even though it was only a half moon. Odd, in spite of its being white, it reminded her of citrus fruit. The curved edge was brighter than the rest and appeared solid like the rind of an orange, and the rest looked textured from the shadows created by the hills and dales on the surface and reminded her of a lemon wedge. In the street, water filled the gutter almost to the top of the curb. The fire hydrant on the corner must have broken.

She glanced up at the moon again. Fairies in a doll house and a citrus moon? Maybe she *was* spending too much time alone. Her self-conscious laughter was the only sound in the stillness.

Chapter Three

Edward heard her screams and leapt out of bed; he stumbled across his bedroom, the floor beneath him swaying violently. Bracing himself between the walls of the hallway, he reached her room just as the temblor stopped. Without a thought, Sara Jane ran and threw her arms around him. "Daddy," she cried.

Wrapping her in a tight embrace, he realized that, at sixteen, she had never experienced a sizable earthquake. Swaying slightly in an attempt to calm her, he said, "It's over, sweetie." He could feel her heart racing as she held on to him for dear life.

"Are you sure it's over?" she asked without moving.

He didn't want to upset her more, but he didn't want to lie either. "The earthquake is over, but there will be aftershocks."

She tilted her head up to him, and he saw the intense fear in her eyes. "You mean little earthquakes?"

"Yes, generally they're smaller."

Tears filled her eyes. "When will they start?"

"There's no time frame, honey. They just happen."

"That was so scary."

"I know," he said, releasing her from the embrace. "Go put your slippers on, and I'll make you a cup of cocoa."

"With marshmallows?" she said looking up at him. In her eyes he saw the little girl she used to be.

"It's not really cocoa if there aren't marshmallows." He smiled. "Now go get your slippers."

Hand in hand they wandered through the rented house. While most of the furniture had shifted to places it didn't belong, actual damage was minimal. A few things were broken, but displaced furniture and accessories were the majority of it, at least as far as he could see. Either the quake wasn't as big as it felt or the house was built on bedrock, which would have absorbed much of the movement.

In the living room, books and magazines were scattered on the floor. Edward wasn't a tchotchke type, so there weren't a lot of "things" to fall and break. Vintage books were his passion. A vase full of tulips and a shattered crystal candy dish lay in a puddle of water on the hardwood floor.

In the kitchen, many of the dishes and glasses were smashed on the granite counter and tile floor.

"Honey, you want to get the broom and dust pan? We'll get this cleaned up before we make the cocoa."

Together Edward and Sara Jane swept up the broken pieces of stoneware and glass and then repositioned all the small appliances on the counter.

Sara Jane pointed to the Viking range. "Look, Dad, the power must be out. The clock on the stove isn't lit. We aren't going to be able to make cocoa." She pouted slightly. He hugged her, knowing the pout was just disappointment that the comfort food she'd hoped for was suddenly out of reach.

Over the top of her head, he looked around and realized the house was illuminated entirely by emergency lights.

He released his daughter. "Wait here a minute." He'd almost forgotten the owner of their rented home not only installed emergency lights, but had a generator. All he had to do was start it, and they'd have electricity. The generator would allow him to plug in the espresso machine to steam milk for cocoa.

"I'm going to call Mom. She'll freak out if she hears it on the news," Sara Jane said as they waited for the water to boil for the steam.

Her smile warmed his heart when she went to her bedroom to get her cell phone. She was a strong little girl. He shook his head and was glad he hadn't said it out loud. At sixteen, Sara Jane was no longer a little girl and would have been humiliated being referred to as such.

She carried the tray holding the cocoa as her father prepared the fire pit on the deck. His hand shook as he lit the paper and kindling he'd laid under the small logs. His daughter took note.

"Are you scared too, Dad?"

He leaned back in the canvas chair gripping one of the mugs in both hands to control the shaking. "Yes. It's been a long time since I experienced an earthquake that big."

She gave him a comforting smile. "I think I'd prefer living where there are tornadoes or hurricanes. At least you know when they're going to happen."

"You get kind of used to it."

She shook her head. "I can't imagine getting used to that."

"You don't get used to the earthquakes, just the fact that there's no warning."

"Looks like the whole city lost power," she said as they both looked out at Los Angeles from the deck of their hillside home. The city lay dark at the base of the Hollywood Hills.

She leaned back in her chair and sipped her cocoa. "This tastes really good. Thanks, Dad."

He smiled at her, put his feet up on the bricks surrounding the fire, and stared into the blaze, imagining toppled buildings, collapsed freeways, and broken water and gas lines. Edward knew that a quake this strong was devastating. But another image, seared into his brain, came back with a vengeance. As a trauma therapist, he'd seen a lot of devastation. But, generally speaking, he arrived in the aftermath. There was one harrowing exception.

The perdition of the Pentagon lay before him. The acrid smoke stung his eyes and windpipe as the gasoline-fed flames leapt high above roof level of the five-sided building. The smell of burning jet fuel and flesh made him nauseous. The black smoke billowing skyward blocked the sun. The sight was horrific yet mesmerizing. Someone calling for a doctor finally brought him out of the trance.

Although his plan when he volunteered to come down here was to help with the emotional needs of the victims, he found himself enlisted to triage the injured. The injuries spanned the gamut from slight smoke inhalation to severe burns and compound fractures to death. Ambulances came and went throughout the day, and as the ambulance carrying his last patient drove off, he became aware of people still wandering aimlessly around the grounds and others staring into the abyss that had been the west side of the massive structure. The line of dead bodies awaiting removal to a temporary morgue was the last thing he saw as he climbed into the taxi.

The long emotional day had brought about a slowing of Edward's movements. He trudged through the deserted Washington, D.C. hotel lobby to the elevators. The floor indicator changed from number to number, the doors opened, and he forced himself inside. He turned around and saw the desk clerks engrossed in watching the never-ending repetition of the day's events. The doors slid shut.

The setting sun appeared black, swallowed up by the smoke that hung in the late afternoon sky. A cynical smile curved his mouth. Legend had it that a black sun was a sign of the apocalypse. While it may not actually have been the physical end of the world, emotionally it certainly felt that way. September 11, 2001, would not soon be forgotten.

A shuddering breath escaped his heat-seared lungs, and he rubbed his face. For some reason, coffee sounded good. Maybe it was the weariness.

When the room service clerk asked if he wanted something besides coffee, he realized he'd eaten nothing since the continental breakfast early that morning, so added a bowl of soup and rye toast to his order.

The hot water felt good on his neck muscles as he turned his head to stretch them. At his feet, the dirt, soot, and blood swirled down the drain. He had been dealing with only the psyches of people for so long that he'd almost forgotten he was a medical doctor and not just a psychiatrist. The water cascaded over his body and for some reason the credo of the City of Hope Cancer Center in California came to mind. He'd attended symposiums there every year since he graduated from medical school and remembered now the saying at the front gate. *There is no profit in curing the body if in the process we destroy the soul.*

For years, he had been treating his patients' minds without ever taking into consideration their bodies or souls. It made him wonder just how effective he'd really been as a trauma therapist. The thought was cut short and forgotten as a persistent knocking on the door forced him from the comfort of the warm water.

"You were thinking about the Pentagon, weren't you?"

Sara Jane's voice brought him out of his reverie. "Yes, how did you know?"

"There's a look you get on your face when you're thinking about the Pentagon. I've seen it all my life."

"Sorry, sweetie."

"You don't have to apologize, Dad. I've seen pictures. It must have been awful. Usually you get there after everything is over, but you were in the thick of it that day." She sipped her hot chocolate. "I'm really sorry you had to go through that."

His "little girl" wasn't so little after all. She really was an amazing young woman. He smiled his appreciation for her understanding and sighed deeply.

The dark blue mug in his hands reflected the fire. The stars, made extra bright by the lack of city lights, shined like sparklers against the black of the nighttime sky. The calmness of their surroundings belied the chaos that he knew must be rampant in the city. He debated with himself about turning on the television to see what was happening. Taking a sip of the cooling chocolate, he opted to stay with his daughter by the fire. There was nothing he could do tonight. They'd finish their drinks and try to get some sleep. Rested, he might actually be of some use to someone tomorrow.

Surrounded by the wooded landscape, it was hard to believe that they were fifteen minutes from Los Angeles, only seven minutes to Hollywood. They would miss this place.

Nestled amongst the trees of Mulholland Drive, the little house was reminiscent of a hunting lodge and may well have been one in the early days of Hollywood. But now it was Edward and Sara Jane's hideaway. They'd looked at three houses but had both fallen in love with this one. The house was all wood and leaded glass with plumbing and kitchen fixtures that were reproductions of hundred-year-old pieces including a pull-chain toilet. They were comfortable here, and he would buy it in a minute if it were for sale, but the actress who owned it was returning to start work on a television series after having spent the past two years in a successful Broadway play. So the hunt for a new house was under way.

"Have you ever felt a quake like that, Dad?"

"Not quite that strong, but in the late '80s and early '90s, there were a lot of earthquakes. The biggest one, was the Northridge earthquake in 1994. I was doing my residency at the time."

"Were you all alone? I can't imagine how scary it would be to be alone."

"I wasn't alone."

"Were you and Mom living together?"

"No. I didn't meet your mother until later."

"Who were you living with?"

"Her name was Toni Rishel, and we were planning our wedding at the time."

"What happened? Why didn't you marry her?"

"It's a long story and it's late."

Sara Jane yawned. "Yeah, I think I'm going back to bed." She went over and kissed her father's cheek. Before she could stand up, an aftershock struck, and she threw her arms around his neck and squeezed. He wrapped his arms around her. It ended before he was able to reassure her in any way. His arm around her shoulders, he walked her to her room and kissed her forehead as he tucked the covers around her.

She smiled up at him. "Thanks for the cocoa, Daddy. See you in the morning."

Edward wished her sweet dreams. Glancing back at her as he left the room, his throat tightened. He loved her so much he was sometimes afraid that he was smothering her in his attempt to keep her safe.

On the deck, his feet propped on the rim of the fire pit, his thoughts turned to Toni. He wondered if things had been different and he'd married her if they'd still be together. Would they have had the four children they'd talked about? He shook his head. Dwelling on the past or what might have been was fruitless. He glanced back at the house. Thinking about the past when the future was asleep inside was just plain silly.

As he enjoyed the restful atmosphere of the yard and sipped what remained of his chocolate, a spider scurried across a web that glistened with tiny drops of dew in the light of the fire.

He'd stopped doing the kind of trauma therapy that took him to the Pentagon in 2001 and had begun teaching. It had started out as a temporary thing, but he liked teaching, and he was comfortable doing it. Ultimately, he took a permanent position on the university faculty so he could stay close to home to be with Sara Jane. The brochures from colleges she brought home a few weeks ago reminded him that she wouldn't be at home forever. College would take her away. Still, he couldn't imagine what it was going to be like not having her in the house. Well, it wasn't something he needed to think about right now.

Instead, he thought about the last conversation he'd had with Jamie, the chair of his department, who had not so gently reminded him that having been made a permanent member of the faculty meant that he had to publish, and publishing meant he would have to do clinical work again, something he'd managed to avoid for the last... well, for a long time. He knew he couldn't avoid it forever but wasn't entirely certain he was ready. *Would he ever be ready?* Maybe fate had taken it out of his hands. The earthquake would leave many people emotionally distraught. He suspected his hiatus was now over.

He looked out at the dark city and could hear no sound. There were no helicopters, no sirens. He didn't see any of the normal things in the sky either. The moon and stars were brighter than usual, but as clear as the sky was, he saw no planes. Even the lights of the jumbo jets he normally saw on the distant horizon, all lined up to land at LAX, were missing. Perhaps the quake was far worse than he imagined. Gulping the last of the cocoa, he went into the house and turned on the television.

Chapter Four

As daylight dawned, Ann knew she ought not venture out when she didn't have anything specific to do, but curiosity got the better of her. Insulated mug in hand, she stepped out into the early-morning aftermath of what the experts were now calling a strong earthquake, a description that seemed something of an understatement.

The neighborhood was quiet except for the water still running in the gutter from the broken fire hydrant. No one else was out, and that made her wonder if her neighbors had not been as lucky as she had.

The few neighbors with whom she was closest were all fine. Even the older couple on the corner seemed to be none the worse for wear. Relieved, she continued her ramble, sipping the coffee as she went. There was a heaviness to the air that was almost ominous. The rising sun appeared red through the thick cloud of dust caused by the shaking earth. Ann turned to head back home just as a strong aftershock struck. She grabbed the street sign and stayed there for a few moments to steady and gather herself after the shaking stopped. On slightly wobbly legs, she returned home.

When Ann opened the child-resistant cupboards, almost everything inside was broken or badly chipped. Very few pieces did not succumb to the violent tremors. She loved the look and feel of stoneware but would replace everything with unbreakable Corelle. Having it all contained certainly made cleanup a lot easier than it might have been. After sweeping the debris into the waste basket, she stepped back. The cupboards hadn't been this empty since they moved in.

The only room left was Alex's office. The small room off the utility area between the kitchen and garage had a three-quarter bath because its original purpose had been the maid's or housekeeper's quarters. Surveying the destruction, she was reminded that even before Alex disappeared they had talked about making it her sewing room. It had been his suggestion since he preferred working on his laptop so seldom worked in the office anyway. When he disappeared, she couldn't make herself change anything. Perhaps fate had taken it out of her hands.

The little room was a mess. The modular shelving had been wrenched from the walls, the brackets now bent beyond any possible usefulness. On top of the mess on the floor was the computer he didn't really use and his N-scale train. Alex had spent days weaving the track around the room on shelves he'd set at shoulder level. He loved that train.

The engine was chipped and cracked as were several of the cars. The top of the caboose was broken off entirely. Unsure if it was repairable, she set it aside. The tracks were as badly bent and twisted as the shelf brackets, with no hope of salvage. She tossed them into the trash can atop the remnants of her dishes. The computer seemed to be intact, but without power she had no way of knowing if it still worked.

Gently, she put the remains of the electric train in a box she retrieved from the garage, and as she began the chore of cleaning up the small room, she glanced over her shoulder. Strange, she was sure someone touched her back and had assumed it was Gigi. Her imagination must be getting the better of her in the stillness. Suddenly, she stood upright and looked all around the room. Someone had touched her, she was sure of it. At the same moment, a framed photograph toppled off of the pile on the floor and lay face up. It was a picture of her and Alex in front of the house, taken the day escrow closed. Was Alex trying to contact her? She laughed. Obviously the quake had put her nerves on end. A ghost. How silly could she be?

It took the better part of an hour, but Ann managed to clear the room of the broken, bent, and generally unusable clutter. She pushed the full trash can out of the room and glanced over her shoulder at the almost-empty space. A file cabinet that she didn't use, a computer desk, and computer (printer too) she also didn't use were all that remained. The lone south-facing window meant the room got lots of light but no direct sun, so really it would make a great sewing room. Guilt washed over her. Even after six years, it felt like a betrayal of hope, and hope was all she had. Whatever she did with the room, it wasn't a decision she needed to make right now.

The hair on the back of her neck stood up. She looked around the small space. She was definitely alone, so why did it feel like someone else was there? She smiled. Nerves, that was all it was.

Ann's office was only two miles from home, but she took her time, wanting to survey the condition of the town. While there was very little traffic, foot or car, nothing appeared badly damaged. Most of the businesses along Lake Avenue had broken windows and signs, but none of the buildings had collapsed. On the other hand, earthquake damage could be deceptive. Unlike the pictures she'd seen of hurricane and tornado damage, after an earthquake, a building could look fine, but the shifting earth could easily make it so unstable that it wasn't salvageable.

As a family therapist, Ann wanted her office to be comfortable, almost inviting, so she chose a building constructed at the end of the nineteenth century that was restored and modernized some ten years ago. The Green Street building was near the area known as "Old Town," and as she turned onto the one-way thoroughfare, she was met with an incongruous sight. A few blocks away, a broken water main was filling the nearest intersection, and an obviously broken gas line was spewing fire through the water. After the initial surprise, Ann realized that her office was probably without electricity, gas, or water, and she wondered how long it would take to get everything back on line.

Stepping into the building's lobby, it was evident that she had been right. The water feature was silent, which indicated that there was no electricity for the recirculation pump and no water. She assumed there was no gas. Her sneakers squeaked on the slate floor as she crossed the atrium-like space.

Inside her office everything atop the desk had either shifted or was on the floor next to it. The plastic paper trays and sorter lay on the floor, cracked and broken. The clock on the credenza had moved but, thankfully, was intact. She was particularly relieved about that. The clock had belonged to her great-grandmother. She loved the whimsical timepiece that once sat on Amo's mantel. As a child, she would watch the girl-on-the-swing pendulum with fascination.

The loft was another story entirely. Almost everything that had been on the narrow bookshelves was now on the floor, mostly books, but she had a few mementos and photographs there as well. Standing in the midst of the debris field, Ann resigned herself to the fact that she no longer had any excuses for not cleaning the books and knickknacks. She'd managed to rationalize the immense job away for months, but now there would be no point putting everything back without cleaning it first. Luckily, she'd rescheduled all her patients for the following week so had more than enough time to accomplish the task.

Stepping over the unabridged dictionary sitting prominently in the midst of the jumble of books, she saw a small cedar box. Nothing special really, the kind of box you find in souvenir shops. Ann picked it up. The green script on the top said Big Bear, and the tiny brass clasp was still intact, keeping the lid securely closed. She flipped it open, and a wave of nostalgia swept over her.

Three small bears filled the box: one hand carved out of pine, one covered in rabbit fur, and the last a miniature stuffed bear. One for each year she and Ted had gone to Big Bear for Oktoberfest. It had been a happy time. She had loved him so much, and she thought he loved her, but she'd been wrong. Ted. The memory of seeing him with another woman just weeks before their wedding still brought tears to her eyes, followed by a rising anger that dried the tears quickly. She slammed the box shut and set it on the closest empty shelf. *Why had she even kept the thing?*

Chapter Five

Wednesday, March 12

Edward got off the freeway at Figueroa Street then turned onto Colorado Boulevard. Three days after the temblor, the thoroughfare that traversed Los Angeles from Griffith Park through Glendale and Pasadena ending in the Victorian village of Monrovia was bizarrely devoid of automobiles. Although Los Angeles was not a walking city, seeing virtually no foot traffic was as unusual as not seeing cars.

The asphalt of the street showed no evidence of the event, but then even at the epicenter of the earthquake the ground had not opened. There were buildings that had major damage while others remained seemingly untouched. A man watering his garden in a small compound of 1940s-era cottages waved as Edward drove by. He raised his arm to return the salute but had to forgo the gesture when he was forced to swerve around a large piece of mirrored glass from a six-story office building on the other side of the street. The façade of smoky gray glass was almost completely gone, the shards and scraps lying in heaps at the foot of the building.

He'd seen on the news that a recently built subdivision in the west valley had incurred so much damage that the entire community had been declared uninhabitable, yet here just past San Rafael Park was a decades-old neighborhood unscathed, as far as he could see. Many of the lovely homes were over one hundred years old and had no doubt seen their fair share of earthquakes, major and minor. *They really don't make 'em like they used to.*

He continued on the circuitous route to the Colorado Street Bridge. It was Colorado Boulevard now, but in 1913 when the bridge was built it was just a lowly street. Colorado Boulevard Bridge just didn't have the same ring to it, so people still referred to it as the Colorado Street Bridge. He'd fallen in love with the landmark when he was a kid, and his family crossed it every time they visited his grandparents in Altadena. It had been the beginning of his love of architecture.

Rising above the Arroyo Seco Riverbed, as there was no water in the river, the monument to early-twentieth-century design was a wonder. The Beaux-Arts structural arches and intricately turned railings along with the massive light standards gave the span an elegant look usually reserved for buildings of the day. Driving across it, he took notice of the barrier embedded into the concrete of the top rail, added to reduce the number of suicides, which he understood it did, however, the nickname *Suicide Bridge* stuck. One of the things he'd learned in his years of trauma therapy was that when someone was intent on ending their life it was impossible to stop them. They would find a way. And so it was with the "suicide barrier." The number of deaths had dropped, but they still happened.

He turned right onto Orange Grove Boulevard. Like Colorado, it was almost devoid of traffic. It didn't look much different than he remembered with the beautifully maintained apartments and condominiums that lined the street. The occasional single-family home from the turn of the twentieth century reminded him that the street had not always been five lanes, and at one time the front yards were deep and wide. He imagined horse-drawn wagons and carriages, bicycles and pedestrians, even the occasional automobile, all jockeying for position on the two-lane road.

He smiled at the thought as he turned onto a narrow, tree-lined street and glanced at his cell phone. The texted address that appeared in the window indicated that this was the right street. He drove slowly, trying to see well-hidden house numbers. He drove past the place twice before realizing it was his destination. In spite of the signs and the Red Cross paved into the front drive, it was difficult to believe the three-story brick manse was home to the San Gabriel/Pomona Valley chapter of the American Red Cross. He'd been in a lot of Red Cross centers in his career, but this was definitely a first. He wandered around the grounds for a few minutes, looking at the house from different angles as it rose into the early spring sky. The mansard roof, mullioned windows, and the gilt wrought iron were reminiscent of a French baroque chateau. It was buildings like this that made him wish, at times, that he'd become an architect rather than a doctor.

The gilded wrought iron filigree of the portico glistened in the morning sun as Edward stepped through the double front doors of heavy leaded glass. He was greeted by a pleasant middle-aged woman sitting in front of a mural (original to the house, he was told) depicting a seventeenth-century French villa which was obviously the inspiration for the home. He smiled, pleased that he'd been right about the origin of the design.

After a short tour that included the solarium, parlor, kitchen, and bedrooms on the upper floor, he was shown a door that opened onto a narrow, musty, enclosed staircase leading to the basement. Edward stepped onto the concrete floor. The low ceiling, gray-and-white walls, exposed pipes, and painted doors looked and felt more like a disaster center than the opulence of the floors above.

He wandered down one short hallway after the other in search of Room 12. In the stale air, he heard a voice, a voice he knew. He stopped and squinted as though it would help him hear. *Could it really be Toni?* He looked around the jamb of the closest door, and there she was. Toni Rishel, his first love, his true love... his only love. He peeked again. She was talking to a small group of people. His heart sped up, and he pulled his head out of the doorway and leaned against the wall, willing his heartbeat to return to normal. His eyes closed. The soothing sound of her voice actually helped calm him. Edward took a deep breath as he continued to listen, remembering the last time he heard her voice. She'd called him a liar and then had thrown the engagement ring at him and stormed out of their shared condo. He hadn't seen her again until this moment.

He opened his eyes and scanned the hallway. He cocked his head and listened, then strode into the room, his voice thunderous as he said, "Silence woman!" His voice, with a slight British accent, resonated in the small enclosed space. His strong arm outstretched, his index finger pointing at her, he challenged her with, "You are accused of sundry acts of witchcraft. Tell me, be you a witch?"

Shocked speechless by both the appearance of the man and his outburst, Ann could do nothing but stare at him.

"How long have ye been a witch?"

Still she said nothing.

"Speak now and answer, insolent cow!"

Snapped out of her amazement by the insult, Ann glanced around the room at the faces looking to her for answers. She had no answers. At once embarrassed and outraged by the intrusion, Ann demanded, "Leave! Now!"

"Leave? Are you mad? What is this impertinence? I will stand no more, I demand an answer. How long have you been a witch?"

A man sitting nearby stood up and placed a hand on Edward's shoulder. "The lady asked you to leave."

Edward's head bobbed almost imperceptibly, but Ann saw it. Something in his eyes changed.

He looked to the left and right without moving his head then directly at Ann. Her eyes were wide. He could see fear and anger. He lowered his gaze to the floor and mumbled, "I'm sorry," and rushed out of the room. In the hall, he leaned against the wall. He'd blacked out. It hadn't happened in years. He glanced at his watch, wondering how long it had been. The look on her face was burned into his brain. What had he done that had caused the fear he saw in Toni's eyes? A shuddering breath was all he could expel. Concerned that she might come out looking for him, he rushed to find the stairs.

Inside the room, Ann was still staring at the door when the man cleared his throat. She looked at him and almost shook her head. "Thank you, Ken."

"Who is he? What was he doing?"

"I don't know." Ann looked over Ken's shoulder to the door then excused herself and went out into the hallway. She walked to both ends of the hall, but he was gone. She stood outside the room to gather herself. Taking a very deep breath and blowing it out slowly, she returned to the small room.

Chapter Six

The cashier behind the bakery display case asked Ellie if she could help, but Ellie saw Ann at a table in the middle of the room when she arrived. Glancing at the young woman, she said, "I see her, thanks."

Ann was staring into her coffee cup, endlessly stirring the strong brew. When she didn't acknowledge Ellie's arrival, her friend slipped into the brown Naugahyde bench, saying, "Hey Annie. What's up?"

Ann did not respond.

"Ann?"

It was a question that received no answer. After several more verbal attempts to get Ann's attention, she finally reached across the table and put her hand on Ann's arm. "Hey, what's going on?"

Slowly, Ann looked up. She looked directly at her friend without seeing her.

"Toni!"

Ann blinked her eyes. "Why did you call me that, *Eloise*?"

"Because you didn't respond to the sixteen times I said Ann."

"Don't exaggerate. I just didn't see you come in."

"Yeah, you do seem to be in never-never land. So what's up? You sounded pretty strange on the phone."

She sighed. "It's nothing, really."

"Come on. You even called me Eloise, which you know I hate."

"Because you called me Toni, which you know I hate. Besides, I don't know why you hate it so much. I think having an unusual name is nice."

"And that's why you call yourself Ann instead of Antoinette?"

Ann smiled. "Antoinette is too long and cumbersome."

"Right. So what's up with you?"

The waitress came and asked if they were ready to order. They came to this Los Angeles landmark diner for the specialty of the house, buttermilk pancakes, so the ordering was quick.

"So why are you acting weird?"

"I saw Ted."

Stunned, Ellie said, "Ted? Like Edward McConaughy, Ted?"

An affirmative nod was the only response Ann gave.

"You saw him across the street, saw him, or you talked with him, saw him?"

"Neither."

"Come on, give me something. What happened?"

"What happened is what has me weirded out."

"Seeing him at all seems pretty weird to me."

"I'm not sure how I would have reacted to just seeing him, but this encounter came out of left field." She took a deep breath. "I was at the Red Cross, giving a few people some exercises for relaxing and calming down because they were very agitated after the earthquake. Ted stormed into the room and accused me of being a witch."

Ellie gave Ann a crooked smile. "How is that weird? You are a witch."

"Very funny. It may sound amusing now, but it didn't feel funny at the time. I wasn't sure what he'd do. He was screaming, demanding that I admit that I was a witch."

Ellie spoke through her giggles. "Sorry, but it does sound funny. I would have loved to have seen that." Ellie cleared her throat at Ann's glare. "What did you say to him?"

"I told him to get out, but he didn't. He kept insisting that I admit I was a witch. One of the men in the group got up and told him to leave, and suddenly he looked around the room like he didn't know where he was, apologized, and ran out. It was very weird."

"Did you go after him?"

"By the time I'd gotten it together, he was already gone."

"You have no idea what it was about? You guys didn't used to play some kind of game that he was reenacting or something?"

"No! What kind of game would that have been?"

"I don't know. I was just trying to come up with a logical explanation."

"Yeah, well there isn't one. Believe me, I've been trying to think of one myself."

The waitress returned to refresh their drinks and to tell them that the pancakes would be up soon. Ann stirred cream into the fresh coffee.

"Why was he there?" Ellie asked.

"I don't know. I suppose it's because of the earthquake. He is a trauma therapist, after all."

"How did he look?" Ellie asked with a raised eyebrow.

"What?"

"How did he look? Good?"

"I don't know. I was so stunned by what he was doing I really didn't notice."

Ellie mumbled something as she stirred sugar into her coffee.

"What?"

"Nothing." She was saved from having to say anything else when the waitress arrived with their food. As Ellie buttered and poured syrup over the stack of three pancakes, she asked, "What are you going to do?"

"About what?"

"Ted."

"Nothing. What is there to do?"

"You could call him and find out what the little scene was all about."

"I'd rather just leave it alone." Buttering her own pancakes, Ann added, "Besides, I don't know how to get in touch with him, and I don't particularly want to see him again."

"Why not?"

"You know what he did to me. Why would I want to see him?"

"That was twenty years ago. Shouldn't you be able to have a conversation with the man?"

"Like I said, I don't really want to. Can we talk about something else? Like what's the verdict on your dealership?"

Knowing that she wouldn't be able to get Ann to talk about Ted, she answered the question. "It's even more of a mess than I thought. The interior is pretty much a total loss. And those glass walls that I thought were so cool-looking are completely gone, and what the falling glass didn't damage beyond repair is now covered in tiny glass shards and dust.

Most of the cars in the showroom were destroyed. The contractor and the insurance adjuster say they don't think much is going to be salvageable."

"God, Ellie, I'm sorry. Is it going to take a long time to rebuild?"

"I'm told the building itself is sound, but the interior has to be gutted. The insurance company has so many claims that it'll probably take a few weeks to determine how much they'll cover. I just thank the Lord I had earthquake insurance. I actually considered dropping it when the recession hit." She grinned. "But I have a witch friend who kept saying that there was going to be a big earthquake, so I bit the bullet and paid the premium. I'm really grateful I did now." Taking a sip of coffee, she crinkled her nose. "Yuck, I let my coffee get cold." She motioned to the waitress and then said to Ann, "You were right."

"Maybe," Ann said, vehemently adding, "*but not* because I'm a witch."

Ellie smiled. "Uh-huh."

"I used to have a bit of second sight, or something, but it hasn't happened in years."

"Well, it happened last year, which is why I bought earthquake insurance."

"There was nothing witching about it. It just seemed like it had been so long since we had an earthquake of any size that we were due for a big one."

"Either way, you were right. How's it going with you?"

"I've got my office almost back to normal, putting the books back on the shelves is all that's left. They still don't know when the water and power will be back on in the building. Should have the house done this weekend, except for Alex's home office, which is a complete disaster. The computer slipped off the desk but seems to be ok. Not sure why. Maybe because it landed on a stack of papers. Anyway, I'm going to have to completely redo it."

The waitress returned to refresh their coffee.

"What are you going to do with the office now?"

"What do you mean?"

"Well, you said you were going to have to completely redo it, and it really is time you did that." Ann made no comment, so Ellie continued. "You've left it exactly the way Alex did six years ago. It's like you thought he was going to walk back in and sit down at the desk, and he didn't even use the desk then.Now you have an excuse to redecorate that room into something you want. You used to talk about turning it into a sewing room. If you did, you'd probably start sewing again."

Ann wasn't at all sure what to say and found herself angry at Ellie's comments. "I want it to be Alex's office."

"Annie, it's been long enough that you could probably have him declared legally dead."

"But what if he's not dead?"

"Well, if he turns up again you can have him declared legally alive. I think the earthquake may be a blessing in disguise. The computer may work, but it's obsolete now anyway. It's time to get rid of it." Ellie reached across the table and took Ann's hand. "Now you can start fresh—new dishes, a sewing room, a whole new life. You really do need to start living again."

Ann withdrew her hand. "That's easy for you to say. He wasn't your husband."

Taken aback and more than slightly offended, Ellie shot back, "No, he was only my brother. You've always acted as though you were the only one affected by Alex's death."

"We don't know that he's dead," Ann said angrily.

"What exactly do you think the chances are that he's not? Do you really believe he walked away from wherever his plane went down and just decided not to come home?"

"Maybe he doesn't know who he is."

"That's a remote possibility, I suppose, but are you willing to wait and see if he suddenly does remember?"

"Anything is possible."

"Okay. What if he remembers but prefers his new life?"

"He wouldn't." Ann bit her lip. "Would he?"

Ellie said quietly, "No, I don't think so. But I don't think he's living somewhere in blessed anonymity either. I'm fairly certain he died when his plane crashed."

"Fairly certain?"

"Annie, there's a part of me that wants him to be alive too. But reality and logic tell me he's gone, and I need to move on."

"How? How do you move on?"

"Just keep living."

"I am living."

"No. You're existing, not living." Ellie stirred a bit more cream into the strong coffee. "You know you've never been in this alone. You act like you are, but there are people just as affected as you are. The first year I was just like you. Every time the phone rang, I ran, hoping it was Alex. Every time a car pulled into the driveway or someone knocked on the door." Ellie stopped talking for a moment. "But it never was Alex, and frankly, I got tired of expending so much energy pretending he would walk through the door when deep down I knew it would never happen. Deep down you know it too. Everyone else has accepted that he's gone, and your refusal to accept it makes it that much harder for the rest of us."

"I'm just supposed to give up so it's easier for the rest of you?"

"You don't need to give up anything. You need to face the facts. Watching you put your life on hold has been difficult for all of us. You're not doing yourself any favors hanging on to a ghost. And Annie, he is a ghost."

"I'm not the only one who thinks he might still be alive."

"Yeah, you are."

"His Civil Air Patrol buddies go out every spring looking for him."

"Annie, they aren't looking for him. They're looking for his plane, and they hope to find his remains when they do. They're like the Marines, never leave anyone behind. They're just trying to give everyone closure, that's all." Ellie shook her head. "You don't really think he's alive either. You just hope he is."

Struggling with the term "his remains" and the truth of Ellie's statement, Ann was unable to control the tears. "Is hope such a bad thing?"

"No, not under normal circumstances, but in your case, it's been debilitating, particularly in the face of reality. You need to let go."

Chapter Seven

Thursday, March 13

The Huntington Research Library was Ted's refuge. He loved walking the paths and byways winding around the two-hundred-plus acres that were once the private home of Arabella and Henry Huntington. After applying the member sticker to his jacket, he headed for the steps that led to the grounds, passing a model of the library's Japanese teahouse and a display of pink rose paraphernalia in the window of the bookstore. He smiled at a string of lights that looked like pink rosebuds. Sara Jane would love them. At the top of the steps, he gazed out at the vista before him.

The gentleman in the ticket booth told him that the library had been extraordinarily lucky, and the earthquake had caused no structural damage to any of the buildings. Even most of the exhibits had been unaffected. After the series of earthquakes leading up to the Northridge quake had caused so much destruction, particularly to the main house, the entire complex was restored and retrofitted so it wouldn't happen again. Some fallen branches and a lot of leaves blanketing the wide expanse of lawn were the only indication that anything had happened. Ted walked down the stairs and headed across the lawn, kicking leaves as he went.

The tropical foliage of the jungle garden created the shelter he was seeking. The sounds of the waterfall, birds, and the rustle of the leaves overhead swirled gently around him. A serene, restful place, it always reminded him of the poem, God's Garden.

> *The kiss of the sun for pardon,*
> *The song of the birds for mirth,*
> *One is nearer God's heart in a garden*
> *Than anywhere else on earth.*

He definitely was closer to God in a place like this than in church. Here it felt like God was all around him. He stretched out his legs and leaned back against the weathered wood of the bench and gazed up into the canopy above.

Ted closed his eyes, recalling the look on Toni's face yesterday, a combination of fear and curiosity that turned to anger. Racking his brain, he had been unable to remember what he had done to cause it. All he knew was that one minute he had been standing in the hall, trying to decide if he should attempt to see her, and the next he was standing in front of her with some man asking him to leave. What transpired in that room?

The incident had been disconcerting, to say the least. The most troubling thing was that it wasn't the first instance of lost time. It happened during his residency after medical school and was very strange. One minute he would be talking to someone, and the next he would be in the same place but alone, or the person would ask for an answer to a question he hadn't heard. He assumed it was stress or overwork. His residency kept him in the hospital for twenty-four to thirty-six hours at a time, and he was usually running on only a few hours of sleep. He'd blown the episodes off. After all, what could he be doing in a couple of minutes? But then it happened again after the devastating loss of his son, and he'd assumed it was caused by the mind-numbing grief. Now, though, there was no easy explanation.

The path leading to the lotus pond was strewn with leaves and twigs, compliments of the shaking earth. Even in Southern California, March was too early for the fragrant flowers to be in bloom, so the only color was the mallard's teal-blue feathers, brightened by the sun as he glided on the surface of the water. Ted looked out over the landscape before him. The ice plant borders of the desert garden looked like pink clouds floating on the ground. Too bad the rest of the desert wasn't as pretty. Looking away from the garden, he found the expanse of lawn and hedges more inviting so took the path leading to the rose arbors and teahouse.

Rambling through the rows of rose bushes, thoughts of how best to approach Toni circled his mind. What would he say when he had no idea what had happened? Would she speak to him at all? The important thing was that he needed to apologize to her. He needed to do it for himself even if she refused to accept it.

The deep, rich colors of the Desert Peace rose stopped him not far from the tearoom. Unlike a regular Peace rose with pale yellow petals blushed with pink, this flower was brilliant yellow painted with a burgundy so deep it looked like velvet. He smiled. It reminded him of Toni, warm and vibrant. A slightly wicked idea flashed in his head.

Looking around, he appeared to be the only person amongst the roses this morning. In the teahouse, he could see a few ladies intent on their various conversations, so he positioned himself with his back to the mullioned windows, his body blocking anyone's view of the Desert Peace rose. Taking a last look around to be sure no one was watching, he plucked a bud from the bush, then quickly but carefully slipped it into the pocket of his jacket.

He hoped that this small token might break the ice and give him the opportunity to explain himself, if he could come up with an explanation.

As he walked past the café and library on his way to his car, he considered telling her the truth about his blackouts. It was a fleeting notion that was swept out as quickly as it had surfaced. She'd never believe it. She'd see it as an excuse for whatever his actions had been.

When he reached his car, he retrieved the rose, taking care not to break the stem. A small fold that caused a crease on one of the outer petals made him realize how delicate the stately flower was and how easily it could bruise. It was bright, vibrant, delicate, and thorny, and that was the reason it reminded Ted of Toni. Her outward strength and fortitude belied the frailty of her emotions. Anger was her thorn, protecting her from pain, unaware that it often caused pain to those around her.

In the car, he laid the rose next to him. It looked all the more fragile alone, engulfed by the bucket seat. He got his cell phone and started to punch numbers but stopped after the fourth numeral and slipped the phone back into his pocket. He was only a few blocks from her office. Catching her unaware was the most practical thing to do if he truly wanted to see her. If he called ahead, she would find any number of ways to avoid such a meeting. With the decision made, he turned left out of the library parking lot and toward what, he wasn't sure.

Chapter Eight

The courtyard of Toni's building was unnervingly quiet. The terrarium-like space with a waterfall-fed pond and stream stood silent and dry. *The earthquake must have damaged the water system in the building.* It made him wonder if Toni would even be in her office. There was no one around, but the faint sound of clanging metal indicated that workers were there.

The door to Toni's office stood partially open. *If she wasn't there, would her door be open?* Perhaps her last patient had left and the next had not yet arrived. His footsteps seemed to echo in the stillness of the landscaped atrium. He stood at the open door, gathering his courage, finally pushing it open the rest of the way.

The office reminded him of a study or library in an English manor house. The centerpiece of the room was a large desk, mahogany perhaps. A dusty rose leather chair sat behind it. At one end of the large room was a conversation area. There was a small oval table separating a loveseat and two comfortable-looking chairs. Knowing Toni, he suspected several of the pieces were antique.

There was no trite theme like "English Country Cottage" and no obvious color scheme either. It wasn't the usual therapist's office with blue or yellow walls and decorations that are supposed to create a calm atmosphere. Like Toni, this room was warm and inviting. It was a gift she had, making people comfortable.

He stepped into the office. At the other end of the room was a spiral staircase of highly polished wood which led to a loft surrounded by railings matching the staircase. He assumed the earthquake had caused the empty shelves that lined the balcony.

He strained to see if she was upstairs and took a few steps backward until he bumped into one of the chairs in the conversation area. There she was, sitting on the floor, stacking books after wiping them off with a cloth. The sun streamed through the skylight, highlighting glints of copper in her hair. She was wearing it up, accentuating the curve of her neck. He remembered how the chestnut tresses looked when they tumbled in soft waves over her shoulders and down her back. He sighed.

He hadn't really seen her yesterday, so he didn't realize how lovely she still was... yesterday! That was why he was here, to apologize for whatever it was he'd done. He sat on the arm of the closest chair and cleared his throat.

Ann glanced over her shoulder, assuming it was one of the workmen who had been coming in and out since she arrived. She couldn't have been more surprised. She got up and went to the railing.

"How did you find me?"

He blew out the breath he'd been holding. "My powers of deduction are quite remarkable these days... you're listed in information."

"Oh." Her stomach was suddenly tied in knots.

"When did you change your name?"

"I got married, if it's any of your business."

"I meant your first name."

"Ann is more professional than Toni."

"Toni suits you."

"It suited the child I was. What do you want?"

"I want to apologize."

"For what?"

"Yesterday."

Eager for him to leave, she rushed to say, "Apology accepted." She hesitated a fraction of a moment. "You can go now," she said and started to turn away.

"I'd like to talk."

"About what?"

"You could tell me what you've been doing."

"I have no desire to have a conversation with you about anything, certainly not about my life." She had the souvenir box from Big Bear in her hand, and she almost threw it at him but controlled herself. "Look, I accepted the apology for your bizarre behavior yesterday, so why are you still here?"

Ted slipped off the arm of the chair into the seat. "Why are you so angry?"

She glared at him from her perch in the loft and could see in his eyes that he really didn't know why. She closed her eyes and took a deep breath, turning her back to the room. Why *was* she still angry after all these years? Uncle Jamie had tried many times to get her to purge the anger, but even through her happy years with Alex she held on to it. If she had a patient doing this, she'd be counseling to let it go. So why couldn't she?

Her thoughts thus engaged and her back to the room, she didn't see Ted move from the conversation area to the foot of the stairs. She turned at the sound of an unfamiliar voice.

"Miss?"

Ann rubbed her eyes dry before turning. "What?"

Speaking with a soft Scottish brogue, Ted said, "I would know your name."

She stepped to the head of the stairs. "What?"

"Your name Miss, what is your name?"

Now, what was happening? Ted was standing there looking up at her, but it wasn't Ted. *What did that even mean?* Assuming it would be like yesterday, she braced herself for another explosive confrontation. She looked into his eyes; it definitely wasn't Ted looking back. What was going on? Whatever it was, she was concerned that he might become as volatile as he had been the day before so thought it best to play along until she could figure out what he was doing.

Slowly she said, "Ann Hart. My name is Ann Hart."

He made a deep bow. "Andrew Mcnaughton, at your service, Miss Hart." His mouth turned into a lopsided grin. "It is Miss, is it not?"

Baffled, but trying to elicit information, she sidestepped his question and asked one of her own. "How do you come to be here, Mr. Mcnaughton?"

Continuing in the Scottish brogue, he hesitantly answered, "The same way you did, Miss Hart. I boarded at Glasgow."

"Scotland?"

He chuckled. Obviously it was Scotland, for where else would they have been? "Yes. We left Glasgow under full sail at eventide yesterday, and with God's speed shall arrive in Antigua three weeks hence." He looked up at her rather quizzically and asked, "Are you in need of the ship's physician, Miss Hart?"

Unsure what to say about any of it she asked, "Why do you ask?"

"As you are aboard a ship but have no memory of it, I thought perhaps you were in need of medical assistance."

Still thinking that playing along would answer some questions she responded, "I am quite well, thank you; however, as you suggest, I do seem to have lost some time. Can you tell me the date?"

"It is, as of the midnight hour, the tenth of May in the year of our Lord eighteen hundred and five."

A loud rap on the open door made both Ann and Ted turn. A man in gray work clothes looked up at her. "Saw your door standing open, Doc. Wanted to check that nothing was amiss." He looked through squinty eyes at Ted. "Are you all right?"

Ann looked down at Ted, who looked up at her. He was back. He was Ted again. She turned to the workman. "I'm fine. Thanks, Sam."

Glaring at Ted, he said, "Okay, just makin' sure." He left, looking over his shoulder as he went.

Once the workman was gone, she asked, "What's going on with you?"

Trying to recover gracefully, from what he wasn't sure, he answered her question with, "What do you mean?" He glanced around. Before Ann could answer him, he said, "How did I get over here?"

"You walked."

"I guess I mean, why am I over here?"

"Well, you should say what you mean, and mean what you say."

"Hmmm, I believe we've had that conversation before." She couldn't help but smile, remembering their first meeting.

She was about to ask him about his odd behavior again, when he cleared his throat and pulled the rose out of the pocket of his jacket. He took a few more steps up the stairs and then held it out to her. "I brought this as a bit of a peace offering. It reminded me of you."

His sporadic and peculiar behavior was pushed to a back burner, and curiosity now replaced her anger. Hesitantly she said, "It's beautiful." It was almost a question. Taking a few steps down, she accepted the proffered bloom. "I've never seen a rose this color. Where did you get it?"

"The Huntington Library."

"I didn't know the Huntington sold individual blossoms like this."

Quietly and with downcast eyes he admitted, "I didn't buy it, exactly."

"Exactly?" Realization struck, and her eyes popped wide open. "You picked it? You stole it from the rose garden?"

He looked, for all the world, like a small boy caught with his hand in the cookie jar. Then she saw a smile come into his eyes that spoke of satisfaction. She couldn't help herself; she laughed.

"I've never been given a pilfered rose before." She smiled.

It was nice that she wasn't angry about it. "I couldn't resist it."

"I could probably have your library membership revoked and have you banned permanently from even being allowed in."

"But you wouldn't, would you?"

Unable to deny her amusement, Ann conceded that she would not. The "girl on the swing" clock chimed the half hour. Ted glanced at his watch.

"I need to go," he said as he took the few steps still separating them. "It was wonderful seeing you again." He leaned in and kissed her cheek then rushed down the stairs. At the door he turned back. "I'll call you," he said and left.

Ann's mind was in complete turmoil. But when she calmed down and thought about it for a second, she found that she really enjoyed the exchange. She sat on the step in the middle of the staircase and inhaled the fragrance of the rose. A pilfered flower. She shook her head, making no effort to stop the grin from spreading across her face. She was amazed at how comfortable it was being with him, but even more amazed that she *wanted* to hear from him.

Chapter Nine

Six-inch-tall letters proclaiming Happy Birthday and a balloon bouquet greeted Ann as she struggled with the front door of her parents' house, juggling a grocery bag, a cake safe, and a wrapped gift.

Leaving her brother's birthday present on the hall tree at the entry, Ann made her way to the kitchen where she deposited her other parcels on the blue granite counter.

"Mom, I'm here," she shouted.

From the back of the house, her mother called, "Hi, honey. I'll be out in a minute. Just running a brush through my hair."

"Don't hurry on my account."

Amid the array of plates, napkins, and silverware on the bar dividing the kitchen from the dining area, Ann placed the cake. Although it was a lifelong hobby, or at least since she was a young teenager, Ann was only really able to pursue baking and cake decorating for gatherings of family and close friends. This time, since her brother loved strawberries, she'd created a cinnamon chiffon cake filled with cut strawberries and whipped cream, then using stabilized whipped cream had decorated it to look like a basket filled with the ripe berries.

Folding the reusable grocery bag and slipping it under her purse on the counter, Ann headed to the entry hall to retrieve her brother's gift and added it to the two from her parents.

Lynn Rishel was one of those women other women hate. She never had a hair out of place, her makeup always looked freshly applied, and her clothes looked as though they'd just come from the dry cleaner. Even tonight, the jeans she was wearing appeared to have been ironed. Of course, she claimed that she never went out of her way to look as she did, and that was what made it so infuriating, even for her daughter. And tonight was no different.

"Hi, doll."

"You look great, Mom."

Ann, on the other hand, as usual, looked tousled and windblown. Mother and daughter hugged.

"Where's Dad?"

"Out with the dogs. They're still a little skittish after the quake."

"It looks like you got the house back together."

"It was mostly cleaning up broken pottery so wasn't much of a project. How about you?"

"I've got everything pretty much done now, cleanupwise. I need to replace the dishes and glasses, though."

"The Pottery Barn is having a sale," her mother offered.

"I love the Pottery Barn."

"I know." Lynn smiled.

"That'll be a fun project for tomorrow." Replacing a few of the strawberries that had fallen off the cake, Ann asked, "When is Tommy getting here?"

"Anytime now," Lynn said, glancing at the kitchen clock. "How did Ellie fare?"

"Her house was almost untouched. Weird, isn't it? The house next to hers collapsed, but she didn't even get a crack. The dealership, on the other hand, lost everything but the walls. She has to completely rebuild the interior."

"What a shame. But at least she has a home to go to."

The back door opened, and Peter Rishel, Ann's father, came in with two golden retrievers. "Hi, Toni."

"Hi, Dad." After hugging him, she bent down and hugged the dogs, Meteor and Star, who greeted her exuberantly.

Ann gathered the dishes and cups from the birthday celebration and carried them into the kitchen, then put them in the dishwasher. Returning to the living room, she hugged Tommy, her brother. "Happy birthday, big guy."

"Thanks. Thanks for the globe. It's awesome, as the kids say. And the cake, as always, was delish."

"You're more than welcome."

She said her good-byes, hugging Tommy's wife, Michelle, their two children, her Aunt Maura, and her parents.

As she was slipping on her sweater, Uncle Jamie came over carrying her cake safe. "Forgot something," he said, holding up the plastic container.

She shook her head. "You wouldn't think I'd forget something that big. Thanks." She reached for it.

"I'll carry it. You have enough."

"I'm okay. I've only got my purse and an empty bag."

"Well, I'll walk out with you anyway."

She said good-bye again to everyone and walked out the door on the arm of her favorite uncle.

Using the remote key fob, she unlocked the car door. Jamie opened it for her, then tossed her cake safe onto the passenger seat. "I understand you saw Ted."

"Yeah." Suddenly realizing that she hadn't told him, she asked, surprised, "How did you know?"

"I talked to him this morning."

"Why?"

"We're friends."

"Friends?"

"We stayed in touch after his residency, and over the years we became friends."

"Why didn't you ever mention it?"

"I didn't think you'd want to know." Ann got a strange look on her face, and Jamie quickly added, "We didn't talk about you either." She was relieved.

"Did he tell you what happened?"

"According to him, not much."

She bit down on her thumbnail and stared at the ground. "Have you seen him recently?"

"Yes."

"Has he done or said anything that seemed strange?"

"No. Why? What happened?"

She thought about it, but couldn't think of a way to explain it. "I'm not sure. He just acted a little weird."

"I suspect he was nervous."

"Yeah, maybe." She turned and kissed his cheek. "Well, thanks for walking me out." She slipped behind the wheel of her car.

Jamie pushed the door shut. *What happened yesterday?* Ted had been cryptic about the meeting too. Jamie shrugged as Ann drove away.

Holding one of the few surviving stoneware mugs in her hands, Ann sat at the kitchen table looking out at her woodland wonderland.

What happened yesterday and at the Red Cross? What was going on with him? How did Jamie not know something was happening when it was so obvious to her? Was she the cause? And why, in spite of his betrayal, did Ted's peck on the cheek tingle? Why had she not wanted him to leave? Why did she want to hear from him again? There were so many questions... but no answers.

She stirred the melted mini marshmallows into the hot chocolate, absently watching the white foam create designs in the thick brown liquid. Suddenly, she realized something quite disturbing; the rest of that day, after he left her office, she had thought of nothing but Ted. Her throat tightened. She had not thought of Alex at all.

Ann shook her head. It was evident that the earthquake had shaken much more than Southern California.

Chapter Ten

Saturday, March 15

The doorbell rang as Ann removed the last of the new glassware from the dishwasher and set the lightly tinted green margarita glasses on the counter. When she was halfway across the living room, the Westminster chimes rang out again. She opened the door to Ellie laden with several bags and boxes. Ann took one plastic bag with a pink box in it and stepped aside to allow her friend entrance.

"What happened to picking up a couple of tacos on your way over here?"

"There are a couple of tacos in there somewhere." On the way to the kitchen, she continued her explanation. "Los Gueros was having a special on the chile rellenos, so I couldn't resist. While I was waiting, I saw a plate of enchiladas go by, and they looked so good I had to get some of those too. Course we couldn't have all that Mexican food and not have beans, rice, and guacamole."

"And this?" Ann asked, removing the pink box from the bag.

"You know that cute little bakery on Hill? Well I figured we needed dessert."

"You didn't get flan?"

"Wanted something different for dessert, so I got chocolate éclairs."

"Well, it's a good thing I got new dishes, or we'd be eating this feast on paper."

"And drinking margaritas out of plastic. By the way, where are the margaritas?"

Sitting in the living room, each sipping her third margarita, Ellie leaned back in her chair and stretched out her legs.

"I'll be glad when they finally get the dealership finished."

Surprised, Ann asked, "Have they started?"

"No, and I have no idea when they will. The insurance company and the contractor said that a car dealership wasn't a high priority."

"Well, there are a lot of people without homes, and some hospitals were damaged."

"I know. It's just weird not having anywhere to go in the morning and not having any idea when it might change. Besides, it seems like businesses that put people to work would be a fairly high priority."

"I suppose it depends on the business. It has only been a week."

"I know, I know. That doesn't make it any less frustrating." Ellie looked out at the backyard as the lights in the garden started to come on. "Quake didn't mess up the fairy house, huh?"

"All the little stuff inside was on the floor, but no, the whole yard was spared. Didn't even lose much water from the pool."

Ellie looked out into the darkness of the coming night. "What's Gigi doing?"

"Patrolling."

"Patrolling what?"

"The yard."

"Seems like she should be in here curled up on the hearth or something."

"Great Pyrenees are bred to be nocturnal guardians. She walks the perimeter of the property, making sure there are no intruders. She'll come in when she's sure everything's okay. She's still a bit edgy. That was her first earthquake. She hasn't been able to relax with all the aftershocks."

"Boy, I know how she feels," Ellie agreed. "Some of them have been pretty scary."

"Want some tea?"

"Sounds good."

Ann took the glasses with her and went into the kitchen.

Ellie looked around the room, thinking to herself that it was a shame Ann lost all the beautiful antique cut glass. Still, it was just stuff, nothing that couldn't be replaced, unlike her brother, whose smiling face was looking at her from the mantel. She got up and took the framed portrait back to the chair. Her throat tightened, and tears filled her eyes as her hand skimmed the glass. She clutched the photograph to her chest.

Ellie looked up as Ann came in with two mugs of tea, her eyes red and cheeks streaked with tears. Ann hurried to put the mugs down and went to her friend.

"Ellie, what's wrong?"

She allowed the framed photograph to fall away from her chest onto her lap. "Sometimes I miss him so much."

Ann sat on the arm of the chair and put her arm around Ellie's shoulder. "I know. Me too."

Gigi trotted in from the kitchen and forced her massive head under Ann's free hand. Ellie smiled through her tears. "Maybe I need a big dog."

Ann scratched the animal's head. "She can be a real comfort."

Ellie took a deep breath. "Enough of feeling sorry for myself." She put the picture on the coffee table. Ann kissed the top of her head and got up, picking up the photo as she did.

Returning it to its place on the mantel, she turned toward her friend and changed the subject in order to lighten the mood. "I saw Ted again."

"On purpose?"

"It was for him."

"What do you mean?"

"He just showed up at my office."

"How did he find you?"

"411."

"Was it like the other night?"

"Part of it was just as weird."

"As weird as accusing you of witchcraft?"

She cocked her head. "Maybe not quite as weird. You know how I said when he did that there was something that wasn't right, a look in his eyes like it wasn't really Ted? Well, something like that happened again. He claimed to be someone named Andrew Mcnaughton and that the year was 1805. The really strange part was he seemed to think we were on a sailing ship. I don't understand what's going on with him."

"Let me get this straight. He just started talking like he was someone else?"

"Yeah, and right in the middle of the conversation. One minute he was Ted, apologizing for what happened the day before, and the next he was speaking with a Scottish accent. Then when one of the workmen came in, suddenly he was Ted again. It was so strange."

"And you're sure it's not some kind of game?"

"I wish it was, but I could see in his eyes that he had no idea it happened. He even asked me why he moved. I can't really be angry with him over it because I think he's as perplexed as I am."

"Wow, the mystery deepens. What did he say happened?"

"Nothing. Like I said, he had no idea."

"Did you ask Jamie about it?"

"Apparently Ted's never done anything odd around him."

"So what do you think is going on?"

"I have no idea." She took a sip of tea. "But that's not the only strange thing that's happened."

"With Ted?"

"No, this doesn't involve Ted at all." She stood. "Come on. I want to show you something."

As Ellie put down her mug, she asked, "Stranger than Ted acting like he's three people?"

Ann hesitated. "Maybe not stranger, but just as strange."

Alex's office was stripped of almost everything but basic office furniture.

Ellie asked, "Where's the train?"

"The track was destroyed, and a couple of the cars broke. One of these days, I'll take it to the Whistle Stop and see if it's salvageable. But that isn't what I wanted to show you."

Ann went to the sleeping computer and moved the mouse. After a few seconds, a website appeared on the screen.

How things work. Reincarnation.

"When did you get interested in reincarnation?"

"I'm not. When the power came back on, I turned on the computer to see if it still worked, and this is what came up on the screen."

"That's interesting, but I'm not sure I'd say it was strange."

"Technically it's not. Except, I didn't search for or go to the site. But this is the strangest part..."

Ann turned off the computer and waited a few minutes then turned it back on. Instead of opening on the desktop or to a browser, it went directly to a page titled *NDE and Reincarnation* that consisted of a few paragraphs and a whole list of links.

Ellie turned away from the screen and asked Ann, "What's NDE?"

"Near-death experience." Ann looked over at her friend and cocked her head. "Well?"

"Well, what?"

"I didn't do that either. It just came up."

"And you didn't bookmark either site?"

"Nope. Until this started happening, I'd never seen them. And it's not finished yet. You might want to sit down for this one."

Once again she turned the computer off and then on again, but this time a video from YouTube began to play. It was a video about a toddler who knew all about World War II airplanes and had dreams in which he was shot down. As the video wound down with a scientist claiming the child was fabricating and/or mimicking what he heard from adults, Ellie sat in silence.

"Weird, isn't it? It happens every time I turn it on or wake it up. It always goes to one of these sites."

"Can you still use it? I mean go to other websites?"

"Yeah, but it always goes back to these when I finish."

Ellie got a quizzical look on her face. "And you've never gone to those sites before?"

"No, I never even gave reincarnation a thought."

"I'll give ya that it is pretty weird. Maybe it was something Alex was researching before he"—she hesitated slightly—"disappeared."

"None of it started until after the earthquake. Besides, he didn't use this computer much after we got him the laptop."

"Do you think the earthquake had something to do with it?"

"Like what?"

"I don't know. Do you have a theory?"

"No, I don't. It's just that there seems to be lots of strange stuff going on. When I was cleaning up in here, I was sure someone touched me. And every time I come in here now, it feels like there's someone else here, that I'm not alone. And now all this weirdness with Ted. What do you think it means?"

"I don't think it *means* anything, but then I try not to overthink things. Did you ask anyone about it?"

"Who would I ask? And what would I say?"

Ellie shrugged. "I don't know. It just seems like there should be someone you could talk to."

"Problem is, do I need to talk to someone about the computer acting weird or someone about reincarnation?"

"Well, that is a dilemma." Ellie yawned. "You don't mind if I crash here, do you?"

"Of course not," she said as she flicked off the power switch on the computer.

After bidding Ellie good night, Ann went into the kitchen to make herself another cup of tea before bed. From the other side of the utility room, she saw a faint light emanating from the office. She must have left one of the small lamps on.

Sure she'd turned the computer off. Ann was more than a little surprised to see the light came from the monitor. She must not have pushed the button in far enough. As she stepped through the door, her breath caught. She looked into every corner of the room, sure someone else was there... but she was alone.

On the computer screen, a single word was bobbing and tumbling: *forgive,* in all lowercase letters was moving on a field of black. Ann turned the computer off, but before she turned around it came back on. After three more attempts, she determined there was a short or something in the power switch and left the machine on. Glancing over her shoulder as she left, the word *forgive* continued its motion on the screen.

Chapter Eleven

Sunday, March 23

The swirled plaster on the ceiling looked like ripples of water in the dim predawn light. Did he imagine water because the dream had been on the ocean? In spite of a yawn coming from deep in his chest, he knew he wouldn't get back to sleep. He'd gone to bed early and couldn't remember waking up in the night so was unsure why he felt exhausted, but it was as if he had not slept at all. Perhaps the strange and emotional dream that kept recurring was the cause. He'd been having this dream, or was it dreams, since he was a kid, but they had never been so intense. Until recently, he never felt like he was part of the dream. Now though, he felt every emotion the men in the dreams were experiencing... good and bad. He threw the covers off and swung his legs over the edge of the bed, rubbing his face with the open palms of his hands. He yawned again. He needed coffee.

On the deck, Ted lit the fire pit and plopped down in the captain's chair feeling more than a little logy. He leaned back and closed his eyes, unable to get the images of the dream out of his head. He couldn't stop the tears that filled his eyes either. This was all very strange. He never understood why he dreamed about people and places he didn't recognize, but it had been going on so long that he'd stopped wondering about it. Now though, it went way beyond the dreams. How, or why, was it possible that he was experiencing the joy and tragedy of the people in the dream to the extent that he often awoke devastated by grief? Why had he developed such a strong affinity for the man when he had no idea who he was?

What did it mean when you dreamed about strangers but had no personal interaction with them? It was like watching someone else's dream. If it was possible to get stranger than that, it certainly had when suddenly the scene changed from a ship to what appeared to be a stark wooden building with benches and more people he didn't know. Standing before the people in the room was a man ranting and raving. Ted thought a moment. What had the man been shouting about? The subject escaped him, but the overwhelming feeling of dread was palpable, and the lingering anger was distressing. In years past, the dreams had simply been dreams with no residual effects. This intense emotional connection to the people was entirely new.

He was ripped from the memory of the dreams when the spotlight of a police helicopter passed over him. He looked out at the city below. It had been two weeks since the earthquake, and the city was getting back to normal. He could see headlights from the cars on the Hollywood Freeway. Where were they all going so early on a Sunday morning?

The cappuccino from the single brewer tasted particularly good this morning, so he went inside to make another. While he waited for his cup to refill, his mind was bombarded with images from his dream. The memory of the second part of the dream was already fading. The only thing he was sure about was that he had not been present in either dream. *Had it been two different dreams?*

He picked up his laptop and mug and went back outside. Signing on to the Internet, he typed into the search engine "dream interpretation," and several websites came up. Hoping for one that would allow him to describe the dream and then have someone interpret it, he was faced instead with dream dictionaries. He sat staring at the alphabet, trying to figure out what he was looking for. The dream seemed to have taken place aboard a ship, but the meaning of a sailboat was different from a sailing ship. Traveling abroad had several different meanings. Water, sea, and ocean all had different meanings as well. His search was getting him nowhere as none of the sites did more than give vague definitions that could be taken to mean any number of things. None of the sites had anything about a dream in which the dreamer wasn't included, so he still had no idea what that meant.

He closed the computer and sipped his coffee. The blackouts had started about the same time the dreams intensified. He leaned forward to put the computer on the table, wondering if the two things were somehow linked. He ran his hand through his hair, then leaned back in the chair and gripped his mug with both hands. *What was that smell?*

Usually the overriding fragrance in the yard was pine and eucalyptus, but this morning he smelled cigar smoke. He looked around, but saw no hint of a burning cigar. He couldn't remember the last time he'd smoked a cigar. Was he just imaging it? Rubbing his forehead, he remembered a scene from his dream with two of the men drinking brandy and smoking cigars. *Had that triggered a sense memory?*

The sky was turning pink and orange as the sun began its ascent in the eastern sky. He closed his eyes, and the images from his dream could not be suppressed.

The young man was dressed in a hunter-green tailcoat and fawn knee britches. The ocean mist made his black boots glisten in the late afternoon sun. Fog swirled around the deck of the heaving ship with his pregnant wife huddled close, his arms tightly around her in an effort to protect her from the chill air. He had not wanted her to travel with him at this time, but she had insisted. Carrying their first child, she was wont to remain in Scotland when an urgent request for her husband's return to Antigua came on the last ship from the Caribbean island. They had already made a home in the island nation, including a room for the nursemaid that adjoined the nursery. With three months until the birth of the child, Catherine was confident that all would be well. His love nestled close to his side, Andrew was overjoyed she was here. Guilt for allowing her to travel with him was fleeting in the warm glow of her love.

He had taken precautions. He made sure that their bedchamber and sitting room had all the comforts (as far as comforts on a ship could be) of home. Most importantly he had been able to convince an old friend from St. Andrews, George Bell, a physician, to accompany them, and the nursemaid was also on board with them. As the sun set on their tenth day of travel, Andrew wrapped his arms around her. Catherine turned her face from the red sky and kissed him. Still surprised by his wife's freely given affection, he was thrilled that after three years of marriage she not only had the desire, but acted on it. He had always loved that about her. He smiled, remembering stolen kisses in the garden even before they were married.

With only a few days left in their journey, Catherine was wobbly. She had felt fine for most of the trip, but today the motion of the ship seemed to be making her feel dizzy. She did not understand why that was so. The gentle and not-so-gentle rocking of the ship had not bothered her before this. The shooting pain in her abdomen had her concerned for the baby, but George told her it was nothing to worry about, that twinges in the late stages of a pregnancy were completely normal. Andrew found her lying down in their bedchamber. The fear that grabbed him at the paleness of her skin was hard to suppress, but he didn't want her to see his anxiety so stood in the doorway collecting himself for a few moments before entering the room.

His wife looked up at him as he sat on the edge of the bed. Her smile melted his heart, but the shadow he saw in her eyes wrapped him in cold fear.

"George says you need to eat something. Do you feel you can?"

"Perhaps some soup."

"I shall bring it to you."

"No, I think I would like to get up," she said weakly.

Leaning heavily on the arm of her husband, Catherine shuffled to the captain's cabin where they had been having all their meals.

As she insinuated herself into the chair, George stood up. "Mrs. Mcnaughton, are you feeling better?"

"I am weak, but Andrew wants me to eat something." She grimaced and bent over; George was immediately at her side.

"What is it?"

"The pains have been far worse today, and I'm feeling dizzy more often than not."

The physician turned to Andrew. "She should be lying down, Andy."

The color drained from his face. "Yes, of course." Gently he lifted his wife into his arms and took her back to their room.

Andrew watched as George tried to make Catherine comfortable. Her scream was like a knife in his heart.

"The baby is coming," George said.

Terrified, Catherine cried, "No! It is too soon."

Andrew rushed to her side and knelt beside the bed. Her small hand was lost in his as she squeezed with each stabbing pain. He brushed the hair from her forehead and kissed her. She released his hand and caressed his face. Suddenly, a pain caused her to cry out. The heart-wrenching cries were hard for him to bear, but he stayed at her side, holding her hand, swabbing her face with a cool, water-soaked linen cloth.

George stood up, the still, lifeless infant in his arms. Tears filled his eyes. "I'm sorry, Andy."

Andrew laid his head on the edge of the bed, unable to stop the tears. It was Catherine's gentle touch that caused him to raise his head.

She whispered, "I am sorry, my love."

"For what, dearest?"

"I promised to give you a son, and I have failed."

"No, my love. We will have sons... and daughters."

George put his hand on Andrew's shoulder. "She needs to rest Andy."

He stood slowly, reluctantly releasing his wife's hand; her weak smile tore at his very soul.

Andrew watched her fade over the next few days, and as the ship approached their island home, he sat on the edge of the bed and held his wife in his arms.

She whispered, "There is one promise I can keep, my sweet husband. I will love you with my dying breath." Although weak, her smile was reminiscent of the radiant smiles that kissed his heart, but this one was filled with sadness. "I am so sorry, my dearest love." She used the last of her strength to reach up and kiss him. "Be happy, Andrew, for me... for us." She closed her eyes and breathed her last. She went limp in his arms. He lay down beside her, holding her as close as he could get her. His gut-wrenching sobs filled the small room.

Ted was overwhelmed with sadness. In spite of trying not to cry, he could not stop his tears any more than Andrew could. *It was so strange. Who were these people?* Why was he dreaming about them? Why did their tragedy leave him so emotionally drained? A grief-stricken sob escaped him as Sara Jane came out of the house.

She rushed to her father's side. "What's the matter, Daddy?" She knelt down next to him, her hands on the arm of his chair.

He wasn't sure what to say when he had no idea what was happening, but he wasn't going to lie. "Had a weird, emotional, extremely sad dream."

"What's it about?"

"A young couple whose baby dies."

"Maybe it has something to do with Josh."

"I don't recognize any of the people. Even I'm not in it, and it seems to take place over two hundred years ago."

"But it makes you feel bad?"

"Yeah. It's like I'm experiencing all of it myself. It's very strange."

Sara Jane's cell phone rang. She stood up and answered it. After a few hurried sentences, she disconnected.

"Jenny and I are going to Santa Monica."

"Not exactly beach weather."

"We're going to the pier. Just need a change of pace. Every day for two weeks at the Red Cross after school was pretty intense."

"I know. Thank you for doing it with me."

"I liked doing it, but I need a break. Are you going to be okay? I don't have to go."

He smiled at her. "It's my job to worry about you, and your job to have a good time. I'm fine. Go."

She bent down and hugged him, kissing his cheek. "Okay, if you're sure."

He kissed her cheek in return. "I'm sure. Besides, I'm meeting Jamie for breakfast."

"Okay then," she said as she ran out. "See you later."

"Be careful," he added as she slipped through the patio door.

As the sun rose higher in the clear sky, he finished his coffee and went inside to get dressed. The shower felt good. He didn't want to get out, but he'd only left himself a half an hour to get to his breakfast. The shower helped to refresh and revive him a bit. He suspected his emotional reaction to the dream was, at the very least, partially responsible for the deep-seated fatigue he felt. Grabbing his keys from the table in the entryway, he ran out the door.

Chapter Twelve

The sun was just cresting the horizon when Ann snapped the strap of her bike helmet under her chin, beginning her weekend ride. Once a competitive cyclist, she now competed mostly with herself. When she did race, it was in the over-forty group, but she could still hold her own. She really enjoyed riding, finding the exercise and experience invigorating. She hadn't ridden since the earthquake, so she wasn't in a hurry. Today was going to be a leisurely ride.

Because it was so early on Sunday morning, she didn't have to dodge much traffic as she made her way to the Colorado Street Bridge. It was such a beautiful old structure, and she couldn't see it, never mind ride over it, without thinking of Ted. His love of the bridge and architecture was something they had shared. Most people thought since they were both in medical school that that was how they met, but it was architecture and not medicine that had brought them together.

It had been one of those warm days near the end-of-June gloom but before the summer heat set in, and Ann was taking pictures of the buildings on the college campus when Ted came up behind her.

"What's ya doin'?"

Without stopping her activity or looking at him, she answered, "Taking pictures."

"I can see that."

"Then why did you ask?"

"Well, I guess I meant why are you taking pictures of buildings?"

"You should say what you mean and mean what you say." She walked away without looking at him.

He thought he was starting up a casual conversation with a very pretty girl, but somehow it got turned around, and now he was watching her walk away. *What happened?* He walked fast to catch up with her.

"So why are you taking pictures of the buildings?"

"Photography class."

"So you're a student here?"

"Yep."

"You aren't very talkative."

"You haven't given me a reason to talk, and I try not to unless I have something to say."

"That's unusual."

"Why?"

"I don't know. It just seems that most people talk without having much to say. So, like I said, unusual."

"I don't like to think of myself as 'usual.'"

"You definitely are not."

Ann turned to him and smiled. "Thank you."

Her smile was radiant. Her chestnut hair tumbled down her back and fell over her shoulders, gleaming in the sun. And her skin was like fine porcelain. His heart sped up, and he felt a tightening in his chest.

He smiled back. "What's your major?"

"Second year med in September."

"I start my residency next month."

She smiled again but did not comment.

"So, why the photography class?"

"I needed a little break from all the science, and I love architecture. Photography gave me an excuse to take pictures of the buildings I love."

"Me too. I actually considered architecture rather than medicine."

"Why did you choose medicine?"

"It wasn't really a choice, I suppose. I've always wanted to be a doctor, so it just never occurred to me not to go to medical school."

"Me too. I didn't consider being an architect, but I always wanted to be a doctor."

"So we have a lot in common."

"Two things."

"That's more than a lot of people."

She agreed.

"Can I buy you a cup of coffee?"

"No." She turned and walked away. He thought things were going well so was surprised by the abrupt rejection. He hurried to follow her, but before he caught up with her she looked over her shoulder at him, her smile beaming. "You *can* buy me a glass of iced tea, though."

They walked across the quad together, and until she broke the engagement they had been together almost every day. Three years that he just threw away for a fling. She started pedaling as fast as she could, setting a two-mile personal record on Los Feliz. Ann continued her ride, making a concerted effort to not think about Ted and his betrayal.

By the time she had gone about seven of the twelve miles on Santa Monica Boulevard, she could smell the ocean. Or at least she thought she could smell it, the salty, fishy smell that seems particular to the Pacific. After another four miles, she tilted her head up and closed her eyes slightly, allowing the soft moistness of the sea air to caress her face.

After waiting for the traffic light to change from red to green, she made the wide left turn onto Ocean Avenue and took the few hundred feet to the pier. The sign that arched over the entrance had been there for as long as Ann could remember, and she'd always wondered if it had ever actually been a marina for yachts and fishing boats as the sign proclaimed.

Once she hit the wooden decking of the pier, she got off her bike and walked. The giant timbers making up the boardwalk were held together by huge steel nails. After all the storms and restorations of the pier, she wondered how much of it was original, if any.

Bubba Gump Shrimp Company was the main restaurant at this end of the pier. *What was it before the movie,* Forrest Gump? She was pretty sure it had always been a seafood restaurant but had no recollection of any of the previous names.

Down a bit farther, just past the stairs that led to the beach, was a rock shop, or at least that was what the sign said. In the window were petrified starfish, sand dollars, and sea urchins, even a sponge, but no rocks. She laughed at the absurdity.

She continued her sojourn of the wharf, passing the arcade, amusement park, and miniature golf course. The few people on the pier were fishermen, none of whom seemed to have caught any fish. The cleaning tables on the lower deck held only soft drinks, coffee, and bait. Catch buckets were empty. She guessed that the mussel shells strewn broken on the deck were deposited by the birds living on the old wooden structure.

At the end of the pier, Ann watched as gulls swam on top of the water like ducks, paddling around the barnacle-encrusted pilings. A few sandpipers were burying their beaks in the wet sand, pigeons were here and there, and one pelican swooped down to catch an early breakfast. There was one strange-looking bird—small, black-and-white with a bill longer than a duck, shorter than a piper—swimming atop the ocean swells, suddenly diving down then surfacing again. The strange animal dove one last time, then disappeared as the pewter waves smashed against the wooden pilings of the pier.

When she arrived, there were very few people, but she eventually found herself having to maneuver around several new arrivals.

Rising above her at the shore end of the pier was the Looff Hippodrome. She'd fallen in love with the carousel housed inside the first time her grandparents brought her here; she'd been eight. Ann peered in at the quiet machine. Built in 1922, it had been beautifully restored in the late 1980s so was particularly beautiful when she and Ted decided to get married there.

Ann had never been one of those girls who dreamt of her wedding and knew exactly what she wanted and how she wanted to look. A lavish, expensive wedding when neither of them cared about it was ridiculous, considering the mounting medical school loans they would have to pay, and getting married in the Looff Hippodrome seemed like a fun place to celebrate their love.

She could still imagine how wonderful the beautiful musical contraption would have been as a backdrop for the wedding and reception. No fancy catering either. They'd planned on having a hot dog cart, popcorn cart, and a cotton candy cart. They would have a cake and champagne, but that was as traditional as it would get. She smiled at the thought of how lovely and enjoyable it would have been.

Slowly she walked around the brown stucco building, stopping at the first of three octagonal corners. The Wurlitzer orchestrion was standing a lonely vigil, its shadow dissolving in the morning sun as the coastal clouds started to burn away. The memory of Ted's insistence that they stay and listen to the entire repertoire of the antique machine was a reminder of how things change even as they stay the same. The mechanical device was still there, but with the belts missing or broken, it no longer worked.

The last corner of the old building was empty. It was where the ceremony was to have been. The painted posts in the dome-like corner were to be festooned with ivy, ribbon, and flowers. She thought about the beautiful silk crepe gown she had made. Its simple elegance made her feel like she walked off the silver screen in the 1930s. Peering in through the salt-frosted glass, Ann wondered if her mother still had the dress, not that it mattered. Glancing inside again, she smiled, remembering that Ted bought a tux, rationalizing that he would need it for medical conferences and other events. She wondered how many times he'd actually worn it.

For the first time, she was filled with sadness rather than anger as she stepped back away from the window and the memories. She leaned on the railing of the wooden stairs for a moment, surprised at her reaction. Anger had been her "go to" emotion for so long that this new wrinkle of feeling sad caught her off guard. She had purposely not come here before because she feared her reaction, but now she wasn't even sure what her reaction meant.

Taking a deep breath, she glanced up the stairs at what used to be apartments above the merry-go-round but now were offices for the pier. She wondered what it would have been like to live here in the heyday of the carousel, the roaring twenties. The thought brought a smile as she stepped out onto the weathered wood of the pier and went to the railing overlooking the beach.

She took several deep breaths, inhaling the salty, mist-filled air. She smiled at the sight of a Newfoundland running along the sand, his black coat stark against the gray ocean and light sand. She laughed out loud as the animal plunged into an incoming wave. She wondered if Gigi would enjoy the ocean too.

"That dog looks like he's having a lot of fun."

Ann turned to the young woman standing next to her, a lovely brunette who appeared to be high school aged. "Yes. I was just wondering if my dog would like to do that too."

"What kind of dog do you have?"

"Great Pyrenees."

"That's the big white one, right?"

Ann smiled. "Most people have never heard of her breed."

"My dad and I watch the Westminster Dog Show every year. It's kind of a tradition."

"I like watching it too."

Watching the famed canine event was something of a tradition for Ann too. Over the years, she'd missed it very few times even though Alex had considered it silly to watch a bunch of pampered pets run around a ring. She had countered that it wasn't any sillier than watching a bunch of souped-up cars run around in circles, NASCAR races being one of his favorite spectator sports.

The two women watched as a golden retriever joined the Newfoundland, barking as he went. Ann asked, "Do you have a dog?"

"No. We rent a house, and the owner wouldn't let us have a pet. But we're getting ready to move, and we're going to buy a house this time, so we'll be able to have a dog."

"What kind of dog do you want?"

"I love goldens. I know it's not very original, but I really like them."

"My parents have two. They're really smart."

"Mostly I like them 'cause they're cute and cuddly."

Ann laughed. And the young woman noticed the bike. "Did you ride here?"

"Yes."

"From where?"

"Pasadena."

"Whoa! That's far."

"About thirty miles."

"So you have to go sixty miles to get home?"

"Yeah. Not that big a deal. I do it almost every weekend."

"I can't imagine that."

"It's exhilarating, for me anyway."

The young woman turned her back to the beach and took in the Looff Hippodrome. "I love the carousel. My dad brought me here a lot when I was younger, and I still love to ride it."

Ann turned as well. "My grandparents brought me here when I was a kid. I haven't ridden it in years. Too bad it doesn't open until eleven. I don't feel like waiting around for it. Is that what brought you down here?"

"No. My girlfriend and I just wanted a change from school and the earthquake."

"The earthquake?"

"We've been working at the Red Cross after school, and it's been pretty intense."

"What were you doing at the Red Cross?"

"We were helping separate all the donated food and stuff for the refugee centers where the people who lost homes or didn't have power and water were staying. I was amazed at how many big grocery stores donate stuff, and not just packaged food, but fresh fruits and vegetables. They donated diapers and formula, paper towels and napkins, all kinds of stuff. Nice to know the big corporations do that."

"Yes, it is."

"You said you live in Pasadena?"

"I do."

"That's where we've been looking at houses. It's really nice there. Dad really likes the... what does he call it, craft houses?"

"Craftsman."

"Yes! I like them too."

"Pasadena is a good place to look. I have one, a Craftsman. Monrovia has a lot of them too."

"I don't think we've ever looked there. I'll have to mention that to Dad."

"It's a cute little town." Ann put on her bike helmet. "Well, I need to get going."

"Yeah, I need to find Jenny. It was nice talking with you."

"Yes, it was. By the way, my name is Ann."

The teenager smiled brightly. "I'm Sara."

"It was nice meeting you, Sara. Good luck with the house hunting."

"Thanks, and be careful riding home."

"I will. Bye."

Chapter Thirteen

Ted was a meat-and-potatoes kind of guy so had never cared much for trendy restaurants. He preferred coffee shops and steakhouses to the more popular cafes frequented by those who considered themselves the erudite elite.

But as trendy restaurants went, The Lotus was one of the best, at least as far as Ted was concerned. It was situated in a beautiful old house built in 1918 as the Craftsman era was gradually becoming the art deco era. The latent architect in him thoroughly enjoyed the beautiful woodwork and arched doorways that made the café a unique location.

The front yard had been landscaped to match the era of the house which included the addition of a small pond filled with the beautiful and fragrant flowers (although they weren't in bloom just yet) from whence the restaurant took its name. The water feature was surrounded by tables and chairs scattered about the lawn. The whole thing created a comfortable environment Ted appreciated. That, and the belgian waffles for which the restaurant was famous.

Ted pushed away from the diminutive table, stretching out his long legs. The small bistro furniture in the garden wasn't designed for a man with a six-foot-three-inch frame.

He reached for the heavy mug containing his second cup of coffee and glanced at this wristwatch.

Jamie was late, not unusual for his department chair. That was okay. It gave Ted the chance to enjoy the landscaped neighborhood. It reminded him of the Pasadena area he'd visited a few weeks before.

In anticipation of the return of Susan Sullivan, the actress who owned the house they lived in, Ted had casually started looking at areas they might like to live. He was leaning toward Pasadena. It had always been a favorite with its old-growth trees and lovely vintage homes. He and Sara Jane went into an open house not long ago after seeing balloons and flags announcing the event.

The street was an old one with the great oaks creating a canopy overhead and jacarandas that would be blanketing the street in purple radiance in just a few short weeks. The house itself was set back on its lot, leaving a large expanse of lawn that was beautifully manicured. It was a Greene and Greene Craftsman, making it well out of his price range, but they stopped to see it anyway. It was a lovely house, and he decided then that he would try to find a smaller version.

Ted breathed in the flower-scented air and sipped his coffee while waiting for his old friend and boss.

His athletic build and full head of salt-and-pepper hair belied his sixty-plus years as Michael James Sullivan stepped out of the shadow of a crepe myrtle tree.

"Sorry, I'm late."

"No problem."

Jamie had been Ted's professor and mentor in medical school and continued to be one of his closest friends and now was his boss as well.

Jamie smiled as he sat. "You look like something the cat dragged in."

"Thanks a lot. You look great too."

"What's wrong?"

Pulling himself upright in the small chair, Ted said, "Haven't been sleeping too well, I guess."

"Maybe you're still recovering from the earthquake. It shook up a lot of people."

Ted chuckled. "Shook up, huh?" He said. "Could be, I suppose. That is when it started."

"If there's anything I can do, let me know." After ordering coffee from the waiter refilling Ted's cup, Jamie picked up the menu. "What are you having?"

"Belgian waffle. Isn't that why we come here?"

Jamie grinned and ordered scrambled eggs with lox. "How's Sara Jane?"

"She's good. She went to Santa Monica today. Between the quake and volunteering with me the past couple of weeks, she needed a bit of a break. Mostly from me, I suspect."

"She's such a great kid."

"Yes she is. Wish I could take credit for it."

"You can. She is your daughter."

"Yes, but she's the way she is in spite of me, not because of me."

They sat quietly sipping coffee, seemingly enjoying the serenity of the garden and the occasional splash from the koi in the pond. Jamie broke the silence. "You're awfully pensive. What's up?" Ted glanced over the edge of his coffee mug but said nothing. Jamie tried again. "Have you seen Ann?"

Ted shook his head. "Not since that day in her office."

"Why?"

"I'm not sure. Guess I'm afraid of what her reaction will be. I caught her off guard that day, and I'm pretty sure that wouldn't work again. Besides, I can't just keep dropping by and pretending that it wasn't planned."

"You could just call her."

"If she doesn't ignore the caller ID, she'll find reasons to avoid seeing me. There's no real point."

"Well, if it's not Ann, what has you so preoccupied?"

Ted looked at his friend. "What do you know about dream interpretation?"

"Not much. Why?"

"I've been having strange recurring dreams all my life, but lately they've been extraordinarily intense. I don't think I'm getting much rest."

"You said dreams. How many are there?"

"Two."

"How strange are they?"

"The dreams themselves aren't particularly strange, but I'm not in them. I'm connected to the men in them, but I don't know how or why."

"What do you mean, connected?"

"I'm not sure. It's like I'm drawn into them. I can feel the anger and pain, the love and fear, but at the same time I'm just a spectator. When I couldn't get back to sleep last night, I got up and did some research on the Internet and found a lot of stuff on dream interpretation, but it's only what they mean when you're in them. I couldn't find anything about a dreamer not being in the dreams."

"I've never heard of anything like that." He watched Ted for a moment. "There's more to it than just a dream. What's going on?" When Ted shrugged the question off, Jamie tried again. "How do the two dreams differ?"

"One is about a young couple on a sailing ship that appears to be the late eighteenth or early nineteenth century, and the other seems to take place in a courtroom in the seventeenth century. But the thing that's bothering me about them is how they make me feel. They're really intense, very emotional."

Jamie thought a moment. "Is Ann in any of them?"

"No. I don't know any of the people. Why?"

"You saw her again about the same time the dreams started, right?"

"Yeah, but all the people in the dreams are strangers. Besides, I've been having the dreams all my life."

Jamie thought a few moments. "You know, dreams are a kind of specialty of Tom Alderman's. I bet he'd have an idea what they mean."

"That's an interesting thought. I might talk to him."

Chapter Fourteen

Saturday, May 10

March comes in like a lion and goes out like a lamb. The old idiom certainly held true this year, not so much in regards to the weather, which was the original meaning of the phrase. But the earthquake felt very lionlike, with the rest of the month being quite mild in all respects, like a lamb. April had been warm and cool by turns, but May so far had been filled with warm days and cool evenings, the kind of weather that made people move to Southern California. The temperature today was supposed to reach the mid-80s, which made it perfect weather for the dinner party Ann was planning, just a few friends to kick off the patio season.

The butterflied leg of lamb was already in the refrigerator, marinating in red wine, olive oil, garlic, rosemary, and mint. The heat of the grill would make all the flavors meld together perfectly. She'd made a trip to the local farmers market to get freshly picked vegetables and fruit. She'd drive into Old Town to get the finishing touches. She needed french vanilla ice cream to go with the pie she made, as well as Yukon Gold potatoes and Maui onions. She'd found a recipe for potato galette that looked absolutely wonderful in the pictures, thin slices of crispy potato and onion browned in butter and duck fat and baked in a spring mold. A recipe with butter *and* duck fat was not for the faint of heart, but she had no doubt that it would taste fabulous. For those who were more interested in what was good for them and not what tasted good, she would have brown rice too. The thought of rendering the duck fat herself lasted for about a half a second, so she'd gone online to find out if she could buy it and where. Luckily for her, Sur la Table in Old Town had it.

The potatoes and onions were in the trunk of her car, now parked in a municipal lot, and tucked in the handled shopping bag she carried was a jar of pure duck fat and a small mandolin so the potatoes and onions could be sliced very thin and evenly as the recipe suggested. She'd wanted a mandolin for a long time, but most of them were so expensive that every time she'd seriously considered buying one she questioned how often she'd actually use it so had never bothered to get one. This was a small and relatively inexpensive tool, so she indulged herself and bought it.

Old Town Pasadena was a nice place to shop even if most of the stores were the same ones that populated upscale malls. Ann disliked enclosed malls because she enjoyed walking outside when going from store to store. She was on her way to her car when she heard someone call her name. In a small sidewalk café, the young woman with whom she'd struck up a conversation at the Santa Monica pier a couple of months before was waving at her.

She stopped at the small table. "Sara, isn't it?"

"Yeah! I'm waiting for my dad. He's in the bookstore across the street. Want to join me?"

"I'd like that." Ann sat down.

"How come you're out here and not in the bookstore? Don't you like to read?"

"I have a Kindle."

"I love the tactile experience of a real book."

"Real books are heavy. With the Kindle, I can have lots of books but not the weight. Recently, though, I've gotten into audiobooks."

"I've never tried one. It always seemed as though it would be boring."

"Not for me. One of my favorite things when I was little was Daddy reading to me. When I was really little, I would sit on his lap. When I got older I would sit next to him, and he would put his arm around me and read. I felt so safe and warm. It's still my favorite place to be, next to him with his arm around me." She sipped her raspberry lemonade. "When I listen to audiobooks, it's like having Daddy reading to me again, and it's comforting."

Ann smiled. "Sounds like your father is a pretty special guy."

"He is."

Ann ordered a raspberry iced tea from a passing waiter.

"You were looking for a house when we met. Have you found one?"

"I think we may have. We looked at this really awesome house today in an area called 'Bungalow Heaven.' Have you ever heard of it?"

"Indeed, I have. It's where I live."

"How cool is that?"

"Pretty cool."

"It's a Craftsman-style like Daddy wanted. It has a pool and Jacuzzi, and the whole attic has been turned into one big room with a huge closet and built-in shelves and drawers and an absolutely awesome bathroom. If we buy the house, the attic will be my room."

"Sounds wonderful." She took a business card out of her purse and wrote her cell and landline phone numbers and home address on the back. "If you do move there, we'll be neighbors, so you'll have to come over for a visit."

Taking the card, Sara said, "Thank you, I will."

"Do you have plans for the summer?"

"I'm doing a theoretical physics class in summer school to try to get it out of the way and will probably spend a couple of weeks with my mother."

"Oh, your parents aren't together?"

"Not for ages. I see her once a year, usually in the summer. She lives in Chicago and travels a lot for her job, so sometimes even when we have plans they get shelved at the last minute. I'll just have to wait and see. Other than that, nothing special."

Sara raised her hand in a wave, and Ann turned assuming it was the girl's father. The women were very surprised when they both said "Uncle Jamie" at the same time. As the man approached the table, Sara explained, "Jamie is one of my dad's best friends."

Ann smiled. "It really is a small world. Jamie is my mother's brother."

Jamie looked at the two women with more than a little surprise on his face. He hugged Ann, then said, "Sara Jane," and hugged her.

Exasperated, she said, "It's just Sara."

"Sorry, forgot." He turned to Ann. "Sara Jane is actually her name."

"Yeah, but I prefer Sara."

Ann asked, "Was your mother a fan of *Gone with the Wind*?"

"I don't know. Why?"

"Sarah Jane Hamilton was Aunt Pittypat's name."

Changing the subject, Jamie asked, "How do you two know each other?"

Sara offered, "We met a couple of months ago at the Santa Monica Pier."

Ann continued the explanation. "And just ran into each other again. She's waiting for her father to come out of the bookstore. They've been looking at houses to buy in 'Bungalow Heaven.' How's that for a coincidence?"

Jamie smiled but didn't comment, just said that he was meeting Maura and some friends for lunch so needed to be off.

Before he left, he hugged Ann again and said, "I know you don't believe in fate, but you may want to rethink that."

"What does that mean? Why so cryptic?"

With a broad smile, he said, "You'll find out soon enough. Good afternoon, ladies."

Ann and Sara looked at each other as Jamie walked away.

Sara asked, "What was that about?"

"I have no idea."

Sara shrugged. "Whatever." Glancing at Ann's shopping bag, she said, "That's one of my favorite stores."

"Sur la Table is one of your one favorite stores? Not The Limited or Forever 21?"

"I'm not really a clothes person, but I love to cook."

"A kindred spirit."

"What did you get?"

"Well, I'm trying a new recipe for a dinner party tonight, potato galette. Thinly sliced potatoes and onions baked in butter and duck fat. I bought a jar of duck fat and a mandolin."

"I didn't know they sold duck fat in a jar. I read somewhere that if you add a couple of tablespoons to pie crust it makes it extra flaky. When I read that I wondered what it would do in biscuits. Is the dinner party for a special occasion?"

"No. I love to cook too and entertain. Tonight is the first of what I call my 'patio dinners.' I do them off and on all summer."

"Does that mean you barbeque or just eat on the patio?"

"Generally both. Tonight I'm grilling a leg of lamb."

"Whoa. Lamb and crispy potatoes. Sounds wonderful."

"And fresh asparagus. I wish I'd seen that article on duck fat and pie crust. I've already made a rustic plum pie for dessert."

"A la mode?"

"Of course, but I also made what I call crème brûlée sauce. It's made with cream, butter, and egg."

"Sounds yummy. I love vanilla custard."

"You and your father are welcome tonight if you'd like to come. There will be more than enough food."

"Seriously?"

"Yes."

"That's awesome, but I don't know if Dad has plans."

"You can come alone if you'd like. I just wanted to extend the invitation to both of you."

"Hey, we can ask him right now."

Ann turned and saw Ted coming toward them. There was a stilted silence when he reached the table. Sara did not immediately pick up on the tension so introduced them.

"Dad, this is Ann. The lady I told you about, who I met on the pier. Remember, the one who rides bicycles long distances?"

He stared at her. Sara cleared her throat, so he finally said, "Yes, I remember." He still had not taken his eyes off Ann so added, "Hello."

A blush colored her cheeks, and she almost whispered, "Hello."

Excitedly, Sara said, "Ann lives in 'Bungalow Heaven.' Can you believe it? And she's invited us to dinner at her house tonight. She's making an awesome dinner. Lamb, your favorite."

"Yeah, it's Ann's favorite too."

Sara looked at Ann quizzically. "It is?"

Grateful for the chance to shift her gaze from Ted to Sara she said, "Yes."

"How did you know that, Dad?"

He hesitated, so Ann answered, "We went to medical school together."

"You know each other?"

Her father finally responded, "We do."

"You're right, Ann. It is a small world. Can we go, Dad?"

Trying desperately to maintain a modicum of normalcy, he turned his attention to his daughter. "I thought you were going to the movies with Tanya and Clara."

"We didn't make any definite plans. We were just talking about it. They want to see the newest Superman movie, and I'm not really that interested in it. So can we go? Please."

"We'll talk about it later, honey."

Ann stood up. "Well, I need to get home to get this 'awesome' dinner started." She turned to Sara. "You have my numbers, let me know what you guys decide so I know how many places to set."

Ann smiled a farewell to Sara and nodded to Ted, then walked away. Ted's heart was racing, so he took a deep breath to calm it. Sara looked at Ann as she walked away then at her father. Something strange had happened, but she had no idea what.

Chapter Fifteen

Ted was more than glad that the car was parked nearby so it only took a few minutes for them to reach the vehicle. He slipped in behind the wheel.

"I thought you were going to let me drive home."

"Maybe next time, kid."

"I'll drive to Ann's tonight."

"You have to have a licensed driver with you."

"You'll be with me."

There was a very long pause before he answered, "Sure, I'll drop you off."

"But she invited you."

"She was just being polite because I was standing there. She invited you, and you should go, but believe me, she'll prefer it if I'm not there."

"But the invitation was for both of us."

"The invitation was extended before she knew that I'm your father."

"I thought so."

"What did you think?"

"The way you looked at each other, I could tell you were more than just classmates. So what happened between you two?"

"It's a long story, honey."

Sara Jane still held Ann's business card in her hand. She read it. "Her name is Antoinette."

Quietly he said, "Toni."

"What?"

"Toni. She used to go by Toni but decided that Ann was more professional."

"Is she the Toni you were living with during the big earthquake you told me about?"

He glanced over at her. "You have much too good a memory."

"So, she is."

"Yes, she is."

They were quiet for a bit. Sara Jane broke the silence, "There's no real reason for me to go."

"Except that you like her and want to go."

"Yeah, but if you don't go, I won't know anybody else, and everyone will be old."

He smiled. "Like me?"

"You know what I mean."

"Well, for what it's worth, Tom, Toni's brother—sorry, Ann's brother. Tom has two boys who are probably fourteen and sixteen now. I'm sure they'll be there."

"Oh. You don't mind if I go? I don't want it to hurt your feelings."

"No. If you want to go, it's fine with me."

Ann found Sara doing dishes when she took the serving platter into the kitchen.

"You don't have to do that."

"I know, but you did all the cooking, so it only seems fair. It's how Dad and I do it. The one who doesn't cook has to clean up."

"Your father cooks?"

"After the divorce, he had to. Josh was four, and I was only two."

"Well, it's very nice of you." She picked up a towel and started drying the silver and serving pieces that Sara had already washed.

"Don't you want to be with your guests?"

"They're having such a good time gossiping about the folks who didn't come that I doubt I'll be missed. Besides, you're a guest too. So how did you get on with Noah and Jacob?"

"They're really nice."

"Sorry they left so early. They're both competitive swimmers and train early in the morning."

"My brother was a swimmer too."

"He isn't anymore?"

"Josh died in a car accident eight years ago."

"I'm so sorry."

"I guess that isn't right, he didn't actually die in the accident."

"Actually?"

"He was barely hanging on when they got to the hospital."

Her stomach tightened at the thought that Ted might have been injured. "They?"

"He was with another team member and his mother. They were pronounced dead in the emergency room." Sara took a deep breath before continuing, "Josh was declared brain-dead the next day."

"I can't even imagine that."

"I think it was hardest on Dad because he made the decision to turn off the machines."

"What about your mother?"

"Mom was on a business trip and didn't get there till later."

"So your father had custody of both of you?"

"Yes. We were so young when they divorced that I don't remember ever living with both of them. Anyway, by the time Mom got there, Dad had made the decision and signed the papers. He waited for her to do it, but she's still angry. She didn't want him to stop the machines."

She looked over at Ann with tears in her eyes. Ann had already said she was sorry and could think of nothing else to say. She wrapped the teenager in a tight embrace.

Sara stepped away and dried her eyes with her hands. "I'm sorry. I'm not being a very good guest."

"You're a great guest. Don't worry about it." Attempting to lighten the mood a bit, she added, "No one else is helping with the dishes."

While Sara rinsed the soapy water out of the sink, she asked Ann, "What happened between you and Dad?"

Ann thought a moment. "I guess it just wasn't meant to be." She continued to dry and put away dishes as she judiciously avoided eye contact with the young woman.

Sara knew that her father's "it's a long story" and Ann's "it wasn't meant to be" meant that neither of them would tell her so said only, "That's too bad."

Ann, unable to keep the sadness out of her voice, agreed. "Yes, it is."

Chapter Sixteen

Thursday, June 5

May gray turned into June gloom and brought with it a storm that had pounded Southern California with rain accompanied by thunder and lightning, a fairly unusual occurrence. Ted left the confines of his office and stepped out into the gray afternoon. Not one to discuss his personal problems with other people, he'd resisted talking to Tom Alderman as Jamie had suggested months ago, but the dreams had persisted. They attacked his sleep at night, and images from the dreams preyed on his mind during the day. He was unsure if talking with someone would help, but Sara Jane had seen the distress the dreams caused, so he could ignore it no longer. Besides, if he didn't do something, he would lose his mind.

The campus clock struck two as he pulled open the heavy bronze door of the century-old building. Finals were over, and the gloom of the storm filled the deserted hallway with a ghostly silence, the only counterpoint the squeaky soles of his shoes on the highly polished floors. The silly thought that he would be unable to sneak up on anyone lightened his strange mood.

The office door was ajar. Hesitantly, Ted rapped on the jamb. Tom looked up from his task. "Ted."

"Have you got a minute?"

"Sure. Come in, sit."

Ted thanked him as he sat in a comfortable side chair opposite Tom's desk.

"What's up?"

"Jamie tells me you do dream interpretations."

Tom smiled. "I guess you could say that. Most of our colleagues don't put much stock in it, including Jamie, and frankly, I'm surprised you're asking about it." He asked jovially, "So what are you doing in your dream? Running naked down the middle of the street? Making love in a hot-air balloon?"

Ted's wan smile made it clear that whatever was happening was serious. "Dreams come from the subconscious so can often help tell us what's troubling the patient." He leaned forward. "So tell me about the dream."

"There are two, I think."

"You think?"

"Sometimes it seems like two dreams that run together, and sometimes it's two distinct dreams."

"And they recur?"

"Yes."

Tom nodded. "So tell me about them."

Ted inhaled deeply, then blew it out. He began, "The first one appears to be the early nineteenth century aboard a sailing ship. A young married couple is traveling to the Caribbean. They have Scottish accents, so I assume they are sailing from Scotland. The wife is pregnant, and before they reach the islands she goes into labor and delivers a stillborn son. Then she dies."

"Are you the young groom?"

"No."

"Who are you in it?"

"No one. One of the really strange things about this is that I'm not in either of them. It's as though I'm looking in from outside and watching it all happen. I seem to have a strong connection to the young man in the one about the couple and one of the judges in the other, but I have no idea why. And even though I know what's going to happen, they still take an emotional toll. I feel the grief that young husband experiences as though a knife is being driven through my very soul."

"How often do you have the dreams?"

"Originally, it was once in a while, but now it's almost every night. Sometimes it's a shortened version, like a movie trailer."

"When did they start?"

"I've had them since I was a kid, but recently they've become extremely intense."

"You mentioned a second dream?"

"When they're combined, at the point when the young man is crying over his dead wife, the image starts to fade, but before it's completely gone, a new one starts to develop and ultimately takes over. Like a fade out and in, in a movie."

"Then what happens?"

"It seems to be a trial. In fact, I'm pretty sure it's the Salem witch trials. All I see is a room with two windows, one on each side wall. There are people sitting on benches. At the end of the room on a raised platform, three men are sitting at a table." He took a deep breath and continued.

The hem of her gray garment gently brushed the rough-hewn boards of the meeting-house floor. The only sounds in the room were the rustling clothes of the spectators, the whisper of the woman's shoes, and the jangle of her iron shackles. A few loose curls escaped her dust cap. Her apron and dress were dirty from the dirt floor of her dank, dreary cell. She held her head high as she made her way slowly down the length of the aisle, finally coming to stand in front of her accusers and judges. Refusing to be intimidated by the men who held her life in their hands, she looked each one squarely in the eyes.

One of the men, all of whom appeared to be judges, raised his voice and said, "You are now in the hands of Authority. Tell me now why you hurt these persons."

"I did not."

He repeated sternly, "Tell me why you hurt these people."

"I am an innocent person. I am a gospel woman."

"You have engaged you will not confess, but God knows."

"So he doth."

"Will you not renounce Satan?"

"I have never accepted Satan, therefore cannot renounce him."

"I find you will own nothing without several witnesses, and yet you will deny all."

"I know nothing of any of it."

"Will you not confess?"

"I have nothing to confess except my love of God."

Angrily the judge raised his voice. "This will not do. You cannot continue to defy this Authority as you do."

After several more hours of examination, the woman was weary, her arms heavy with the iron restraints. Refusing to let them see her fatigue, she forced her head up and stiffened her back. Frustrated by the woman's contrary and argumentative testimony, the judge ordered that she be returned to her cell. On his command, she was unceremoniously rushed out of the room between two burly men.

In her cell, the bonds still heavy on her arms, the woman fell to her knees and prayed, beseeching the Lord God first to make the judges see the error of their way so that no more of the innocent should be found guilty and put to death, and secondly, to make her strong, to help her through the trial and empower her to accept the coming verdict which she knew in her heart would be guilty. Her last walk would be to Gallows Hill.

She covered her face with her hands as the bitter tears turned to uncontrollable sobs.

"Considering the subject of the trial, I think you're right about it being the Salem witch trials." Tom queried, "You aren't in that dream either?"

"No, but the anger I feel from one of the judges is so intense that when I wake up my fists and jaw are clenched." His shoulders sagged as he unclenched his fists. "What do they mean, Tom? What does it mean that I'm not in them? Why is this happening?"

"From what you're telling me, I think the dreams are memories."

"Memories of what? I didn't live in the seventeenth, eighteenth, or nineteenth centuries."

"Perhaps, you did. I believe they're memories of past lives."

Chapter Seventeen

Coming through the front door, Ted asked, "What are you squinting at, sweetie?"

Sara Jane was on the couch, her computer on her lap. She glanced up at her father, her eyes slightly glazed over. "Studying for a calculus final and everything is kind of merging into a blob."

"Calculus? I didn't take that until college."

She smiled at him. "I guess it was easier to get into good schools in the olden days."

"You're right, it was much easier. I only had to compete with dinosaurs." He met her smile. "Perhaps you need a break."

She closed the lid of the computer. "Thanks, I needed that."

"Needed what?"

"Permission to stop."

"Permission has been granted." He kissed the top of her head. "You're nuts, you know."

Her grin was a bit lopsided and her eyes bleary. "Isn't insanity inherited?"

"Very funny." He ruffled her hair. "How do you feel about going out tonight? I've been in the mood for prime rib."

"Sounds really good, particularly the going out part." She moved her computer and books to a nearby table. "Can we go to Outback? I feel like a Bloomin' Onion." When he didn't answer, she looked up at him. He was staring at the wall. "What's going on with you, Dad?"

Her question jolted him out of his daze. "Nothing's going on with me."

"You've been acting strange lately. I thought maybe it was because you saw Ann, but it really started right after the earthquake."

He considered telling her their meeting in the café wasn't the first time he'd seen Ann but didn't really see the point, and it would raise even more questions he didn't care to answer.

"It's nothing really, just that weird dream I told you about. It keeps recurring, and I don't know why or what it means."

"My psychology teacher said a dream that you're not in is a memory."

He was surprised by the statement, and now wondered if Tom Alderman was right. But for Sara Jane he said, "Pretty sure that's not the case. The dream seems to be more than 200 years ago. I'm old, but I'm not that old."

Sara giggled and got up, yawning and stretching. "So can we go to the Outback?"

"Sure, kid."

In the car, Sara Jane suggested they go to Pasadena for dinner.

"Burbank's closer."

"Yeah, but since you don't want to live in Ann's neighborhood, we can drive around and maybe find another area with the crafty houses you like so much."

"Craftsman, not crafty."

"Whatever."

"All right, Pasadena it is."

After dinner, Ted pulled into a parking lot Sara Jane didn't immediately recognize. "What's this?"

"Vroman's"

"That's a bookstore."

"I know."

"I don't want to go to a bookstore."

"Hey, we went to the Outback because you wanted onions. We came to Pasadena because you wanted to drive around looking at houses. Now I want to go to the bookstore. It won't kill you to look at a few books. But if you're that opposed, stay in the car." He got out of the vehicle.

She heaved a sigh and got out too.

While Sara Jane sulked in the gift-book section, Ted moved among the shelves and rows of books in an attempt to surreptitiously find information on past lives and reincarnation. Most were new-agey trash, but one got his attention. He was thumbing through it when Sara Jane rushed up to him.

"Daddy, look at this. It's so cool."

He hurriedly closed and hid the book on reincarnation and looked at the purple book in his daughter's hands. In what was supposed to be someone's handwriting it said *Fairyopolis - A Flower Fairies' Journal.*

"Isn't it amazing? It's a journal supposedly written by a woman who was documenting the activities of the fairies in her garden. It's like a scrapbook with stuff in it."

He slipped his book back onto the shelf and looked at the fairy book more carefully.

Sara Jane continued enthusiastically, "See, there's a library card and a map of her town. There's a train ticket and something called fairy dust." She looked up at her father. "Can we get it? Please."

"Yes, dear, we can get it."

She held the book to her chest. "Thank you."

Sara Jane reached for her tea, being careful not to spill it on her new book. She was reading all the handwritten entries of the fictitious journal, spending extra time on the scrapbook-like additions.

Her father joined her on the couch while she was reading a small booklet inside the journal called "A Field Guide to Fairies."

"It says here, 'a fairy is a tiny being in human form that possesses magical powers.'" Sara Jane looked at her father. "It also says that fairy comes from the French word that means fate. Interesting, huh?" She moved the book so he could see it too. "It tells about flower fairies, elves, pixies, goblins, and gnomes."

From a small envelope inside the book, Sara withdrew a card purporting to contain a fairy wing. "Isn't this cute? She wrote that it's really fragile."

He smiled. "It's charming. This, my dear, is why you need to go to bookstores with me more often. You never would have been able to put this on your Kindle or iPod."

"Yeah. I've never seen anything like it."

"'Cause you always fight with me about going into bookstores."

She giggled. "Well, I won't next time." She took a sip of her tea. "Ann would love this book."

"What makes you think so?"

"She has a fairy house in her garden. It has miniature furniture, dishes, and books in it. It's very cute."

Ted's only response was "Hmm." He drank the last of his coffee. "Are you going to do any more studying tonight?"

She sighed. "I don't think so."

Ted yawned as the end credits rolled for a television movie about the murder of Amish school children. Sara Jane's left elbow was propped on the arm of the couch, her index finger resting on her lips. She was staring down, at what, Ted couldn't tell.

"What's up?" He got no response. "Sara Jane?"

Slowly she turned toward him, her eyes brimming with tears. He reached over and put his arm around her shoulders, pulling her close to him. She laid her head against him.

"What's the matter, baby?"

"Sometimes I miss Josh so much."

"I know. Me too." He leaned his cheek on the top of her head.

"Sometimes I see him. He'll be sitting next to me or across the table." She looked up at her father. "Pretty silly, huh?"

He squeezed her shoulder. "No. I imagine I see him sometimes too."

"If time heals all wounds, why does it still hurt so much?"

"Time doesn't heal the pain so much as lessens it. In time, the hurt isn't as intense or as frequent. I'm pretty sure it never goes away entirely."

They sat quietly, Sara Jane's head nestled against Ted's shoulder. "When did you start smoking again?"

"I haven't."

"Your shirt smells all smoky," she said, letting him know he was busted. "A couple of days after the earthquake I got up in the middle of the night, and you were on the deck smoking a cigar and drinking brandy."

"You saw me smoking?"

"I've seen you a couple of times."

"Why don't I remember that?"

"Maybe you were sleepwalking."

"Could be, I guess."

"Did you ever talk to Uncle Jamie about the dreams?"

"I mentioned them to him."

"Well, maybe you should mention the sleepwalking too."

He squeezed her again. "You're way too smart. Are you sure you're my progeny?"

She reached up and kissed his cheek. "No doubt about it. I have your nose." She sat up and smiled at him. "But maybe genius skips a generation."

He laughed. "That must be it."

Chapter Eighteen

Friday, June 13

Unlike earlier in the month, the June gloom had burned off, revealing a beautiful, sunny day. The campus hummed with end-of-the-year activities. Hammers clanged against nail heads, and drills whirred bolts as Ted and Jamie walked by the bleachers being dismantled after graduation.

"So you're still not sleeping. Are the dreams keeping you up?"

"I am sleeping, but the dreams seem to keep me from actually resting. When I wake up, it's as though I've been up all night."

"Did you talk with Tom Alderman?"

"Yeah." Ted laughed.

"Can I assume he didn't help?"

"He thinks the dreams are memories of past lives."

"You don't agree with him?"

"Past lives? I wasn't really expecting much help, but past lives? Come on."

"If you don't have another explanation, then how can you dismiss it out of hand?"

"Jamie, you're a psychiatrist. As a scientist, how can you even ask?"

"I've been around long enough to know that not everything is easily explained and that there's far more we don't understand than we do. You've been around long enough too."

"Yes, but reincarnation?"

"Millions of people the world over accept reincarnation as a fact of life."

"As part of a superstitious religious dogma, not real life."

"Religion is very much part of real life for the vast majority of people on the planet."

Ted's mind was reeling, and he wasn't even sure what to say. How was it possible that his friend and mentor believed he might be experiencing past lives, that he had been reincarnated?

"Okay, let's say you and Tom are right and the dreams are memories of past lives. How does that explain the blackouts?"

"Blackouts? You never said anything about blackouts."

"This time I've only had two, as far as I know, and they were only a couple of minutes each." He didn't bother to add that they both occurred when he was with Ann.

"This time? Ted this could be serious."

"I know, but it's not. There's no physical cause."

"How do you know?"

"I saw a neurologist. She ran every test under the sun. There's no tumor, no physical anomalies, nothing. In fact, she thinks it's stress related."

They sat on a nearby bench. Jamie asked, "The blackouts just started out of the blue?"

"No, not exactly."

"What do you mean, not exactly?"

"They've happened before." He could see the questions on Jamie's face so expounded without prompting. "When I was doing my residency, I'd experience small lapses in time. I'd be having a conversation with someone, and suddenly they'd be saying something that made no sense based on my last memory, or they'd ask a question that I couldn't answer because I didn't remember what we were talking about. A couple of times, I would be talking with someone and the next thing I knew, I was alone."

"You and Ann were living together then, right? What did she say about it?"

"I never told her. I assumed I was just overtired. She was finishing medical school and planning the wedding."

"I know. You didn't want to worry her."

Ted shrugged. "It happened again after Josh died, and grief seemed the logical explanation. Both times it only lasted a couple of months, so I didn't give it much thought."

"How is this time different?"

"The intensity of the dreams, mostly. Although I have no idea if they're connected to the time lapses." He stared at the grass, trying to decide how much to divulge, finally admitting, "Sara Jane says she's seen me smoking and drinking brandy in the middle of the night. Needless to say, I was stunned. I have no memory of it at all."

"I thought you stopped smoking."

"I did."

"I don't understand. Was Sara Jane seeing things?"

"I don't know. She thinks I'm sleepwalking."

"If you stopped smoking, where would you have gotten cigars?"

"That's the only easy answer in this mess. My folks took a Caribbean cruise last year, and Dad brought home a box of cigars. He left six with me, ostensibly to have on hand when they come to the house. I think he was secretly hoping I'd start again so he wouldn't be the only one smoking."

Jamie grinned. "Sounds like your father. Are any of them gone... the cigars?"

"I don't know. I didn't look. I figured Sara Jane was dreaming or something. It does make me wonder if the time lapses happen when I'm sleeping."

Jamie nodded. "Or maybe you're sleepwalking when you have the lapses."

"So, you think it's all related then: the dreams, sleepwalking, time lapses?"

"Yes, I do. It's just too coincidental not to be."

"Yeah."

The men got up and continued to walk, and Jamie asked, "What made you see a neurologist this time?"

"A combination of things really. I was hoping to refute Tom's assessment, and the dreams are driving me crazy, but mostly because Sara Jane is more than a little aware that something is wrong. Particularly now that she thinks I'm sleepwalking."

"Does she feel better now that you've seen a doctor?"

"I didn't tell her."

"Why?"

"There isn't really anything to tell her at this stage, and she's only sixteen years old. She shouldn't be worrying about me."

"So you're protecting her by not telling her the truth? Is that how you counsel your patients, lie?"

"It isn't a lie."

"At sixteen, she isn't a little girl anymore, and she's already worried. Besides, it's a lie of omission."

"Jamie, I need help with the situation, not a critique of my parenting skills."

"Or lack thereof." Jamie asked, "Do you have a theory?"

"I think I need to seriously consider the possibility of dissociative identity disorder."

Jamie laughed. "I think we can pretty much rule that out."

"Why?"

"Even documented cases of DID have several comorbidities. Can I assume you don't have a substance-abuse problem or seizures or any of the other medical or mental conditions associated with dissociative identity disorder?"

"So I'm told."

"What's left?"

His throat tightened, and he felt as though he might cry in frustration. Finding another bench, he sat down. "I'm scared, Jamie. What am I going to do?"

"Did Tom have any suggestions?"

"He thought that hypnotherapy might help." He scoffed. They sat quietly for a few moments. Then he admitted, "But I am considering it, for Sara Jane's sake."

"Does that mean you've looked into it?"

"I've done some research online, but that's it."

"Why is that it?"

"You know me, not the most trusting person in the world. Who would I go to for hypnosis?"

Jamie started to say something, but Ted stopped him. "I know, I know. That sounds ludicrous since I expect patients to trust me. And I can't explain it, but I just can't seem to let go with complete strangers. Does that make me a horrible therapist?"

His old friend smiled. "We aren't here to critique your therapy skills." He squinted in the bright sunlight. "I do have a suggestion you probably won't like, but I'm going to make it anyway." He hesitated slightly before offering, "Hypnotherapy is one of Ann's specialties."

Ted's head almost swiveled on his neck. "You don't expect me to get into all this with Ann, do you?"

"You're the one with trust issues, and you do trust her, don't you?"

He had to admit that even as angry as she still was, he would trust her with his life.

Ann stepped into the room and looked around. The strange feeling that she wasn't alone every time she was in Alex's office persisted. Why did she only feel it in this room? She looked into every corner just to be sure something wasn't lurking in the shadows, but she was alone. She shrugged.

It didn't really matter whether she turned it into a sewing room or not. She had to do something with it. She either had to get new brackets and rehang the shelving or she needed to take the uprights off the wall, which meant she would need to spackle the screw holes and paint. But then she never had liked the almost-red walls. Alex thought it was vibrant and fun, while she found it dark and foreboding. But it had been his office, so red it was. Now though, she could change it. Would changing it mean she had accepted that he would not return?

She sat down at the computer. Over the months since the earthquake, she had changed the screensaver several times, but it always came back to the black screen and the tumbling *forgive*. She had even downloaded new screensavers and installed them, but it made no difference. *Forgive* kept coming back.

The reincarnation websites still came up every time she turned on the computer too, even though the only reason she sat down at the old desktop (she had a new laptop and tablet) was to see if it would keep happening and was frustrated when every time it did.

Her thoughts went back to the possibility of a sewing room when the phone rang.

"Hi, Jamie."

"Hi, lovey. How're you doing?"

"Good. Just trying to decide what color to paint the office. So what can I do for you this bright, almost-summer day?"

"I have a huge favor."

"You know I'll do anything for you."

"I hope so, because Ted is going to call you, and I want you to see him."

"No!"

"You just said you'd do anything for me."

"Yeah, well, I didn't think it would be that."

"Just hear me out, please. He's having a pretty serious problem." Ann's throat tightened. "He's seen doctors who say it isn't physical, and one of the therapists here at school suggested hypnotherapy. You know Ted. He's grudgingly willing to give it a try, but it isn't going to work if he doesn't trust the therapist. That's where you come in. He trusts you."

"Yeah? Well, we know I can't trust him."

"Antoinette!"

Jamie, like her mother, always thought she overreacted to the incident, so she apologized. "Sorry."

"I've often wondered if you've stayed angry because you were afraid you'd forgive him if you didn't. And then you might fall in love with him again."

Unwilling to admit the possibility was true, she insisted, "That's ridiculous."

"Good. Then there's no reason you can't help him. You don't need to trust him. He needs to trust you."

"Maybe, but I don't want to get involved."

"So don't get involved. Just help him."

"If he wants my help, why isn't he the one who called?"

"Because he's sure you would ignore the caller ID if you saw it was him or refuse to help him if you did answer. So I'm trying to pave the way."

She had to admit that he was right. "And he's okay with this? I know how he feels about hypnosis. He thought it was stupid when I got interested in it at school."

"Well, I wouldn't go so far as to say he's okay with it, but he's willing to try because Sara Jane is very concerned about him and he wants to put her at ease."

Ann thought about it for a few moments. The part of her that wanted to run screaming from the situation was suddenly overcome by the part of her that wanted to see Ted again. Besides, maybe the "problem" had something to do with his odd behavior two of the times she'd seen him recently.

"Annie?"

Finally, she conceded. "All right, I'll see him... for Sara." After a slight hesitation, she added, "And you."

"Good. I'll tell him he can call."

Sara Jane was a lovely girl. Ted had done an amazing job rearing her. She wasn't really surprised. She'd always thought he'd make a great father, and obviously she'd been right. Sadness crept into her mood; they'd planned on having four children.

She pushed away from the desk, staring at the *forgive* that continued to bob on the screen. She looked down at her hands. She was twisting her wedding ring around her finger. Was the pain in the pit of her stomach guilt because she wanted to see Ted while she was still married to Alex? Was she still married to Alex?

Chapter Nineteen

Wednesday, June 18

Ann was miffed. After agreeing to see Ted, he hadn't bothered to call, so she was a bit surprised to find a message from him on her office voice mail. Ted said in his message that he assumed she would prefer to keep things on an entirely professional basis, so he hadn't wanted to disturb her at home. As much as she wanted to be angry at him, it was actually very thoughtful. She'd arranged her schedule so she could see him that afternoon and found that she was looking forward to it and was almost angry at herself for it.

This time the water feature in the lobby of Ann's building was working, and a gentle waterfall cascaded over resin rocks, splashing gently into a small pond and stream that wound its way around the atrium-like space. Ted stood and stared at the garden; the look and sound was very soothing. As mesmerizing as the scene was, he knew that he was actually using it as an excuse to delay going into her office. His stomach was in knots, and he wasn't sure if it was because he'd be seeing her or because he would now have to tell her what was happening, the thought of which embarrassed him. Both, he supposed. Delaying it wasn't going to make it any easier, so he took a deep breath and went to her door. It was closed this time, so he knocked.

"Come on in," he heard through the door. He greeted her as he entered the office.

She rose from behind her desk. He hadn't given any thought to how she might be dressed but was surprised that she was wearing a sun dress. Professional for Ann had always meant a suit, but the pale yellow sundress hugged her body, showing off her still-youthful figure, and accentuated her light olive complexion and dark hair. She looked amazing.

A smile brightened her beautiful face when she said, "Come over here and sit down." She went to the conversation area as she spoke. He thanked her and sat on the loveseat.

"Would you like tea?"

"Iced?"

"Hot tea is more relaxing."

"If you think tea will do the trick."

While she waited for the tea to brew, she turned and leaned against the sideboard. "The last time you were here, you said you'd call."

It wasn't a question, but he felt compelled to answer it. "I didn't think you'd actually want me to."

Not sure herself, all she said was, "Hmm," and went back to making the tea.

Did her asking mean she wanted him to call and was disappointed that he didn't? He considered asking but was afraid of what the real answer would be so dropped it.

"I know this is hard for you," she offered as she set the mug on the table in front of him.

"I'm sure you do. Unfortunately, you knowing doesn't make it any easier." He picked up the steaming china mug.

Inhaling the light orange and pungent spice of the tea, he tilted his head and smiled at her. "You remembered."

Ann's shy smile almost made him forget why he was there. "Of course." Looking away, she sat down. "I want to thank you for allowing Sara to come to dinner. I really enjoyed having her there. You've done an amazing job with her."

"I wish I could actually take credit, but she's just a great kid."

"She is, but she didn't get that way on her own. Don't sell yourself short."

He smiled at the compliment but said nothing.

"I'm really sorry about Josh. I can't imagine how horrible that must that been for you."

"It was a very dark time. As a matter of fact, it was the second time I experienced the blackouts."

"Blackouts?"

Confused, Ted said, "It's one of the things I'm experiencing. Didn't Jamie tell you?"

"No. He didn't tell me anything, just asked me to see you because someone suggested hypnosis as a possible remedy for what ails you."

"But nothing about what it is?"

"No."

"Well, I guess that's where we should start."

"You're having blackouts?"

"Well, they're really more like short lapses of time. They never seem to last more than a few minutes. Anyway, the story behind all this actually started when I was doing my residency."

After a rather lengthy explanation, Ted sighed. "Well, there you have it."

Ann was trying to process it all, past lives, reincarnation, dreams, blackouts.

Ted gave her a lopsided grin. "How you doing?"

"I'm not sure." She swallowed her own disbelief. "You believe all of it?"

"If you mean, do I believe in past lives and reincarnation, then no. But I've had every test there is, and they can't find anything physical. Jamie is certain that it isn't dissociative identity disorder because I don't have any of the usual maladies that accompany it. That said, I'm not left with much in the way of an explanation except for reincarnation."

"No, I guess not," she said absently.

"May I have more tea?"

She didn't seem to hear.

"Ann?" He got up, and the movement snapped her out of her own thoughts.

She looked up at him. "Are you leaving?"

"Just getting more tea."

"I'll do it." She took the mugs to the antique sideboard, and while waiting for the water in the electric pot to boil, she turned to him. "You said that the second time you had the blackouts was when Josh died. When was the first?"

He hesitated. He hadn't told her at the time because he hadn't wanted to seem weak, but there was no point avoiding it now. "When I was a resident."

"When we were together?"

"Yes."

Stunned by the revelation, she couldn't help but ask, "Why didn't you tell me?"

"I just assumed I was overworked. Besides, I didn't want you to think I was a wimp. You know, I wanted to be the 'big, strong' man, and at the time I didn't consider it particularly important. I was sure I could handle it myself."

She took a deep breath. "Physician, heal thyself?"

"Something like that."

It was so typical of him. "Did it last all during your residency?"

"No."

When he didn't continue, she prompted him. "So when did it stop?"

He looked down at his hands and nervously flicked his fingernails.

"Ted?"

He looked up at her and then looked away. "Not long after you left."

More than a little surprised, she was still able to ask, "Do you think it was something I did?"

"No, Toni, no."

Ann took a deep breath. She pushed the thought that she might have been the cause out of her mind. "The second time was after Josh died?"

"Yes. And like the first time, it was small bits of lost time which I assumed were caused by grief. It only lasted a few months, and then everything went back to normal."

"Are the dreams the only difference this time?"

"I've had the dreams most of my life, but the intensity of the dreams is part of what's different this time. There is one other thing that seems to be different. Apparently I'm sleepwalking. Sara Jane has seen me a couple of times in the middle of the night in the backyard, smoking a cigar, but I have absolutely no recollection of it."

"Maybe the time lapses happen during sleep as well."

"I hope that's all it is. I gave up cigars years ago."

"You said there isn't a physical cause. How do you know?"

"I saw a neurologist. Since she found nothing physical, she has attributed it all to stress." He looked at her over the edge of his mug, trying to read her mood but with no success. "It's far more intense this time, mostly because of the dreams, which are making me crazy. There are two, and I have them over and over."

"Tell me about them."

A second lengthy explanation followed. Ann could see that even talking about the dreams was disturbing to him.

She smiled at him. "Besides crazy, how do the dreams make you feel?"

After several moments of thought, Ted said, "The one with the young couple leaves me devastated. The grief is very real for me, as though the loss is mine. The other one is likely the Salem witch trials and makes me feel extremely angry. Rip-your-throat-out kind of angry. It's very disturbing."

"Because of the subject matter?"

"No, it's like I believe the woman is a witch, and I'm angry that she won't admit it." He drank some tea. "Sometimes I'm almost paralyzed with the anger and grief, so that I can't even force myself to get up. Other times I can't wait to jump out of bed just to end it all. It's ridiculous. I have no idea who these people are. Why are the dreams affecting me this way?"

"I assume that's a rhetorical question. Do the blackouts always coincide with the dreams?"

"No. The blackouts, as far as I know, are random, occasional, and sometimes last only moments. But the dreams are almost every night, and sometimes it feels like they go on forever."

"Do the sleepwalking incidents happen every time you have the dreams?"

"I don't think so. The only reason I know for sure it's happening is because Sara Jane's seen it."

"The only reason you know for sure? What does that mean?"

"I didn't realize I was smoking cigars, but I have noticed that my clothes sometimes smell of cigar smoke. I assumed I'd been somewhere people were smoking, and I just hadn't noticed." Ann sat staring at the table that separated them, saying nothing. "Ann?"

Slowly she raised her eyes to meet his. "You said one dream is the Salem witch trials?"

"I think so, why?"

"The day we saw each other at the Cravens, the Red Cross center, did you have a blackout?"

At the time, he never would have admitted it, but with all that had happened since, he saw no percentage in hiding anything. "Yes. How did you know?"

"First, tell me why you came the next day and apologized?"

"Well, I have to admit that part of it was simply because I wanted to see you." He smiled at her. "But the apology was because I'd seen fear on your face. I couldn't imagine what I'd done to cause it, but I knew I couldn't let it go."

Ann, astonished by his revelations, was bewildered by them at the same time. She took several deep breaths, her mind reeling.

"The other dream is about a young Scotsman on a ship?"

"Yes."

"You had a blackout the day you were here too, didn't you?"

Hesitantly, he said, "How do you know?"

She inhaled very deeply, then blew the breath out. "I think I've seen two of the people from your dreams. That day at the Cravens, you stormed into the room, accusing me of witchcraft. I knew something really strange was going on because I could see in your eyes when he left and you came back. Then the next day when you were here, you asked how you'd gotten over to the stairs from the chair. Do you remember?"

"Yes."

"You did it as the Scotsman who was on a ship in 1805. He said his name was Andrew Mcnaughton. Just like the day before, he suddenly disappeared and you were back."

"My God!"

"Yeah. If I hadn't seen it in your eyes, I would have assumed you were fooling around." She paused slightly. "Jamie said that Tom Alderman suggested hypnotherapy. Do you know why?"

"He said something about integrating the past lives into my subconscious. How is that for strange?"

"What I find really strange is that you seem to agree with him."

"I actually don't. But when I realized how concerned, almost fearful, Sara Jane was, I had to do something."

Ann's mind was suddenly flooded with all the information she'd seen on the websites about reincarnation, and images started flashing in her mind like a slide show. What was happening? She had been certain that the strange goings-on with Alex's computer were related to him. Was it possible they were somehow linked to Ted?

She chose her words carefully. "Tom may not be as far off as you think. Strange as it seems, reincarnation may be the most logical explanation."

"Did Jamie tell you he thought that too?"

"No, like I said, he didn't tell me anything."

"Do you think hypnotherapy will help?"

"I really don't know. Let me do some research and see if there is a technique of some kind."

"What do you mean, technique?"

"I've taken courses that teach age regression, but I only use it to help patients recapture childhood memories."

"You mean repressed memories?"

"No, no. I definitely don't buy into that. But often adults will dwell on the darker things that happened in their childhoods and allow it to color their entire lives. I use hypnotherapy to get them to remember the good things that happened in the past. Anyway, I'd like to be sure there isn't something special I need to do for past-life regression."

"How long do you think it might take? I haven't been getting much rest, and I'm not sure how much longer I can do this."

"I'll look into it this afternoon. I want to call Tom Alderman and maybe do a bit of online research. Can I call you this evening?"

"That would be great."

Ann sat quietly, twisting the ring on her left hand. Ted knew from the look on her face that whatever was on her mind was something serious, and that made him nervous. She looked up at him.

"There are a couple of things we need to discuss."

He nodded and held his breath.

"The idea of you being a patient is weird for me."

Relieved, he let the breath out. "Me too."

"So how do you want to deal with it?"

"I'd like to think we're still friends." When she said nothing, he continued. "So you're just helping out a friend."

When she still didn't respond he asked, "Does that work for you?"

She hadn't really paid much attention to what he was saying after she heard the word "friend." All she could think of was that he had once been her best friend, but now she didn't know what he was.

"Ann?"

She gave him a half smile and absently said, "Yeah, friends. Okay."

"You said a couple of things, what's the other one?" His question brought her mind back to the conversation.

"How much, if anything, do you want Sara to know?"

"She knows something strange is happening to me. What do you think?"

"I'm not a parent, but as a family counselor I'd say to at least tell her what we think and what we plan to do. The more she knows, the less she'll worry."

"Of course, my reaction is not to tell her anything, to protect her from all of it. But you're probably right about her worrying." He stood to go. "I look forward to hearing from you." At the door he looked back at her. "Can you believe all this is happening?"

She smiled. "Well, you never did do anything halfway."

Chapter Twenty

Sara Jane trudged into the house and dropped her backpack on the floor near the door, then collapsed onto the couch next to her father.

"Do I have to go to summer school?"

"I thought you wanted to get theoretical physics out of the way."

"I did, but it's only been a week and I feel like I've been in school all year. I'm tired."

"Honey, you are the overachiever in the family. I'd be happy if you spent the summer at the beach. You should be doing what sixteen-year-olds do. Surf, shop, go to parties."

"Yeah, but I want to get into to a really good college."

"Baby, you get straight As, you've won every academic award out there plus awards for community service, and you still have two years to add to all that. You're going to get into every university you apply to, so spend the summer having fun. Don't throw this time away. You only get to be a kid once, and you need to enjoy it."

"So you don't mind if I drop the class? I mean you did pay for it."

"It's just money. If you don't want to finish the class, don't finish it."

She threw her arms around his neck and kissed his cheek. "Thank you, thank you."

He hugged her in response. "Hey, kid, we have a dinner invitation. Feel like going out?"

She leaned back and looked at her father. "Is Mom in town?"

"Not as far as I know."

"Then who, where?"

"Ann has invited us to her house."

"Both of us?"

"Yes."

"And you're willing to go?"

"Yes."

"Why suddenly are you willing to go when you wouldn't last time?"

"Things change. So do you want to go?"

"Of course. I really like her, and she's a great cook. Should I make dessert to take?"

"If you'd like. She says we're welcome any time after five, although she's planning dinner at seven."

"This is so cool. I knew you guys still liked each other." She jumped up and headed to the kitchen, not giving him the opportunity to deny it, and added, "You'll love her house."

Sara got up and started to gather the dishes. "Should I put on a pot of coffee?"

"As your hostess, I really should do that."

"It doesn't matter who makes the coffee, does it?"

Ted glanced at Ann with a raised eyebrow and a slight tip of his head.

Ann sighed. "Okay, as long as you don't mind."

Sara almost skipped into the house, Gigi following close behind. Ted and Ann continued to sip their wine.

"She's quite a girl."

"Yes, she is. She's going to be off to college soon, and boy am I dreading that. I can't imagine her not being in the house."

"Maybe she'll go to school locally. There are a lot of good schools here."

"Yeah, but she's looking at Yale, Princeton, Columbia, even Trinity in Dublin. Ireland. She can't get much farther away than that."

"You do have to let go eventually."

"Just not ready yet."

"Lucky you don't have to yet."

"So when are we going to talk with her?"

"Since she made it, I thought we'd wait until after dessert, when we're all relaxed and calm."

"As relaxed and calm as I ever am these days."

A warm smile spread across her face. "I'm really sorry you're going through this."

"Thank you." With a raised eyebrow, he said, "But I would have thought you'd be thrilled."

She wasn't proud of the fact, but admitted, "I might have been if I hadn't seen how much pain you're in because of it."

Ted broke the slightly awkward silence that fell over them. "Jamie said you were widowed." He reached over and squeezed her hand. "I was sorry to hear that."

"I'm not sure I am widowed."

"What do you mean?"

"Alex was a pilot, private pilot. He went flying one day on a search-and-rescue mission and didn't come back. They've never found the plane or him. His Civil Air Patrol unit goes out every year after the first thaw, but they've never found anything."

"How long has it been?"

"Six years."

"How long were you married?"

"Four years."

"Oh." He assumed she'd gotten married shortly after they broke up, perhaps because he did. In fact, he married less than six months after their breakup.

"That was kind of an odd 'oh.' Was there a deeper meaning in it?"

"More surprise than meaning. I assumed you got married a long time ago."

"It feels like a long time ago."

Ted felt her grief. "I can only imagine how difficult it is to grieve when you don't know what happened." Under his breath, "It's hard enough when you do know."

"It has been hard. Still not sure I'm ready to let go entirely, and not having a grave or ashes or anything makes it harder. Daddy says that funerals are for the living so they can see that it's real, that the end arrived, but I haven't had that."

Ted reached across the space separating them and held her hand. "If there's any way I can help, tell me. I'll do anything."

His hand sent a small electric charge through her body, so she quickly withdrew it, awkwardly trying to find something to do with it. She finally allowed her hand to drop into her lap. "Thanks, I appreciate that." Changing the subject, she said, "Sara's been gone a while."

"I'm guessing she put the coffee on and then did the dishes."

Ann jumped up. "I don't want her to feel like she has to do that."

Ted stood just as quickly. He put his hand on her arm to stop her from going into the house. "Don't."

"Why?"

"It's something we do, and she's fine."

"I know. She told me that whoever doesn't cook does the dishes, but she's a guest here and I should be doing the dishes." She took a step, but Ted did not relinquish his grip.

"What you're really doing is trying to get away."

She looked into his eyes, unable to deny it. She took a deep, shuddering breath and dropped into the chair again with Ted sitting opposite her.

"I'm sorry if I upset you. It wasn't my intent, but I don't want you ever to feel the need to run away from me." With a slightly amused look on his face, he said, "Seems like I've been apologizing to you a lot lately."

Her emotions were roiling, but she managed to say, "You don't need to be sorry for anything."

Ted had hoped he'd have the opportunity to broach the subject of their breakup, but before he had the chance, Sara Jane came out with two steaming cups of coffee. She set the tray with cream and sugar on the table and sat down. Gigi lay down at her feet.

Her father asked, "The dishes all done, sweetie?"

"Yep."

Ann felt awful. "Thank you so much, but it wasn't necessary."

"Maybe not, but I figured you two might have things to say that you wouldn't if I was sitting here."

Ted looked at Ann and shook his head. "You are way too smart, my dear."

Sensing the tension between them she said, "I guess I was wrong, though."

Unable to look at either of them, Ann almost whispered, "Not really." Wanting to change the awkward atmosphere, she asked, "So when do we get the fabulous dessert?"

"I like to wait a bit after dinner to have dessert, but we can do it now if you want."

"Later is fine with me."

After partaking of the sticky toffee pudding Sara made for dessert, Ann was surprised to discover that the young woman planned to be a research scientist and not a chef. The warm brown sugar and butter sauce drizzled over the pudding and topped with a dollop of sweetened whipped cream made her baby back ribs pale in comparison.

"I think you're missing your calling, not becoming a chef."

"No, cooking is just a hobby. I love it, but would never want to have to make a living at it. It wouldn't be any fun then."

Ann laughed. "I know just what you mean. People are always telling me I should open a bakery, but if I *had* to do it, I wouldn't enjoy it anymore."

Ted scraped the last bit of sauce off of the plate and leaned back in his chair. Ann had refilled their coffee, which he sipped as he watched the two women finish their pudding. He felt a pang of regret seeing them sitting together, regret that Ann was not Sara Jane's mother.

The thought evaporated when he heard Ann say, "Sara, your father and I need to talk to you about something."

Sara's face lit up, and she rushed to say, "You and Dad are going to try to make a go of it again?"

"Sara Jane!" her father almost yelled. He took a deep breath. "Let Ann talk."

"Sorry. I was just hoping."

Ann tried again. "This has nothing to do with us as a couple."

"You're a couple?"

"Sara Jane, please."

Ann took a deep breath. "How much do you know about what your father is experiencing now?"

Sara looked at both of them and quizzically said, "You mean the dreams?"

"That's part of it. It actually started twenty years ago." She hesitated. "When your father was doing his residency, he had short lapses in time that he attributed to overwork."

Sara looked over at her father. "Are you okay now?"

"Well, honey, that's kind of why we're here."

Ann continued. "Along with the recurring dreams he's having now, he's also having similar lapses in time."

Sara Jane's voice started to sound anxious. "What do you mean, lapses in time? You mean like fainting?"

"No. I don't lose consciousness."

"I don't understand."

Ted was quick to answer. "Occasionally I'll find that several minutes have passed, but I have no memory of it. Other times, I'll lose track in the middle of a conversation I'm having with someone." He paused seeing the concern on his daughter's face. "It's nothing serious, but when the dreams got so intense, I decided I needed to do something about them since I'm not sleeping well, and we think the blackouts and dreams may be linked somehow."

Sara went over to her father and wrapped her arms around his neck. "Daddy, I'm so sorry. Are you sure it's not serious? Maybe you should see a doctor."

Ted tried to calm her. "I did, sweetheart. I saw a neurologist who ran every test imaginable—MRI, PET scan,

CT scan, everything. There were no anomalies, no abnormalities. Nothing physical that can explain what's happening."

Still kneeling next to his chair, with her arms around him and his around her, Sara Jane became alarmed by the information. She stood up and stepped away from him. "You had a bunch of tests and didn't tell me? What if they'd found something? Were you just going to spring it on me?" She stood with her hands on her hips. "Why didn't you tell me? Don't you trust me?"

Ann got up and gently put an arm around the girl's shoulder. "It has nothing to do with trust. It has to do with the fact that he didn't want you worrying about him if there was no reason to worry."

Sara shrugged Ann's arm off of her shoulder. "Well, I'm not a baby, and you shouldn't treat me like one."

Ann took Sara's shoulders in her hands and guided her to sit. "You need to calm down. We're trying to tell you what's going on."

To her father, Sara said, "I just don't understand why you didn't tell me before."

Ann answered before Ted could. "Your father needs to be in total control of himself at all times, and this situation makes him feel completely out of control. Something that is very hard for him to deal with."

"What situation?"

"The dreams, time lapses, and sleepwalking."

"What does the sleepwalking have to do with it? A lot of people sleepwalk."

"Yes, but we think they're all connected."

"How?"

"We don't know, but it all started about the same time."

"After the earthquake."

"Yes."

In a rather snippy tone, the teenager asked, "What is it you're going to do to help if you don't know what's happening?"

"Sara Jane, you're a guest here!"

Ann reached over and squeezed Ted's hand. "It's okay. Sara, our intent here is to tell you as much as we know, so here goes. One of your father's colleagues believes that the dreams are memories of past lives, that your father has lived before as other people."

"My psychology teacher said that too. So does this mean you guys think Dad's been reincarnated?"

Ann smiled. "I wouldn't go that far, but we have decided it's worth delving into the possibility. Tom, your dad's colleague, thinks hypnosis is the best way to do that."

Ted offered, "It's one of Ann's specialties."

"How is it supposed to help?"

Ann shook her head. "I'm not really sure."

Angrily, the young woman asked, "Then how can you say it might help?"

"SARA JANE!"

Ann put her hand up to stop Ted from saying anything else. "Truth is, I've been asking myself that same question. At the moment, my plan is to talk with Tom Alderman and see why he thinks hypnotherapy will help. I tried to get in touch with him this afternoon, but he wasn't available. Since he's the one who suggested reincarnation as the cause and hypnosis as the cure, perhaps he can offer some insight into what we need to do and how I might be able to help."

Sara Jane looked at Ann and then at her father, finally saying, "None of this seems real."

"I'm with you there kid," Ted agreed.

Chapter Twenty-One

Thursday, June 19

The light, soothing scent of lavender filled the air of Ann's office and mingled with the pungent aroma of chamomile tea. The butterflies in her stomach were going nuts. Was he as nervous as she was? The leather of her desk chair was cool and soft as she leaned back and closed her eyes, breathing in the essence of lavender in an attempt to calm herself before he arrived. As she finally felt the tension leaving her body, she was startled by a knock on her office door. Her eyes popped open. "Come in," burst from her mouth as she jumped to her feet. So much for staying calm.

Ted, apprehensive, acknowledged her with a simple "Hi" as he closed the door behind him.

"You didn't have to knock."

"I didn't want to interrupt anything."

Gesturing to the conversation area, Ann asked, "Shall we sit over here?" At Ann's request, Ted sat in a Queen Anne wing chair. "It's a recliner, so you can relax."

"I'm not sure relaxation is a possibility." Before joining him, Ann locked the office door. Ted's face brightened with mischief. "Locking the door. Are you planning to make advances?"

Ann blushed a bright red. "I just don't want anyone barging in."

Unable to stop grinning, Ted's only response was a raised eyebrow and "Mm."

She hurried to the sideboard and with her back to him asked if he wanted tea. He said yes. While she continued her preparations, a slightly awkward silence fell over the room, broken after a few minutes by Ted.

"Is that lavender I smell?"

"Yes. It has calming properties." She turned holding two china mugs.

"Calming properties, huh?" He gave her a roguish smile. "Apparently you didn't see the study that men find the fragrance of lavender and the aroma of pumpkin pie arousing."

Once again a blush rose in Ann's cheeks, and she imagined a far deeper red than she would have liked as she placed the mugs on the table separating them, then sat on the loveseat.

Ted reached for the delicate vessel and brought it to his lips, inhaling the fragrance of the brew. The mischievousness danced across his features. "Good thing it's not Constant Comment."

"Why?"

"It has the same spices as pumpkin pie. Who knows what that might have done to me."

As her face flushed for a third time in a matter of minutes, she pleaded, "Would you please stop? You're making me blush."

His smile went from playful to warm. "I see that. It's quite fetching."

Taking a deep breath, Ann changed the subject. "How is Sara?"

"She's calmed down a lot. Still ticked off that I didn't tell her what was going on, but she's accepted your explanation about my needing to be in control."

"Good."

"She seems to understand my *failings* better than I do."

"I noticed that."

"Sometimes it feels like she's the parent and I'm the child."

A smile lit Ann's face. "I'm not at all surprised."

Through a chuckle, Ted said, "No, I don't imagine you are."

Ann took a sip of her tea and asked, "Did you have the dreams last night?"

"Yes. It's pretty much every night to some degree."

"What do you mean, some degree?"

"It isn't always both dreams. It can be just one or the other, or even flashes of either or both."

"Was last night both dreams or flashes?"

"Both dreams, entirely unedited, and I'm drained."

"That may be a blessing."

"Why?"

"If you're tired, you won't be able to fight the hypnosis as hard."

"You expect me to fight it?"

"Yes."

"Why?"

"Because I know you." She put her mug down on the table. "My plan is to use self-hypnosis."

"I don't know anything about self-hypnosis."

"I know. I'll guide you, talk you through it. Eventually, you'll be able to do it yourself. But in the meantime, I'll lead the way."

He smiled. "You know I'll follow you anywhere."

Ann blushed a very pretty pink.

"How or why is hypnosis supposed to work?"

"Well, according to Tom Alderman, if you know who these people are and understand them, then eventually you'll be able to accept that they're a part of you. It's my job to bring them out so you can learn whatever you need to know in order to do that. I don't understand that fully, but that's what he said."

"How does the regression work?"

"I contacted one of the professors who taught me hypnotherapy, and he told me that we need to take you back to your childhood and infancy, your time in utero, and then to whatever came before that."

"I'm supposed to remember being in my mother's womb?"

"They say everything is there somewhere. My job is to find it, whatever and wherever it is. Something else he mentioned. Normally a subject won't remember the regression, so I'm going to make the suggestion, while you're hypnotized, that you remember everything."

He finished his tea. "Okay, let's do this then."

"One more thing before we start. I thought background sound might be helpful. I have rain, ocean, and babbling brook because I know you like water."

"You're the one who likes moving water."

She smiled, mostly to herself because he remembered. "But you like the ocean and rain storms."

"I'm surprised you remember that."

"So, have you a preference?"

"The brook would be nice." Ann got up and turned on the CD. As she went back to the conversation area she said, "First of all, I'd like you to recline the chair."

"Why?"

"Hypnosis is deep relaxation. If you're reclined, then theoretically, relaxation will be easier."

"You're the boss." He pulled the lever on the side of the chair and pushed back.

"And close your eyes."

"Yes, ma'am."

"Focus on your breathing and try not to think about anything."

His shallow breathing was indicative that he wasn't relaxing, so she suggested, "Imagine black velvet, feel it, sink into the darkness, the softness. Allow it to caress you."

He smiled, thinking that he'd much rather she was caressing him and not black velvet.

She saw his smile. "You're supposed to be thinking about velvet."

He raised his head and looked at her. "How do you know I'm not?"

She shook her head and smiled. "You keep forgetting that I know you. Now lie back, close your eyes, and think about black velvet."

He did as he was told.

She began, "Take a deep breath."

He turned his head and looked over at her, a playful grin curling his lip.

"Do you want to do this or not?"

"Yes, yes. Sorry."

Ann took a deep breath, then began again. She spoke, the sound of a mountain stream under her low, even tone.

"Concentrate on your breathing, allowing yourself to go deeper and deeper into a relaxed state."

She paused as his breathing finally deepened.

"Relax the muscles in your face. The jaw is the location of much stress and tension, so concentrate on relaxing your jaw."

Ted stretched his jaw, and Ann smiled.

"Neck and shoulder muscles also harbor a lot of tension, so concentrate on relaxing your neck and shoulders. Allow the muscles in your arms, hands, and fingers to loosen to the point of almost melting into the chair."

Ann waited a few moments before continuing.

"Breathe deeply and relax the muscles in your back, chest, and abdomen. Keep breathing, going deeper and deeper."

After a few minutes she continued.

"Allow your legs to relax completely, first your hips." Softly and slowly she added, "Now relax the muscles in your thighs." After a short pause, she said, "Now your knees, your calves, and feet. Go deeper and deeper into that completely relaxed state."

The soothing tone of her voice was calming, so he was actually relaxing. His feet started to tingle, and he felt himself drifting, almost floating.

"Ted?"

"Yes?"

"There is a light above you, and it's going to enter your body. Allow your heart to gently pump the warm and healing light throughout your body." She waited. "The light surrounds you now and helps you go deeper and deeper into a serene place where you are at peace." After a few minutes she asked, "How do you feel?"

"Wonderful."

"I'm going to count backward from ten to one. As I do, you will attain a deep peace, and with each number back you will go deeper and deeper into that place of peace and tranquility." A look of calm contentment spread across his face, and she could see he was completely relaxed. "I'd like you to visualize a peaceful place, a garden perhaps."

"A secret garden."

A knowing smile curved Ann's bow-like mouth, although Ted didn't see it. *The Secret Garden* had been one of Ann's favorite books as a youngster, and when the film came out in the early '90s, she and Ted fell in love with it together. "Does the garden have a wall?"

Even in his deep, relaxed state, he smiled. "Of course. It's a secret garden."

"And a hidden door?"

Seriously, Ted insisted, "It wouldn't be a secret garden if it didn't have a hidden door." In a tranquil voice he added, "And it's a wonderful weathered gate, with iron hinges and latch." Now he got a quizzical look on his face. "There are two more doors—one is barn red and very old-looking. The other is forest green."

Ann watched his body stiffen. "What is it, Ted?"

"Just looking at the red door angers me."

"Does the green door do the same?" she asked.

"Not anger, but overwhelming sadness. What does it mean?"

"I don't know. Shall we proceed?"

He took a deep breath. "Yes."

Chapter Twenty-Two

Ann leaned back into the corner of the loveseat. Ted looked so peaceful. It reminded her of the times she would watch him sleep after he'd worked a long shift. He'd said that being with her banished the stresses of the day, and he was content to simply lie next to her. The reverie ended when Ted sat bolt upright, forcing the recliner into a sitting position. In a booming but lightly British-accented voice that was definitely not Ted, he sternly said, "What evil spirit have you familiarity with?"

"What are you talking about, Ted?"

He almost screamed, "Ted! You dare speak to a magistrate of the court in such a way?"

"Magistrate?"

"Do not play coy with me, madam. You know well that I am John Hathorne, magistrate of Salem Village. Now tell me what evil spirit guides you."

Concerned that he might become erratic, she reached over and touched his hand. The accent, the timbre of his voice, but mostly the look in his eyes made Ann recognize the man who interrupted her session at the Red Cross several months before.

"How far have you complied with Satan whereby he takes this advantage against you?"

Ann tried to calm him, but his reaction to her use of his given name was extremely volatile.

"You will not speak to me in such a way, wench." Then his tone and manner softened considerably. "How can you say you know nothing, when you see those who are tormented?"

Ann got up and put her hands on his shoulders. Forcefully he shrugged her off.

Afraid to use his first name again she tried, "Please, Mr. Hathorne, sit back and close your eyes." He turned and looked at her with such hatred that her stomach tied in a tight knot, but something took hold of him, and she saw Ted return. He fell back into the chair and closed his eyes. After a few minutes, his labored breathing became deep and even.

She blew out the breath she'd been holding and went back to the loveseat. She sat for a few minutes and took several deep breaths, but before she had a chance to gather herself or speak, Ted opened his eyes.

Saying not a word, he casually put the chair upright again and stood. He smiled at her as he sat on the opposite end of the loveseat, leaning against the corner of it and stretching his legs full length until his feet were under the table, almost touching hers. She moved as far away as she could get without leaving her seat. He lounged there, his left arm flung carelessly over the arm of the small sofa, his hand cupped as though it held a brandy snifter. With his right hand he pushed the hair off of his forehead. He raised a single eyebrow as he gazed at her.

The look she saw was one of evocative familiarity that was definitely not Ted. There was an intensity that suggested power and control, and it made her uncomfortable but fascinated her at the same time. She asked, "Ted?" Receiving no response she ventured, "Mr. Hathorne?"

Rubbing the crease in his chin with his index finger then resting his jaw on his fist, he watched her. The look in his eyes made a light blush color her cheeks.

With a Scottish brogue Ann had heard before, he said, "Mr. Hathorne, Ted. I fear I know neither of these men."

"Who are you?"

"Andrew Mcnaughton. Do you not remember me, Miss Hart? We met earlier today."

Of course. This was the man she met in her office several months ago. He thought they were on a ship that sailed from Scotland on the way to Antigua, just like Ted's dream.

"Yes, of course. Nice to see you again, Mr. Mcnaughton."

A roguish grin played on his lips. "So, Miss Hart, what takes you to Antigua?"

While Ann tried to determine the best way to answer his question she was startled by the sudden motion of him sitting upright and pulling his legs out from under the table. In the earlier British-accented voice he said, "How can you say you know nothing, when you see these tormented people who accuse you?"

Hathorne was back. Knowing that she had to respond in some way but not wanting to antagonize him, she said, "What would you have me do?"

"Confess if you be guilty."

"I am not guilty."

His menacing look changed suddenly to a softened, playful one. In the gentle Scottish voice he said, "Guilty of what, Miss Hart?"

Startling her, Hathorne returned, saying furiously, "Why do you hurt these folks?"

Andrew slipped back in with his soft brogue and intoned, "Of what are you not guilty, Miss Hart?"

Becoming more and more agitated, Hathorne stood. Pointing at her, he angrily said, "We do not send for you to go to prayer. I demand you tell me why you hurt these people."

Completely confused by this strange cacophony of back-and-forth voices, entities, past lives or whatever was happening made Ann jump up and shout, "Stop!"

Even in his agitated state, her shout startled him, and he quickly sat down. She could see that Hathorne and Andrew were gone and Ted was back.

"Close your eyes and visualize the garden. Find a bench and sit down." She waited a few minutes. "Now take a deep breath."

The room was calm for the first time in several minutes, and Ann took the time to pull herself together, repositioning herself on the loveseat. Having finally regained her composure, she asked, "Ted?"

"Yes."

"I'm going to count backward from five. When I reach one, open your eyes. You will feel calm and refreshed and will remember everything that happened."

Ted brought the chair to an upright position. "That has to be the strangest thing I've ever experienced."

"I'll buy that. I'm not even sure what happened, but if you have no objection, I think we should talk to Jamie and Maura about it."

"Wouldn't Tom Alderman be the one to ask?"

"He didn't seem to have any better grasp of this than I do."

"But you think Jamie and Maura will?"

"Maura, mostly."

"Why?"

"A few years ago, her mother was diagnosed with lung cancer. Maura was at her bedside for all the chemotherapy, radiation, and surgery. When her mother went to hospice care, she started looking into what might be on the "other side" by reading about near-death experiences and reincarnation, hoping to ease the transition for her. So she actually knows a lot about it."

"That explains why Jamie accepted Tom's theory so readily. Did the research help her mother?"

"She seemed fairly peaceful at the end, but who knows why. It might simply have been that she was ready. But it definitely helped Maura, so she continued studying even after her mother passed."

"And you think she can help?"

"She isn't an expert, but I think that actually makes her more open to possibilities than 'experts' tend to be."

"Experts like us, you mean?" He smiled.

Chapter Twenty-Three

Maura opened the door to her niece. "Hi, Annie. Come on in. Jamie's on the patio with drinks. Samantha just picked up the grandkids, so I'm definitely ready for a drink."

Ann set her things down on the table in the entry and hugged her aunt. "Thanks for letting us barge in like this."

"It's not barging. You can come anytime you want."

"Yeah, but inviting myself and a friend to dinner at four in the afternoon is a little much."

"Well, I'm guessing what's in the box will make up for it."

"I stopped at the Cheesecake Factory," she said apologetically.

"I made a Cobb salad, so any dessert is welcome, homemade or not. Besides, I like Cheesecake Factory cheesecake."

"And I like your Cobb salad."

She followed her aunt to the sliding glass door leading to the brick patio. Ann loved this house. It was one of the places where she felt completely comfortable. Of course that was mostly because of the wonderful relationship she had with Jamie and Maura. But still, the 1950s ranch house on a quiet cul-de-sac was one of her favorite places. The large lot seemed like a mini ranch, sans horses. The expanse of lawn was always manicured to perfection, and the house itself had been modernized so it had the newest of everything while still retaining the charm of Southern California at the middle of the last century.

The past century. It sounded so strange. She'd been born not far from the middle of the last century, and she certainly didn't feel old, but she supposed she was getting there. She waved to her uncle who stood at the wet bar that had been built before she was born, mixing Long Island Iced Teas. He handed her one of the tall, frosty glasses. "Here you go, kid. Tall, lean, and cool, just like you." He smiled.

She sat in one of the comfy chairs tucked in under the glass-topped table. The sound of the water falling from the Jacuzzi into the pool was refreshing and relaxing at the same time. She smiled when Jamie came to the table with two more drinks and sat down.

"So, what brings you to our neck of the woods?"

"Ted."

"Suspected as much."

"It's so strange. I do wish you'd have told me a bit more about all this."

"Why? Would it have made a difference?"

She sighed. "I guess not."

"So what's the problem?"

"Ted's coming, and I'd like to wait until he's here before getting into it. Besides, I want Maura to hear it too."

"You recorded the session?"

"Yes."

Jamie waved, and Ted came through the sliding glass door as Ann turned. "Got your iced tea right here, so come sit." As Ted approached the table, Jamie queried, "Where's Sara Jane?"

"She's out with friends tonight, and frankly, I would rather she not hear this." Ted smiled at Ann as he sat down next to her.

Jamie said, "Boy, you guys are certainly being mysterious about this. How bad can it be?"

Ann and Ted looked at each other before she answered, "It's not bad, just weird, and we're not sure what to do about it."

"Well, let me hear it."

Ann asked, "What about Maura?"

"We'll play it again for her. I want to hear it."

Ann pulled the recorder out of her pocket, and turned it on. Jamie listened intently as Ted became John Hathorne and then Andrew Mcnaughton several times and then Ted again.

"So what do you think?" Ann asked.

"Well, you're definitely right about it being strange." He turned to Ted. "And you're not faking it?"

Emphatically, he said, "No!"

Ann came to Ted's defense. "When it's happening, you can see in his eyes that he's not faking it." After a moment she asked, "What do you think we should do?"

"I have no idea. Why don't we mull it over for a bit, and then we can discuss it after dinner."

As if on cue, Maura came out with a wheeled trolley laden with a large monkey-pod bowl filled with the promised salad, a basket of pumpernickel-parmesan toast, a pitcher of iced tea and one of lemonade along with dishes and silverware. She pushed the cart up to the table and sat down.

"Figured I'd just bring it all out, and we can eat and drink as we want." She leaned back and sipped her libation from the tall, frosty glass. Taking note of the recorder on the table, she asked, "What are we listening to?"

Jamie answered, "Ted's session with Ann."

"Can I hear it?"

As Maura heard Ann counting backward to bring Ted out of the trance, she got up and returned to the house. Ann and Jamie looked at each other and then at Maura as she slid open the glass door and went inside. Before the other three could say anything, Maura came back outside with her electronic tablet.

"Well, the first thing to do is determine if the men are or were real or if they're figments of Ted's imagination." She grinned at Ted.

Ann was baffled. "Real?"

"Absolutely. If this is a case of reincarnation, then the men should be real. They had to have existed. So, now we can find out." She hit the Google app on the screen and then typed as she said, "The name was John Hathorne, right?"

Ann, still confused, nodded.

Maura looked up at her three dinner companions and smiled brightly. "And here we are. John Hathorne was one of the judges at the Salem witch trials." She looked to Ann. "Explains why he's insistent that you're a witch. He thinks he's in his court or wherever they held the trials." Maura continued. "He must have been really awful. His great grandson was Nathaniel Hawthorne who added the 'w' to the spelling of his last name because he didn't want people to know they were related. Apparently the name was originally pronounced Hathorne, like Hathaway. By adding the *W,* Nathaniel changed the spelling and pronunciation to Hawthorne, like the tree." She swiped the screen of her tablet. "Interesting, huh?"

Ann agreed it was interesting. "How does that help?"

"Well, we know for certain that it is reincarnation." She went back to the tablet. "What was the other name?"

Ann offered, "Andrew Mcnaughton."

Maura typed the name into the tablet. She scrolled through the list. "There's a Canadian scientist, an executive at some company, a guy in Chicago, an Australian musician, a chef, a photographer, and a university professor in England. No Scotsman." She looked up. "He said something about Antigua."

Ann explained that he'd told her that he was from Scotland, going to Antigua in 1805. "He thinks he's on a ship."

Maura typed Antigua and went to several websites about the island country. "I can't find anything about him specifically, but historically it was a British colony, so there were folks from the United Kingdom there in the early nineteenth century. Originally, tobacco was the cash crop, but in the seventeenth century it changed to sugar. So it's altogether possible for Andrew to have actually existed." She set the tablet aside. "Let's eat." She began to serve the salad.

Chapter Twenty-Four

Ted licked the back of his fork. "The sauce is amazing, Maura."

"I'm glad you like it."

Ann added, "It really is good. Did you make it for something special?"

"You know me, waste not, want not. I had some overripe raspberries. If you hadn't brought the cheesecake, I would have made crepes."

"It certainly made the cheesecake better."

Dessert eaten and coffee being sipped, a comfortable quiet fell over the group. Jamie ended it. "So how can I help?"

Ted and Ann looked at each other, then Ted answered, "We actually came for Maura's help, not yours."

Jamie's lower lip quivered with feigned hurt feelings as he sniffed uncried tears. Ann got up and put her arms around his neck and kissed his cheek. "We still love you, even if you can't help."

Waving her aside, he said, "Yeah, yeah."

Ted smiled at Ann and Jamie and then turned to Maura. "Ann told me that you've done a lot of research into reincarnation. So what do you make of all this?"

"Do you mind if I listen to it again?"

Ann took the recorder out of her pocket again and switched it on, leaving it in the middle of the table. Just before it ended, Maura started it from the beginning. Ted got up from the table, and began to pace.

After listening to it this time, Maura said, "It's interesting that you didn't need to do the regression."

Seeing Ted's distress, Ann answered, "I thought that was weird too but I never got the chance."

Ted asked, "How is this happening? I don't understand it."

Jamie reminded him, "Like I said, there is a lot we don't understand. Although I must admit that their showing up at the same time seems odd. Considering your garden-wall visualization, perhaps all the doors were open, which is why you all came together."

"I'm guessing that isn't what he meant," offered Maura, who turned to Ted and continued. "Like with everything else, your past lives are part of your subconscious, which is generally separated from your conscious mind by a... a sort of wall, in your case, a garden wall. For reasons we will probably never know, stress seems to open the doors of the wall, and that allows your subconscious to mingle with your conscious."

Ted sat again and shook his head. "It just doesn't seem possible. What *is* going on?"

Sympathetically, but pragmatically, Maura said, " *What's* going on doesn't really matter. Deciding what to do about it is the important thing."

Ted took a deep breath. "You're right. I'm sorry."

"Nothing to apologize for, Teddy. I do think Jamie's right. All the doors were open, allowing the convergence. So the simple answer seems to be to close and bolt the doors."

"That's it?"

Jamie offered, "That's up to you."

"What do you mean?"

"It's your subconscious. You need to find out why your past wants to invade your present." He poured himself more coffee. "It's not unlike childhood memories infecting adulthood. You can't let something that happened in the past control your future or, in this case, your present."

Ted looked at Jamie then at Ann. "Just how am I supposed to do that?"

"That's what I use hypnotherapy for. No matter how bad your past, there's always some good in it, and hypnosis can help bring that forward, pushing the negative things into the corners."

Jamie added, "I'm guessing it's the reason Tom suggested it."

Ted turned to Maura. "We came mostly to get your take on this, and you haven't said much."

"I figured I'd let the experts do the talking."

"Yeah, but they... we aren't expert in what's happening, and you are."

"I wouldn't go that far, but I do have some thoughts."

"Please, I'd very much like to hear them."

"It appears to me that stress and grief are the triggers for you. Based on what you said, the first time any of this happened was when your grandfather had his stroke. Yes?"

Ted almost did a double take. "I can't believe you remember that."

"It was a particularly hard time for you. Deep into your residency, planning the wedding, and then Deke having the stroke. The two of you were so close. It was upsetting seeing you in so much pain."

Still more than a bit surprised, Ted said, "I'm astonished."

"I remember things about the people I love." Maura reached over and squeezed his hand. "Moving on. The second time was when you lost Josh. I can't think of anything as stressful or that would cause more grief than losing a child." Ted squeezed her hand, but said nothing.

"This time seems a bit odd, but it is possible that the earthquake shook things up more than you imagined. It was stressful for all of us, and I think"—she turned and smiled at Ann—"seeing Ann again was the emotional trigger."

"But you said it was grief."

"I could be wrong, but I believe seeing her again brought back the grief of losing her."

Ted felt the need to get up and move. He desperately wanted to control the tears that were threatening. Ann started to get up, but Maura stopped her with a light touch of her hand.

She cleared her throat. "The trigger is less important than how best to fix things. Because emotions seem to play a big part in this situation, I don't believe that simply bolting the doors is going to be a remedy. You need to find out from these men why your grief keeps them coming back."

"How?"

"Talk to them."

From the shadows he said, "If they're my past lives, doesn't that indicate they've lived their lives? Whatever they did is done, right?"

"Einstein believed that time is relative. There is no past or future, that it is all happening right now."

"Then why are they called past lives?"

"Because we need to put labels on everything, and that's the label we chose for this situation."

Ted began pacing again, finally stopping at the table. "I really appreciate all the help you guys are trying to give me, but my head feels like it's going to explode. I think I need to go home." He bent down and kissed Maura's cheek. "Thank you, dear." He shook Jamie's hand. "Thanks for having me." Jamie started to rise, but Ann jumped up.

"I'll walk him out."

As they headed to his car Ann asked, "Will I see you tomorrow?"

"I guess." He looked directly into her eyes. "Do you understand any of this?"

"No, but I'm sure everything will be fine."

He kissed her cheek. "Thanks for the lie. See you tomorrow." As he got into the car, he added, "Maybe." She watched him drive away and questioned if she really could help him.

Chapter Twenty-Five

Friday, June 27

Arriving at her office later than she anticipated after lunch with a friend, Ann rushed to prepare for Ted's session. She was at the sideboard plugging in the electric kettle when she heard the door open. She turned as the metallic sound of the dead bolt extension slipped into the strike box. His playful look embarrassed her for some reason.

She was suddenly nervous but forced a weak, "Hi," as he walked toward her. She glanced over his shoulder at the locked door. *Why had he locked it?* She didn't have to wait to find out.

"Don't want anyone barging in," he said with a raised eyebrow and impish grin.

She swallowed the lump in her throat. "Oh."

He sniffed the air like a bear in the woods. "No lavender today?"

With a nervous giggle, she said, "I got back from lunch late and haven't had a chance to do it."

"I do so enjoy the scent of lavender," he teased.

Ann saw the medical student she'd fallen in love with so many years ago. He hadn't really changed. Had she? She was being silly and almost shook her head. "Would you like tea?"

"Sure, let's do the whole thing. I'll even light the candle in the infuser."

He stood next to her and lit the tea light under the essential oil, then sat in the recliner. Bringing the tea with her, she sat on the loveseat.

Ted said, "I was thinking about it after I left last night, and I almost wish you'd video recorded it so I could see what was happening."

"We can this time, if you want."

"I *almost* wish it. Not sure I actually want to see it."

The small recording device was sitting on the table in front of him. He reached out and turned it on. After listening intently, he turned it off.

"How will you keep them separate, since they're both me?"

"Believe it or not it's easy. It starts with body language. Hathorne is imposing and intimidating. He stands straight and uses broad hand gestures. His voice is a low baritone with a slight British accent. Andrew's body language has a casual elegance to it. His voice is similar to yours, but there's a different cadence to his speech, and he has a fairly strong Scottish brogue. Then there's you, American as apple pie." She smiled at him. When he didn't respond in any way she added, "And there's something in your eyes that's different with both of them. I can tell when you've returned."

"I meant how are you going to stop them both from showing up at the same time?"

"Maura and Jamie suggested that we make sure one of the doors is closed so only one can be there at a time."

"Oh, right. I forgot." Ted stared at his hands.

"What's wrong?"

He looked up at her. "Nothing."

"You were cheerful when you came in, and now you've turned"—she hesitated slightly—"dour."

"Yeah. I blocked it out for a while and then just ignored it, but now that I'm here the reality is setting in again, if it is real."

"You still question it?"

He shook his head. "I don't know. Tom said it was reincarnation. Jamie and Maura seem to agree with him. Even Sara Jane's teacher said it was reincarnation. But I never actually thought it would be reincarnation. I don't believe in reincarnation so am finding this very hard to accept."

"I didn't believe in reincarnation either."

"You do now?"

"I'm not sure. It's getting hard not to."

"And therein lies the problem. We don't know." He took a deep breath. "Maura said we need to talk with them to determine why they're hanging around. What are you going to say to elicit the information we need?"

"After you left last night, Maura told me that, with luck, a casual conversation might trigger what we need."

"So we're just leaving it to luck?"

The question was one she couldn't answer. "I'm not sure what other option we have."

He sat looking at her without really seeing her and finally said, "Would you mind terribly if we waited to do this next session?"

"Why?"

"Since you're not sure what our next move should be, and I have no idea what we're doing, maybe we should wait a while. You know, get our bearings before we enter the breach. I'm going to be busy the next few days, so we won't be able to keep whatever momentum we get going. In a few days, we can do it and see what happens."

Ann picked up her china mug and sipped her tea. Part of her didn't want to deal with it at all and was more than willing to wait, but that niggling voice in the back of her head wanted to know what would happen next with the past lives and Ted. She also suspected that Ted was simply trying to avoid the situation, but she conceded. "I have no problem with waiting." Her warm smile made him relax just a bit. "In fact, I can use the time to find out as much as I can about reincarnation and past-life regression."

He smiled. "Sounds like a plan." He watched Ann put her mug down and stare at it, her thumbnail clenched firmly in her teeth. He smiled. Some habits are never broken. "You're very contemplative. What are you thinking about?"

She tipped her head and looked at him. "What does it feel like when you're one of the lives? Maybe feel isn't the right word. I'm not sure. What do you experience? Is it like watching a movie or being in a play?"

He thought about it. "Neither. It's all happening around me. I'm in the middle of it, but just watching. I can't stop or change anything either. At least when I tried to stop Hathorne, I couldn't. You had to do it."

"With both lives?"

"Yeah. In fact, I tried to go from one to the other but couldn't."

"How?"

"I know what they're thinking, so I concentrated on being the Scotsman while I was Hathorne hoping that would make him go away. It didn't. I'm the one in my body, but I have no control over what I say or do. It's very frustrating."

She smiled. "That must be really hard for a control freak like you."

"I'm not a control freak."

She raised an eyebrow, and he knew instantly that he had no defense. He was, after all, a control freak, at least a *self*-control freak.

After a few quiet moments, he said, "I've been thinking about letting Sara Jane hear the recording."

"What made you change your mind?"

"You said that the more she knows, the less she'll worry."

"That's funny, I started thinking you were right to not say anything about it."

"Why?"

"Well, we don't really know what's happening or what any of it means, so what do we tell her? It might be more confusing than anything else."

"Now, I'm even more confused."

Ann giggled. "Sorry."

Chapter Twenty-Six

Saturday, June 21

"Okay, sleepyhead, time to get up," Ann said as she clipped the leash onto Gigi's collar. "You've been way too lazy since the earthquake. We're going to the park to work out. I've got the Frisbee and Foxy Loxy, so come on and get your fuzzy butt off the bed."

On the front porch of her Craftsman home, she shrugged on her backpack. Scratching the top of the dog's head, Ann asked, "Isn't it a beautiful day, fur face?" At six o'clock, the cool summer morning was comfortable enough for exercise, and the pair walked briskly to the corner where they stopped to let a large truck cross through the intersection. "Looks like somebody's moving, Gigi." They watched the moving van turn onto the next street.

In the park, the great white animal ran after the Frisbee and played with her unstuffed fox, returning the toys to her mistress so many times she was panting heavily. Ann bent down and hugged her pet. "You just aren't made for Southern California summers, are you? Let's cool off a bit and then go home." At a concrete drinking fountain, Ann filled a plastic bowl. Together they walked to the sheltered shade of an old-growth oak. Gigi lapped up most of the water, then lay down in the cool grass next to Ann.

The broad trunk of the old tree acted as Ann's backrest in the early morning calm. She closed her eyes, breathing in the smell of the freshly cut lawn as her meeting with Ted yesterday filled her thoughts. Part of her was glad he wanted to wait for another session, as he had said the previous one had been rather disturbing. Still, there was a part of her that didn't want to wait, but she was almost ashamed to admit it was because she wanted to see him again. The feelings he was stirring in her were a bit frightening, mostly because she had thought she was over him. Was it possible she was still in love with him? How could she love a man who betrayed her? She stood up and ran her hand over the dog's back. "Come on, Gigi. We're going home." The big animal rose slowly to her feet, still worn out from the rigorous play. The pair headed out of the park not quite as briskly as they had entered it.

Gigi's lumbering gait suddenly stopped, and Ann could feel the tension in the animal along the length of the lead. The dog started barking and pulling on the leash in the direction of an SUV turning the corner a half block ahead of them.

"What is it, girl?" The dog was so strong that Ann had to run to keep up with her pet. As they rounded the corner, she saw the reason for the dog's animated display. Sara McConaughy was on the sidewalk a short distance ahead.

Sara stopped and turned at the barking dog. "Ann!" She bent down, and hugged the dog's broad neck, "Hi, G."

A bit taken aback by the seemingly sudden appearance of the young woman, Ann said, "Sara, what are you doing here?"

Pointing up the street to the moving van Ann had seen earlier, Sara explained, "We're moving in. Remember that house I told you about with the great attic room? Well, Dad bought it. Didn't he tell you?"

"No."

"He told me that you didn't do the hypnosis thing yesterday because he wanted to wait until we made the move, so I just assumed he told you or I would have called you."

"All he told me was he wanted to wait a few days because he was going to be busy."

"He's weird sometimes. You want to see the house? I have coffee."

"I'd love to, but it would seem your father doesn't want me to know about the house. How is he going to react?"

"I don't think his not telling you means he didn't want you to see the house." She added almost conspiratorially, "I think it's because he didn't want you to think we bought the house to be close to you." She smiled brightly. "But don't worry about it. He's not there anyway."

"Where is he?"

"I left him at home, the other home, sleeping and met the movers here myself."

"I thought you couldn't drive alone."

"I can't. I didn't want the movers handling our electronics, so a couple of my friends helped me disassemble everything last night. One of them has an SUV, so we put it all in that, and now they're going to help me put it all back together. They picked me up this morning so I could meet the movers." Gesturing to the SUV Ann had seen, Sara continued. "Nick went out for doughnuts, so I came out to the corner to be sure he found us again. Come on."

A single dormer, almost the entire width of the roof, rendered the hundred-year-old Craftsman unique. Towering ancient pines on either side of the house, accompanied by the smell of the fallen needles, lent an air of forest glen to the landscape. The woodsy feel of the property was enhanced by a river rock planter the length of the front porch. Butterfly bushes interspersed with small rose trees screened the expansive lanai from the street. A delicate blanket of purple and white sweet alyssum covered the ground of the planter. Two concrete strips separated by a single strip of grass created the driveway leading to a stand-alone garage. A third concrete strip was a walkway to the porch.

Glancing in through the large window as they made their way down to the front door, Ann could see boxes and some furniture. The leaded glass of the door was probably original to the house. The beautifully beveled pieces separated by beads of lead didn't often survive to this century, and she knew it was the kind of thing that would have drawn Ted to the house.

The living room was much like hers, except the hardwood floor appeared to be several different kinds of wood while hers was all mahogany (which scratched far too easily). She knew too that the beautiful built-in bookcases that lined the far wall in the living room would have been a major attraction of the house for Ted. Even as a struggling medical student, he had managed to find the money to buy some special edition of a beloved novel to add to his already-sizeable collection. She smiled at the memory but was brought out of her reverie by Sara.

"Come on, I want to show you my room. It's so awesome." They walked through the living room and dining room that, like Ann's, had built-in glass-fronted cabinets. Sara opened a door in the hall that looked like a coat closet but opened onto a narrow staircase with a low ceiling. "The hidden staircase makes it almost like a secret room. It's so cool," exclaimed the excited teenager.

On the stairs, Ann realized that she only cleared the ceiling by a few inches. "Your father must almost double over to go up these stairs."

"Yeah. It was one of the things that kind of held him back from buying it until I badgered him into it. I kept telling him that he wasn't going to need to use the stairs often enough for it to make a difference."

The stairs opened onto a room half the size of the first floor, making it unquestionably the largest room in the house. Light filled the space from the row of windows in the extended dormer. The built-in drawers and bookcases, as well as a desk, ran along the wall opposite the windows. At one end of the room was the large walk-in closet and private bath with both a new claw-foot tub and a stall shower. Without a doubt, this was a teenage girl's dream room. Aside from the size and storage, it was away from the rest of the house and not easily accessible.

"You are definitely right about the room. It's truly amazing," she said, thinking to herself that the wide desk and lots of indirect sunlight would make it a really great sewing room for a true seamstress. Alex's office was more than enough for hobby sewing, which is what she did. The thought stopped her cold. Alex. Here she was in Ted's house, and her only thought of Alex was that his office would make a good sewing room. Trying to block the thoughts entirely, she asked Sara, "Can I see the backyard? It seems like you mentioned a pool when you first told me about the house."

"Yeah. It's nothing like yours. It's just a pool, but it's nice. There's even a deck. Hey, we can have our coffee out there."

Sara was right. While she and Alex had created a woodland backyard, this was more like a cottage garden, informal, almost wild-looking. Tucked in the far corner was a small pool lined entirely with dark blue tile so it appeared to be bottomless. Redwood decking wound around the pool to an elevated deck which included an honest-to-goodness hot tub. Sara said they planned to replace it with a Jacuzzi. There was a small wrought iron table and two matching chairs.

"The furniture isn't very comfortable, but we can have our coffee out here. I'll be right back with it." The teenager rushed off.

Ann skirted the pool. The unseen depth made her stomach jump since all her life she'd been afraid of deep water. Her mother attributed it to having almost drowned in a hotel pool when she was three. It was an event of which she had no recollection, but her subconscious had apparently retained the fear she experienced.

Sara returned carrying a tray with two large cups and saucers, a sugar bowl, and a plate with a few doughnuts she cut into quarters. She set the tray on the tiny table then reached down to pet Gigi, who had been following them around the house and yard but now lay at Ann's feet.

"Made lattes. Hope that's okay."

"It's wonderful. Thank you."

They talked of the house and what Sara planned to do with her room, the kind of furniture she wanted for the deck, the Jacuzzi they found that looked like the hot tub but had jets. The two women sat quietly, each in her own thoughts. Ann was thinking what a wonderful job Ted had done rearing his lovely daughter, and Sara was wondering how best to broach a subject she'd wanted to talk with Ann about for a couple of weeks.

Finally, she broke the quiet. "Can I ask you a therapy kind of question?"

Assuming it had something to do with her father's situation, Ann readily agreed.

Sara bit her lip. "I'm supposed to make my yearly trek to Chicago to see Mom."

"You expected that."

"Yeah."

"When?"

"Next week."

"How long will you be gone?"

"Well, that's the problem. Mom wants me to stay for two weeks but..." She hesitated.

"But what?" Ann prodded.

"Is it awful that I don't want to spend that much time with her?"

"Why don't you?"

"A lot of little things. Most of the time, I won't actually be with her because something will happen at work and she won't come home. Some of the time, she'll complain about Dad and how he killed Josh. And the rest of the time, she'll feel like she has to entertain me, so she'll drag me all over Chicago." She sighed. "I really love her, but she makes me crazy if I spend too much time with her."

"Your mother thinks your father killed your brother?"

"It's kind of a weird situation. Dad was scheduled to pick the boys up from swim practice that afternoon, but there had been an apartment fire in downtown LA, so he called and asked Tommy's mother to do it. Mom said if Dad had picked them up like he was supposed to then Josh would still be alive. But I've always thought that I might have lost Josh and Dad. And she's never really forgiven him for turning the machines off. Anyway, do you think it's really awful that I don't want to see her?"

"You don't want to see her at all?"

"I don't know. I mean I'm always excited when I first get there. But then a couple of days in, it all starts. I end up sitting in her condo alone or having to grit my teeth to not get into an argument with her."

"What did your father say?"

"He says I should go because if I don't I'll regret not having a relationship with her when I'm older. Do you think he's right?"

"Pretty much. Have you ever discussed it with her?"

"What am I supposed to say? 'Hey, Mom, you make me crazy, so I don't want to come this year'?"

"No. Tell her you're looking forward to seeing her and want to make the trip, but ask if she'd mind if it was only for a few days instead of two weeks. Maybe suggest that you could see her more often during the year a couple of days at a time rather than trying to cram it all into one two-week period every year."

"I should have thought of that. She's always apologizing when she has to work."

"That would allow her to arrange her schedule differently if she knows it's only going to be for two or three days."

"That's a great idea. I'll call her tonight. Thank you so much."

"I'm glad I could help." Ann stood up. "I have stuff I need to do today, so I'd best be on my way. Thanks for the tour and coffee."

Sara stood too. "Before you go, can you tell me what happened yesterday? Why didn't you guys do a hypnosis session?"

"Your father wanted to wait because he was going to be busy."

"Yeah, that's what he said too, but it felt like he was holding something back."

"All we did was talk about what was happening. I think he really did just want to wait until the move was over."

"I think he's hiding something. I wish he'd stop treating me like a baby."

"He's just trying to protect you, sweetie. Don't be too hard on him. I really need to go. See you later. You're welcome to come by anytime."

Sara hugged her. "Thanks again."

"You're more than welcome."

Chapter Twenty-Seven

At home, Ann did the mundane chores that had become her Saturday morning routine—cleaning the kitchen and bathrooms, changing the linens on her bed and towels in the bathroom, dusting and vacuuming the rest of the house and then her laundry. It never took more than a few hours, and generally it made her feel like she had accomplished something, but today it just felt like the same ol' same ol'. She was in a rut. When had she allowed her life to be so entrenched by a nonexistent schedule? The dog park, cleaning, cooking for the week on Saturdays, and Sundays always started with a ride and ended with an allotted time to read. Even reading wasn't for fun anymore. Most of the time, she read journal articles and books written by other psychiatrists. She'd always had some structure in her life but not to the exclusion of everything else. *How had that happened? When did it happen?*

She put the stack of warm towels in the linen closet, shut the door, and leaned her head against it. She couldn't stop thinking about Sara Jane McConaughy. The lovely young woman was a reminder that Ted moved on after their breakup and lived his life. She had thrown herself into

school and work. *Why was she comparing her life to Ted's?*
She pushed herself away from the cupboard. She needed to
do something physical.

Gigi watched from inside the air-conditioned house as
Ann dove into the pool. She didn't count the laps; she just
swam. When her arms started to burn, she pulled herself up
onto the rock ledge and sat with her feet in the water. She
leaned back, hoping her body would absorb the sun's healing
rays and bring some sort of balance back into her life.

The sun glinting off the window of the fairy house
caught her eye. She smiled at the miniature furniture and
accessories inside, courtesy of Maura and Jamie's youngest
child. Grace loved to make miniatures, and after she saw the
thatched-roof cottage had gifted them with interior decorations. There was a mission-style table with two chairs (to
match theirs), a stove and dry sink for the kitchen, one
upholstered chair, and a rocking chair with a table near the
fireplace, and then there was the bookcase. Most of the
books were simulated, but Grace had actually made three
books with printed covers and pages. There was *Forever
Amber*, Ann's first foray into nonrequired reading; *Twilight
Eyes* by Dean Koontz, Alex's favorite book; and then there
was *Pride and Prejudice,* Ann's very favorite book. But the
things Ann loved the most were the dishes Grace made, cups
that looked like bluebells with saucers and plates in the
shape of leaves and flower petals. Ann had added the
furnishings that last afternoon, so Alex had never seen them
inside the house. His favorites had been the miniature
books. Her smile faded when the memories of Alex with his
fairy house and thoughts of Ted (which she seemed to have a
terrible time controlling) collided. She pulled her feet out of
the water and stood up.

The shampoo swirled around and down the drain; Ann ran her fingers through her wet hair. When she was a little girl, her mother taught her that if her hair squeaked, then she'd gotten all the soap out of it, and now her hair was squeaky clean.

Freshly showered and her hair dry, she put on one of her favorite "around the house" dresses. Simple high-waisted dresses that she'd been making since her parents bought her the sewing machine when she was seventeen. When she first made a dress from the pattern, it was called Empire, but now she noticed in magazines and on television the style was called Regency for the era between 1790 and 1820. Whatever it was called, the gowns were easy to make and very comfortable. This one was aqua gingham and made Ann feel cool and fresh.

After slipping on a pair of white ballet-type slippers, she went to the dresser. The Sarah Bernhardt pin dish had held her everyday jewelry ever since Tommy gave it to her for her fifteenth birthday when she'd been infatuated with the famed French actress. It had broken into two pieces in the earthquake, but she had lovingly glued it back together and now removed the topaz cross that had been a wedding gift from Alex and carefully clasped the delicate gold chain around her neck. She picked up her wedding ring. For six and a half years, she'd put it on every day. She looked at it. Was she even still married? As much as she loved Alex, she was tired of not knowing, of wondering... of pretending. She dropped the ring back in the dish and walked away.

Taking her iced tea into Alex's office, she sat down at the computer. The silver three-dimensional word *forgive* continued to tumble on a field of black as it had been doing since the earthquake. She'd given up trying to figure out what was happening with the machine. Here it was four months later, and it continued to display one of several websites and blogs that were related to reincarnation or past lives. So she decided to take advantage of it. Whatever the reason it was happening, maybe she could glean some information from these sources that would allow her to help Ted.

She pushed away from the desk and rubbed her eyes. She would need to start wearing glasses if she was going to spend time on the computer. Five hours had gone by while she was sitting there, at least according to the altimeter clock on the wall. It was too late to bake a potato or grill a steak, her usual Saturday dinner. How lame was it that even her meals had gotten regimented? Pushing aside the absurdity of it, she took a sweet-and-sour-chicken dinner out of the freezer, popped it in the microwave, then poured a fresh glass of iced tea. The sound of the tea falling over the ice was refreshing. She ran her index finger around the edge of the tall, slender glass listening to the hum of the "Radar Range," a modern reproduction (although much smaller) of the original microwave. The timer buzzed, announcing the completion of her instant meal.

The black plastic plate was all that was left of her dinner. She dropped it in the wastebasket on her way to the backyard. The moonflowers were opening on the vines, glistening in the warm summer evening. She couldn't help but think of Alex when she saw them. Planting them was something else they'd done that last day, so he'd never seen them in bloom.

Until she'd run into Ted, or he had run into her at the Red Cross center, she hadn't really thought about him, but now he was ever present in her thoughts. Even before Jamie asked her to see him, she'd been thinking about him—even dreamt about him. Suddenly, she got up and went back into the office, returning with a single sheet of typewritten paper.

Every website she went to during her research seemed to have a quote in the header, and like the websites themselves, they all seemed to be aimed at her. She read the first of the quotes she'd printed out. "Forgive the past. Not letting go limits your future." But the one that seemed to hit home the hardest was, "It is not the broken heart that kills but broken pride." Had Ted simply wounded her pride when he cheated on her and not broken her heart? Was that why she had been so angry once the hurt had passed? Wounded pride? She tossed the paper onto the table, and memories of Alex flooded her mind.

These memories weren't the kind that brought tears to her eyes. Tonight she was remembering the differences between Alex and Ted. They really were polar opposites. Was that what attracted her to Alex, that he was so different? In her mind she began to enumerate the differences, their looks notwithstanding. Alex was an extrovert, Ted was not. Alex was very much into physical activity, exercise, triathlons, marathons. He loved to hike and camp. Ted kept in shape, but that was it as far as physical activity went. Alex liked science fiction; Ted preferred political thrillers. The one thing they both liked that she did not was slapstick comedy. The Westminster chimes of the front doorbell brought further comparisons to an abrupt end.

Bill Wyman stood in a pool of yellow light as moths darted in and out of the darkness. Ann hugged Alex's Civil Air Patrol flight commander. "It's been so long." Releasing him, she invited him in to the house.

Gesturing to a chair, Ann insisted, "Come in, sit down. Can I get you something to drink?" She could tell his smile was forced when he refused the refreshments. He was tense and didn't meet her eyes. She was sure he came to tell her that they'd decided to stop looking for Alex, and she readied herself for it, but the information he imparted took her breath away.

He took a deep breath and blew it out. "Doug Wellman, do you remember him?" She nodded.

"He took his sons and a couple of their friends up to Lone Pine for a camping trip. On one of their hikes, they found the wreckage of an airplane. Apparently the earthquake shook stuff loose." He paused, and she knew what was coming, but she said nothing. "It was Alex's plane."

What difference did finding the plane make? "What about Alex?"

The blood drained from his face. "They found his remains too."

"Remains." Ann fell back against the chair. She'd wished and hoped, but all for naught. He'd been dead the whole time.

"You okay, Annie?"

She looked up at him. "Yeah, I guess."

"We're going to do a memorial at the tie-down. Are you going to do the funeral at Sawtel?"

She gave him a blank stare.

"Too soon?"

"He wanted to be buried at the National Cemetery, so I suppose I'll look into it."

"Well, you have some time. The find was yesterday, and the Inyo County Coroner has to examine... has to do his examination, and the NTSB has to do their thing."

"The NTSB?"

"Anytime a plane crashes, they investigate. It shouldn't take long. It was clearly an accident." When Ann didn't respond, he asked, "Do you want me to call someone for you?"

She shook her head. "No, thanks. Did you tell Ellie?"

"Doug is over there now, talking with her."

Ann stood up. "I think I'll go to her house."

"Do you want me to drive you?"

"No, I'm okay. She only lives a few miles away." Ann walked Bill to the door. "Thanks for coming by and telling me in person. I'll let you know when I've made the funeral arrangements."

"And I'll let you know when we set a date for the memorial." He kissed her cheek. "I'm sorry, but at least we know now, so it's finally over."

She nodded in agreement. "Yeah, it just feels weird."

Chapter Twenty-Eight

Wednesday, July 2

Ted was making tea while she finished an insurance form for her last patient. It had been eleven days since she'd seen him. In spite of the summer heat, he had opted for hot tea rather than the freshly brewed iced tea she had prepared for their session. He said he found hot tea comforting.

Ann picked up the hand-painted china mug and as she sat down across from him asked, "Has Sara gone to Chicago?"

"Not yet. She leaves tonight. Thanks to you, she'll only be there three days."

"So her mother didn't object to the shortened time?"

"No. As a matter of fact, Melinda was thrilled. Turned out she felt the same way Sara Jane did... not that Sara Jane makes her crazy, but she felt guilty when she had to work and thought she needed to entertain her with nonstop activities when they were together."

"Why hadn't she said something about it before?"

"Melinda was afraid Sara Jane would think she didn't want to spend time with her."

"Well, I'm glad it worked out."

Ann seemed to drift off as he responded. "It did. Thank you for that." She was lost in another world. "You seem to be a bit distracted? Is everything okay?"

She looked over at him. "They found Alex."

He assumed it was Alex's body they found, but she didn't say anything else. It took a moment for him to think of a question that wouldn't ask it outright. "Where? When?"

"About ten days ago, in the mountains near Lone Pine. He was with the wreckage of the plane."

"Toni, I'm so sorry. After all this time... would you rather not do the session today?"

His question drew her attention from her tea to his face. "No, I'm okay. It's just that I've had to make cremation and funeral arrangements, which has been strange. He's been gone so long."

"When is the funeral?"

"August 2."

"Why not sooner?"

"When you're dealing with the National Cemetery, it takes time. I had to find his discharge papers and prove I was his wife, and there's a waiting list. I was just going to inter him, and skip the whole funeral thing, but his Marine Corp buddies want to have an honor guard, flag, and "Taps." Of course, none of that happens until the NTSB signs off on it."

"The NTSB?"

"National..."

Interrupting her, Ted said, "I know what it is. What do they have to do with it?"

"They investigate every plane crash. They have to say it was an accident."

"Is there a reason to assume it wasn't?"

"No. They've already told me it was, but it's a federal agency, so nothing happens quickly. I'm waiting for the paperwork." She sipped her tea. "Let's talk about something else. Why didn't you tell me about the house?"

It was a bit of a jolt to suddenly jump to the new subject. Before he said anything, she said, "Sara thinks it's because it's in my neighborhood. Is she right?"

"Yeah, I guess she is. I just thought it might be weird, but Sara Jane really wanted that house. We kept looking but never found anything we liked as much. When the house was still available a month later, she was sure it was a sign that it was meant for us."

Ann's face brightened with a radiant smile. "Well, I'm glad you decided to buy it."

"You are?"

"Yes. It's a lovely house, and when I was inside, it felt like you belonged there."

"It feels that way to me too." A playful grin curved his mouth. "Maybe one of my past lives lived there."

She grinned. "Could be."

"About that. You said you were going to do some research. Did you find anything?"

"I researched a whole lot of stuff. I went online to find out as much as I could about reincarnation. That led to near-death experiences. I got a couple of books, even went to a place in West Hollywood that specializes in past-life regression. I also did some reading about the Salem witch trials and Antigua."

"You didn't have to go to that much trouble."

"It wasn't any trouble. I like doing that kind of research and investigation."

"I do remember that. Did any of it help?"

"I'm not sure. The only thing everyone agrees on is that the dreams are memories of the past lives. In fact, it's quite common for people to dream about past lives. Some people have been known to speak, read, and write in languages they've never learned. Children sometimes impart knowledge they've never been taught, and there is a persistent theory that our deepest fears and phobias come from something that happened in a past life. Like the fear of water might be attributed to a past life having drowned.

"The main problem I've run into is that none of the websites, books, or past-life therapists have ever heard of past lives coming to the surface like this. One of them described it as manifesting in a physical form. But whatever it's called, no one had ever heard of or seen it."

"So, does that mean that's not what's happening?"

"Just because no one's ever heard of it doesn't mean it isn't happening."

"What *does* it mean?"

"I don't know."

Ted got up and began pacing. After a few moments, he stopped and looked at her. "This just seems to get stranger and stranger, don't you think?"

"Yes, I do."

Ann explained that the past-life therapists she talked to agree with Maura that finding out as much as they could about the two men would allow Ted to come to terms with what was happening. "Generally that would mean researching the subjects of the dreams, but we can actually talk with them. Hopefully, then you'll be able to lock the doors on them."

"And that will get rid of them permanently?"

"That's certainly the hope."

"Why don't we just lock the doors and be done with it?"

He sat again, and Ann smiled at him. "I asked Maura the same question, and she said that since stress seems to be the trigger..."

"And grief."

"Yes. If we don't find out why they keep invading your present, she's convinced they'll keep coming back." She stopped but didn't take her eyes off of him.

"What?" he asked.

"She said that it appears things have escalated over the years, so she's concerned that the next time will be even more intense."

"I'm not sure that's possible." He took a deep breath. "So the plan is for you to talk to them and figure out why?"

"Yes. At least with Andrew Mcnaughton."

"Not Hathorne?"

"We already know who he is, and I'm guessing he simply wants to keep finding and persecuting witches. So I think we should lock him away as soon as possible. All we need to do is find out which door is his." She added almost under her breath, "Although I suspect it's the red one."

"Why?"

"Red just seems like the right color for the evil bastard."

Startled, Ted said, "Why Dr. Hart, such language." He smiled at her.

"Sorry, but he really was awful."

"He was indeed." Ted sat looking at nothing in particular and saying nothing else.

"What is it Ted?"

"It all seems so surreal, particularly since I don't believe in reincarnation."

"Not believing it doesn't make it any less true."

"Okay, then, tell me how locking an imaginary person behind an imaginary door in an imaginary wall is the answer?"

"We know that Hathorne isn't imaginary, but he's living in your imagination, so you need to close the imaginary door. Somehow or other your mind is allowing him to exist, so your mind has to get rid of him."

Ted resigned himself to never fully understanding what was happening but was happy to let Toni... Ann, try to fix it.

"Okay. Let's do it."

Chapter Twenty-Nine

The hypnosis went far more smoothly than Ann expected. "Are you in the garden?" He did not respond. "Ted?"

Once again, regression was unnecessary. Ted sat upright, his presence imposing and intimidating. But this time, John Hathorne's voice was soft and low. He leaned forward just a bit when he said, "Did you not say you would tell the truth? How come you to the knowledge?"

Questioning if she should answer, she finally responded with, "I didn't say anything." She saw anger in his eyes, but he continued quietly.

"Is it not a solemn thing that last Lord's Day you were tormented, and now you are become a tormentor yourself so that you have changed sides. How comes this to pass?" When she said nothing, he continued a bit more aggressively. "You are now before the Authority. I expect the truth. You promised it. Speak now and tell."

Ann ventured, "Tell what?"

The look in his eyes made her stomach tighten. "What? Have you resolved you will not confess?" In an artificially conspiratorial tone, he asked, "Hath anybody threatened you if you do confess? You can tell."

"Confess what?"

His voice began to rise. "Attempt no lies with me, madam. Your husband committed murder and has a covenant with the devil."

Confused, Ann questioned, "Murder?"

Hathorne became extremely agitated. "Hold your tongue, witch. You know well your husband committed such a crime and that you be the wife of a witch, and now you have become a tormentor yourself!"

"Tormentor?"

He rose to his feet and stood over her. A look of pure evil filled his eyes. "Confess now!"

She pushed herself as far into the corner of the loveseat as she could and almost whimpered, "I have nothing to confess."

Throwing his arms wide, he shouted, "You dare thus to lie in all the assembly."

Ann clenched her jaw and with as much determination as she could muster, raised her voice, and said, "Ted, can you hear me?"

"Yes."

"Sit down, please." He did.

Gathering her strength, she stood and went to the side of Ted's chair. There she laid her hand on his shoulder. "Lean back and close your eyes." After a brief respite, she added, "Go to the red door, make sure it's closed, and then throw the bolt." After a few moments, she asked, "Is it done?"

"Yes."

"Good. Maybe that will keep him under control."

"Yes."

"Do you want to continue?"

"No."

"Okay."

After sitting quietly for a few minutes, Ann counted backward from five, and at one Ted opened his eyes and looked over at her.

She asked, "How do you feel?"

"Horrible. I know what he was thinking, and it's far worse than anything he said." After a momentary pause, he asked, "Didn't you say you found information on this guy?"

Ann got up and went to her desk. "There's lots written about the Salem witch trials. I printed some of it out." She returned with several typed pages and began to read. "The afflicted girls accused Giles Corey of witchcraft in April of 1692. He refused to be tried by the court which, in his view, had already determined his guilt, so he stood mute rather than 'putting himself on the court.'" She stopped reading. "That means he didn't declare himself guilty or not guilty." She continued, "He was sentenced by Magistrate John Hathorne to *peine forte et dure*, even though it had been deemed an illegal punishment by the government of Massachusetts. Corey ended up being torturously crushed to death on or before September 18, 1692." She looked up at him.

"What was the punishment?"

"*Peine forte et dure*. It consisted of binding the person and laying them on the ground, supine. Of course, they were stripped naked first."

"Why of course?"

"As far as I can tell from the trial transcripts, most of the documented punishment and torture were sexually motivated. Even how they made the determination that someone was a witch seems to have been sexual in nature."

"That explains some of his thoughts."

"Like what?"

Ted took a moment before answering quietly, "Suffice it to say that I feel the need of a hot shower and a strong scrub brush." He couldn't look at her.

It was obvious that he wasn't going to say more, so she continued. "Anyway, they would then set a board on the chest of the person and put stones on the board. They kept putting more and more weight on until the person confessed or, as in Giles Corey's case, died. His wife, the woman Hathorne thinks I am, was hanged as a witch three days later."

"How many people were killed because of the trials?"

"Nineteen."

Ted bowed his head, locking his hands behind his neck. "You're wrong about his being just an evil bastard." He heaved a sigh. "He was a sanctioned serial killer."

"He didn't do it alone."

"So they were all sanctioned serial killers. That doesn't make him any better."

"They may have been, but that doesn't make you one of them."

"No. John Hathorne did that by himself."

"But you are not John Hathorne."

"Part of me is, whether it's psychosis or reincarnation."

"Try to keep it in perspective. It was 1692."

"What does the date have to do with it?"

"Belief systems were different then. Witchcraft was a perceived reality."

"That doesn't absolve him. He abused the power he was given, whether he really thought they were witches or not. He was a monster."

She didn't want to agree with him, but she could see his distress, so she tried to allay it. "Like I said, you are not John

Hathorne. In fact, some of the research I did indicates that he may have been mentally ill, caused by the toxins in the rye flour they used for bread. Because of the way they stored it, it often got damp and grew mold like Stachybotrys. As we know, when toxic molds are ingested, they can cause irrational behavior and even death. Some people think it may be the reason for the delusions the young girls had that started the whole witch hunt."

"It doesn't really matter why he was the way he was; I can't stop thinking that he's a part of me."

"Maura says he's probably the reason you're a trauma therapist. You're helping traumatized people to counteract the trauma he caused."

Ted became disturbingly quiet, staring down at what she wasn't sure. His entire look, body language, even the pallor of his skin, made her think of the word wretched. He looked like he felt wretched.

"I need some time to... to... I don't know what I need." He rose and looked down at her. "I don't even want to think about it." He clenched and unclenched his fists. "But I suspect it's all I'll be thinking about." Slowly, he made his way toward the door. Quietly, he added, "I need to figure out a way to get past it."

Now *she* felt wretched. Had she made things worse?

"Ted."

With his hand on the doorknob, he turned back to her.

"Are you sure you'll be okay?"

"Physically."

She wasn't sure how to respond so simply asked, "Will I see you tomorrow?"

Heaving a sigh, he said, "I suppose so." He left.

Staring at the door, Ann felt like she should have apologized, but she didn't know for what.

Chapter Thirty

Ted was determined not to show his daughter the torment caused by his session with Ann, so he entered the house cheerfully calling, "Sweet pea, I'm home." In spite of his forced cheerfulness, he got no response. A cursory look around the house and quick scan of the backyard from the kitchen window made it appear that he was alone. He didn't remember her saying she was going anywhere, but his mind didn't always grasp things these days. With a sigh, he got a can of Coke out of the refrigerator and headed to his office. As he stepped into the hall, the door from the attic swung open, missing him by mere inches.

"Whoa."

"Dad! Sorry, didn't hear you come in."

"And I didn't think you were here."

"I've been packing."

"Are you finished?"

"Yeah."

"Good, 'cause I had a thought. Why don't we head down to the airport now and find someplace for a nice leisurely dinner and avoid sitting on the freeway for an hour and half?"

"Sounds like a good idea. What happened with Ann?"

Hoping to avoid it altogether, Ted put his daughter off with, "Later. I want to get moving. So get your stuff together, and let's get out of here."

The car ride was taken up mostly with innocuous discussions of Sara Jane's travel plans and the already-known excursions with her mother. Sara Jane knew her father was avoiding talking about his meeting with Ann, but it was obvious that whatever happened disturbed him. She let it slide until they got to the restaurant.

After they ordered dinner, she said, "Now you can tell me all about what happened when you saw Ann." Stopping his protests even before he had a chance to say anything, she added, "I'll worry about it the whole time I'm gone if you don't tell me, and my imagination will make it much worse than it actually is."

"I'm not sure that's possible, but there's really nothing to worry about."

"Great! So there's no reason not to tell me."

He sighed. "Honey, I'd really rather not talk about it."

"Dad, I already know that whatever it is upset you badly..." She raised her hand to stop his denial. "Come on, you know you can't hide that stuff from me. What happened?"

He sat looking at her, tapping his lips lightly with his index fingers.

Sara Jane watched him for a moment. "It can't be as bad as all that."

"As bad as what?"

"I knew something was wrong when you got home, but you only do that thing with your fingers when something has really stressed you out. So spill."

Ted leaned back in the booth and looked into his daughter's lovely brown eyes. She truly was a remarkable young woman. Would he ever get used to the idea that she was no longer his little girl?

Heaving a deep sigh, he said, "One of the past lives was a judge at the Salem witch trials in 1692. The one who ordered the torture and death of nineteen people. A monster who hid behind the robes of justice."

Sara Jane watched the blood drain from her father's face. "You're not anything like that."

"I know. Ann says it's why I'm a trauma therapist. If you believe in that sort of thing, I'm trying to make up for what he did."

"She's probably right."

"Right or not, it's disturbing to think that the guy is a part of me."

"He's a part of your past not a part of you."

"What difference does that make?"

"Haven't you always said that we should never regret anything in our past because it makes us who we are now?" He nodded his agreement. "Wouldn't that apply to past lives too?"

Ted had no answer. As so often happened of late, his daughter's wisdom left him speechless. The arrival of the food caused enough of a break in the conversation that it became unnecessary for him to think of something to say.

Ellie sat on the pool's edge, her feet in the water, making lazy circles. "The water feels so good I might go in." She looked over her shoulder when she got no reply. Her friend was staring intently at the burning charcoal in the barbeque. "Ann?"

Nothing.

"Ann!"

Still Ann remained quiet, her eyes fixed on the red embers.

Ellie kicked her feet, splashing wildly in an attempt to attract Ann's attention.

Nothing.

She pulled her feet out of the water and stood, not forgetting her glass of wine, and walked over to the grill. "Annie."

Ann looked up, but as far as Ellie could tell she was still in never-never land. "The meat cooks better if you put it on the heat."

"What?"

"I think the coals are ready."

Ann glanced down at the grill. "Yeah, sorry," she said, reaching for the plate of marinated boneless chicken thighs.

"Still dealing with the whole Alex thing, huh?"

"Yeah, I guess. I'm waiting for the documents I need, but everything seems to be on track. It does feel strange making all these arrangements now when he's been dead the whole time."

"I know what you mean. I've spent the past six years telling myself he was dead and would never come back, and I was sure I really believed it. But when Doug told me about finding him, I didn't know what to feel. I realized that there was a part of me that held on to the hope that he was alive, because when I found out he wasn't, I felt crushed."

"For me it was just the opposite. I was so invested in believing that he was alive that finding out he wasn't was like a tidal wave of"—she bit her lip—"relief. As though finding him gave me permission to stop pretending, to accept reality. Does that sound awful?"

"No, I completely understand. And like Doug said, at least we know now, and it's over."

"Yeah, at least the wondering is over." Ann flipped the marinated chicken pieces on the grill.

"The rest will be soon." Ellie set her wineglass on the table. "I'm going in to put on my swimsuit."

"Not now. The chicken's almost finished cooking."

"Okay, I'll swim after dinner."

Ann smiled. "You have to wait an hour."

"Very funny."

Ann stacked the dinner dishes and stood up. "Are you still going to swim?"

Ellie leaned back in the chair. "Sounded like a good idea at the time but not so much now."

"How does an Irish coffee sound?"

"Got anything to go with it?"

"As a matter of fact, I do. I'll be back momentarily."

Picking up the wineglasses, Ellie said, "I'll help."

In the kitchen, Ann put the coffee to brew and got cups and plates out while Ellie rinsed and put dishes in the dishwasher. Continuing the chore, she asked, "Have you seen the kid again?"

"The kid? You mean Sara Jane McConaughy?"

"Yeah. Ted's kid."

Ann nodded. "Yes, I have."

Ellie closed the dishwasher, turned her back to the counter, and leaned against it. "So?"

"So what?"

"Aren't you going to tell me about it?"

"What do you want to know?"

Exasperated, Ellie said, "Come on. You've developed a relationship with the daughter of a man you almost married, so spit it out."

"I don't have a relationship with her. They came to dinner a couple of weeks ago."

"They?"

"Sara and Ted. Ted wanted me to tell her what was happening with him and what we planned to do. So nothing too exciting. Then I saw her again a while ago when Gigi and I went to the park."

"What was she doing at the dog park?"

"We ran into her on the sidewalk on our way home."

"Again, why was she in the neighborhood?"

"They were moving into their new house," she said, "a block away."

"Ted and Sara?"

"Yes."

"A block away from you?"

"Yes."

"Doesn't that bother you?"

"No."

Ellie took note that Ann wasn't looking at her but finding things to do so she could avoid eye contact. Ellie queried, "You aren't angry with him anymore, are you?"

"No."

"Have you forgiven him?"

"No, just not angry."

Ellie suspected there was much more to it but also suspected she wasn't going to get any more out of her friend. "Are we having our coffee outside?"

"Sure." Ann picked up the tray she'd been preparing while they talked and carried it out to the patio as the lights in the garden flickered on.

Chapter Thirty-One

Thursday, July 3

Ted was in a far better mood than Ann had expected. She'd been dreading seeing him, assuming he would be surly. She wouldn't describe him as cheerful, but he seemed quite calm.

"How are you feeling today?"

"Not too bad."

"Glad to hear it. When you left yesterday, you were pretty distraught."

"Yeah, well, with a teenage daughter who's much smarter than I am, it's difficult to mope around."

"So you told her what happened?"

"Yes, I did. She told me that my past has made me who I am, so I shouldn't be upset. Once again, I had no argument."

"Good for her. Did she get off to Chicago okay?"

"Yep. And while she's enjoying fireworks over the lake, I'll be all alone by myself."

She smiled at his mock self-pity and turned on the CD of a mountain stream, then lit the tea light under the lavender essential oil. So they began.

From his place in the armchair, Andrew looked around and then rose. As he moved across the room, he asked, "Is this your stateroom?"

Puzzled, she said, "No." Then remembered that he thought they were on a ship.

At the foot of the stairs, he stopped and surveyed that end of the room, including the loft.

"A sailing vessel with a library. Unusual, but quite pleasant." He turned and leaned languidly against the newel post. "So what takes you to Antigua, Miss Hart? It is *Miss* Hart, is it not?"

She lowered her eyes from his playful gaze and in a hushed voice said, "No, it is not."

"I see, and why are you going to Antigua?"

Suddenly Ann realized that she and Ted had never discussed how she should handle the specifics if it came to that. All she could do was play along. Her mind flipped through the web pages she'd looked at in her research, but at the moment all she could remember was that Antigua grew sugar, tobacco, and had several military forts.

Not able to come up with anything else, she said, "A visit with my aunt and uncle."

"How long will you be staying?"

"That hasn't been decided yet."

Lightly he touched the back of her neck as he passed behind her on his way back to the love seat. Unconsciously, she shivered at his touch. He sat, and with a slightly roguish grin asked, "Are you traveling with your husband?" She shook her head.

"Your husband is a fool, Mrs. Hart."

The fact that she didn't actually have a husband didn't stop her from demanding, "What do you mean, a fool?"

With a lifted eyebrow, he said, "Any man who allows you to travel alone is a fool." She didn't know if she was insulted or flattered, but before she was able to decide, he added, "If you were my wife, I'd never leave your side."

She could think of nothing to say except, "My husband is dead."

With more sincerity than she would have imagined, he said, "I am sorry."

Quietly she thanked him.

He leaned back, lounging, completely comfortable. With his elbow propped on the arm of the loveseat, his gently clenched fist tucked under his chin, he watched her. His eyes never left her face, which made her self-conscious, but it also made it impossible to avoid meeting his gaze.

"Alainn," he whispered in his native Scottish.

Her eyes narrowed. "I beg your pardon?"

His obvious self-confidence, on the verge of arrogance, tightened her stomach.

"Lovely. You are quite lovely."

Ann looked away but could feel him watching her, the knowledge causing the heat that now rose in her cheeks. Quickly she got up and walked to the desk. Leaning on it with her back to him, she took a deep breath.

What was he doing? It almost felt as if he was trying to seduce her. Her mind reeled. In 1805, wealthy men were gentlemen, weren't they? Then she remembered that even Jane Austen had at least one scoundrel in her books, and they were all gentlemen, as well as seducers of women. Gathering herself, she turned and found him watching her.

"Are you married, Mr. Mcnaughton?"

With a lazy smile, he said, "No, I am not."

"And your home is in Scotland?"

"My home is Antigua." Stretching his arm out in a welcoming gesture, he requested, "Please, sit with me."

The suggestion made her uncomfortable, but she could think of no rational reason to stay on the other side of the room so slowly made her way back to one of the Queen Anne chairs. His eyes followed her progress. Casually he leaned back and stretched out his legs.

Afraid he would seize the conversation again, she rushed to ask, "So how long has Antigua been your home?"

"Eight years."

Continuing with her make-believe trip story, she queried, "This is my first trip. What's it like there?"

He closed his eyes, visualizing it. "The air is soft and warm. The soothing trade winds never allow it to get oppressively hot. The water is a blue-green unlike anything else in nature"—he opened his eyes and engaged hers—"with the possible exception of emeralds, and it is so clear that you can see the fishes."

A playfulness danced across his face as he spoke of vibrant colors and exotic flowers that perfumed the night air. He leaned forward a bit.

"The white sand of the beaches is so fine that it puffs when you step on it, as if you are walking on powder. In the moonlight, it glistens as though diamonds have been cast upon it."

He leaned back with a sigh and smiled at her.

Caught up in his poetic description she said, "It sounds enchanting, quite romantic."

With a raised eyebrow and smoldering eyes, he said, "And so it is."

It felt like his eyes were boring into her very being. Flustered by the sensation, Ann hurriedly asked, "What made you move there?"

Aware that she wanted to keep the conversation away from herself, he decided to go along. *They would be at sea for some weeks; there was more than enough time to become familiar with this intriguing woman.*

"I inherited the stewardship of my father's West Indies properties when I was twenty-five."

"I'm sorry for your loss."

He looked at her quizzically. "My loss, Mrs. Hart?"

"Your father's death."

Curiously, he said, "My father is very much alive."

"But you said you inherited..."

"As the eldest son, I inherited the *stewardship,* not the property. I am responsible for the plantation, the slaves, and the crops."

Stunned, she asked, "Slaves?"

"Yes."

"But slavery isn't legal, is it?"

"Legal?"

His single word question reminded her that the year was 1805 for him, and that was some sixty years before the Emancipation Proclamation, which wouldn't have affected Antigua anyway. She vaguely remembered that even England didn't outlaw slavery until the 1840s. The thought that this man trafficked in human beings turned her stomach.

He saw her body almost recoil. "What is it, Mrs. Hart?"

Her back stiffened. "I am an abolitionist."

With a raised eyebrow, he said, "I see. So, I am a dastardly villain, am I?"

"Slavery is evil and immoral. So yes, you are."

"I agree, not that I am a villain, but that slavery is immoral."

"If you agree, then why don't you free your slaves?"

"I am afraid, Mrs. Hart, they are not mine to free. My father owns them, and you must understand that our economy is based on slavery. The cost of cotton, indigo, sugar, and the things made from them would be exorbitant if the people who worked the fields were paid wages."

Finding herself getting angry, she said, "So you wouldn't free them even if you could because it would destroy your profit margin."

"Not just mine."

"But they're people."

"So they are."

Frustrated and disgusted, she lashed out. "How can you say that? How can you think they are people and that slavery is evil but abuse them anyway?"

"I do not abuse my slaves, Mrs. Hart, and..."

"You said the slaves weren't yours."

He bowed his head in concession. "My father's slaves. I do not abuse *my father's* slaves."

"Making them work without compensation is abuse."

"There is some truth in what you say, but it is the way of it, Mrs. Hart. There will always be some form of slavery, even if only to money."

"It doesn't have to be that way. People like you could change it."

She was unable to read his expression, but his remark, "This is not a subject for polite discussion and certainly not with a lady," only irritated her further, and she slipped into silence.

Andrew watched her for a moment then leaned his head back and closed his eyes. When Ann looked over at him again, Andrew was gone. "Ted?"

"Yes."

"I'm going to count backward from five. When I reach one, you will awaken and remember everything that happened." She swallowed hard, hoping against hope that he hadn't noticed her awkward reaction to Andrew's attentions early in the session. "Five, four, three, two, one."

Ted opened his eyes and sat upright. He looked down at the loveseat and then over at the chair in which he had started the session. "Curious."

"What is?"

"Seems Andrew prefers the loveseat to the chair," he said with a knowing smile.

A small smile crossed her lips as she avoided eye contact. "How do you feel?"

"Ok, I guess."

"Well, it must be a relief to know that he isn't an axe murderer."

"We don't really know that, do we?"

"What do you mean? He's a charming, well-educated, and wealthy man."

With a raised eyebrow, Ted asked, "Charming?"

"He's a cad. His wealth and charm make him think he can have anything he wants."

"Or any*one*."

She couldn't tell if it was a question or a statement so chose to ignore it.

"Well, at least you know he isn't evil."

"I don't actually. And you think he is."

Suddenly, Ann rose and hurried away. He stood and watched. She turned when she reached her desk. "Well, not because he kills people."

"How do you know he doesn't kill his slaves?"

"Why are you doing this?"

He smiled at her as he approached the desk. "I'm not *doing* anything."

As he got closer, she moved around and sat behind her desk. He stopped where she had been standing and looked down at her. "Feel safe now?"

She glanced up at him and then quickly looked away. Her heart raced, and her stomach turned over. "Not particularly."

Ted broke the uncomfortable silence that followed the exchange. "Are you upset because Andrew came on to you or because you think I did?"

After having judiciously avoided eye contact, she looked directly at him. "Neither!" she said adamantly.

"You are clearly distressed by something. You backed away from me and hid behind your desk like you thought I might attack you. Are you suddenly afraid of me?"

Feeling silly for reacting exactly as he described, she reluctantly said, "No."

"What then?"

"I don't know."

Ted would have liked to press the issue to find out what was going on with her, but he knew it would make her shut down even more. "So when do you want to meet again?"

Surprise filled her eyes when she looked up at him. "You want to do this again?"

"I thought the whole point was to find out why he persists in invading my dreams so we can get rid of him permanently, and we haven't bolted his door yet."

She rushed to apologize, then offered, "Of course, you're right. Tomorrow?"

"Tomorrow is the Fourth."

"Right. When then?"

"How about next Tuesday?"

"Sure, whenever is good for you."

He started to leave, but turned back. "I didn't mean to frighten or upset you. I was just teasing. Are you going to be okay? Can I do anything?"

She couldn't help herself and smiled. "You've done enough, thanks."

He returned her smile, then, making a slight bow reminiscent of Andrew, said, "Until we meet again, Mrs. Hart."

Mrs. Hart. Shouldn't she feel guilty? She enjoyed Andrew's attention. Or was it Ted's attention she enjoyed? Had she betrayed Alex by enjoying it? The questions made her head swim.

Chapter Thirty-Two

T ed was following what had already become his regular
morning routine in the new house—shower, shave,
dress, and breakfast in the backyard. Sipping the strong
coffee he'd prepared for himself, he thought of his dream.
He had not dreamt of John Hathorne since bolting the door.
Had locking the imaginary door worked? He certainly
hoped so. But the Mcnaughton dream returned last night,
with a vengeance. The gut-wrenching dream had once again
left him weary, even after a full night's sleep. It motivated
him to want this resolved and done away with if that was
possible. In the meantime, Maura suggested they find out as
much as they could about the Scotsman. As he popped the
last bite of bagel into his mouth, he hit the Google app on his
electronic tablet.

Sifting through several websites, he finally settled on one
that gave the address, phone numbers, and e-mail contacts of
the Antiguan Embassy in Washington, DC.

Ann didn't have to be in the office until ten, so shutting off the alarm, she allowed herself the time to wake slowly and luxuriate in her freshly laundered sheets. She turned onto her side and came face-to-face with Gigi, who licked her nose.

"I love you too, fur face."

As her head started to clear, she stretched and got out of bed. Her slippers whispered against the parquet floor of the hall as the big white dog trotted ahead of her. She opened the kitchen door, and Gigi ran outside. Standing at the sink, waiting for the coffee to brew, Ann watched the dog romp in the beautiful summer morning. She smiled at Gigi's attempts to tree a squirrel, but the tiny creature was much faster and far more agile than the lumbering dog.

Taking her coffee outside, she sat in the rocking chair. The dog came over and put her head in Ann's lap. Absently rubbing Gigi's head, she couldn't stop thinking about her dream. Andrew Mcnaughton kissed her—or was it Ted?

Ann got to her office only moments before Ted arrived. She was excited to see him, and that disturbed her a bit. She took a deep breath. As she slipped her purse into the credenza, her back to the door, he walked in. She turned around to find him standing at her desk holding a box.

"Greetings, fair doctor."

Looking at him and grinning slightly, she said, "Hi. What have you got there?"

"It's a desktop fountain." Looking at the outside of the box, he read, "For interior environmental serenity."

He smiled and stretched out his arms, offering it to her. "It's for you."

She didn't accept it, and warily asked, "For me?"

"Yes." He set it on her desk.

"Why?"

"No need for suspicion. When Sara Jane and I were at your house, I noticed that you still like copper. I noticed also that, even though you like the sound of moving water, you don't have a water feature here in your office." He glanced around the room. "I just happened upon it this morning, so I got it for you. Don't you like it?"

"It's lovely." She looked down at it and then at him. "I don't know what to say."

"Thank you would suffice."

Flustered, she hurriedly said, "Yes, of course. Thank you. It's very thoughtful."

He smiled. "Let's set it up, and you won't have to use the CD of the mountain stream."

She pulled it out of the box and assembled it on the credenza while Ted got water from the water cooler. Together they watched the water bubble up out of the center stem, spilling onto the lily pad–like leaves that spiraled down to the rock-filled oval bowl at the base.

She looked up at him. "I love it. Thank you."

"You're welcome." He turned and made his way to the conversation area. "You don't accept gifts any more graciously than you do compliments. I thought you might have outgrown that by now."

She had an overwhelming desire to throw her arms around him and kiss him but controlled herself and said simply, "I know. I'm sorry."

Ann generally sat on the loveseat and Ted in one of the recliners, so when she approached the conversation area and saw him on the loveseat, she had a very quizzical look on her face. He answered the unasked question. "Seems Mcnaughton prefers the loveseat, so I figured I might as well start out here. Of course, it may have nothing to do with the furniture, and may simply be because it's where you usually sit."

The butterflies darted about in her stomach as she went to the sideboard to make the tea.

Ted asked, "Do you actually believe in reincarnation?"

"You don't after all this?"

"Do me a favor. Since I'm not actually a patient, don't answer my questions with questions. Do you believe in reincarnation or don't you?"

"I didn't before this, but it's hard for me not to believe now. You still have questions?"

"It goes way beyond questions. I always thought that reincarnation was nothing more than wishful thinking by desperate people. I can't suddenly believe in something that I was sure was just delusional fantasy."

"Like I said before, you don't have to believe in it for it to be true."

"I suppose."

She took a sip of her tea. "I have a couple of questions. Since we're doing this for your peace of mind, is there something specific you'd like me to ask or say?"

"Not really. I'll leave it to you. See where the conversation takes you."

"And you don't want me to steer it in any particular direction?"

"No." When she didn't say anything else, he asked, "You said there were a couple of things."

"We didn't discuss how to handle the whole traveling in 1805 thing, so I just sort of winged it."

He raised one eyebrow. "I know."

She flushed pink. "Would you rather I take a different tack?"

"No." And that single word ended the conversation.

Ted drank the last of his tea, leaned his head back, and closed his eyes, visualizing their secret garden.

Chapter Thirty-Three

Ted's breathing went from the regular, rhythmic breaths of wakefulness to the deep breaths of complete relaxation. There was a calmness in him. He seemed so peaceful. Then something changed. She felt her stomach churn and realized that Andrew Mcnaughton was entering the room.

He sat upright and looked at her, then glanced around the room.

"You spend much time here in the library, Mrs. Hart. You enjoy reading."

It was a statement that didn't really require a response, but she agreed. "Yes, I do."

"Who do you read?"

The first name that came to mind that she was sure would fall into the proper time frame was, "Mary Wollstonecraft."

Andrew did nothing to hide his surprise, but all he said was, "Interesting."

Ann suddenly remembered that the mother of Mary Shelley had been a feminist writer who believed in free love. In the late eighteenth century, it went beyond scandalous to believe in and live a free-love existence. The look that accompanied his single word response was more cunning than the playful grin of previous meetings. She swallowed hard, then quickly added William Blake and Shakespeare to her repertoire, hoping to take his mind off Wollstonecraft.

Andrew cocked his head and watched her, trying to discern if her rush to cover her interest in Wollstonecraft was embarrassment or fear. Deciding it was embarrassment since she was obviously a lady, he rose and walked around the office, casually inspecting the art hanging on the walls. Near her desk, he turned, casting a curious glance her way.

"Which poem is your favorite?"

"Poem?"

"You said you read Blake. Which of his poems is your favorite?" A raised eyebrow with the question made it clear that he didn't believe her claim.

Suddenly, she felt as though she'd painted herself into a corner. And the grin that now curved his lips was almost a sneer, telling her that he enjoyed her obvious discomfort. A fact that steeled her resolve to find a way to extricate herself from that corner.

Remembering back to her English lit class in college, she blurted out, "A Poison Tree," silently acknowledging it was the only one she remembered.

Again, "Interesting," was his only response.

He turned away and walked to the other end of the room. Ann watched him as his eyes scanned the bookshelves. He was infuriating. In no more than a few words, he had managed to make her feel silly, inadequate, and rather stupid. By accomplishing that, he had once again taken control of the situation, and she still wasn't sure how to reverse it.

He pulled a book off of the shelf. She could see that it was one of Alex's. She had moved all his books here after the earthquake destroyed the shelves in his office. Blake had been one of Alex's favorite poets, and this book contained what he had considered the writer's best works including reproductions of the etchings Blake, a gifted artist as well, had done to illustrate the poems.

Andrew slowly returned to the conversation area, flipping through the volume as he went. Sitting down, he looked up from the page and stared at her for a moment. Ann was unable to read the look. Turning his attention back to the open book in his lap, he read aloud.

> *I was angry with my friend:*
> *I told my wrath; my wrath did end.*
> *I was angry with my foe:*
> *I told it not, my wrath did grow.*
>
> *And I watered it in fears,*
> *Night and morning with my tears,*
> *And I sunned it with smiles,*
> *And with soft deceitful wiles.*
>
> *And it grew both day and night,*
> *Till it bore an apple bright,*
> *And my foe beheld it shine,*
> *And he knew that it was mine,*
>
> *And into my garden stole,*
> *When the night had veiled the pole.*
> *In the morning, glad I see*
> *My foe outstretched beneath the tree.*

He ended the reading by looking at her and asking, "What intrigues you about that?"

In college, they had discussed just that question, and Ann had remembered it because of its obvious message, obvious to her in any event.

"The depiction of the destructive nature of anger."

Closing the book, he traced the gold letters on the cover with his index finger. He didn't look at her when he said, "Is anger always destructive?"

There was something behind the question that she couldn't quite figure out. "Extended anger, never getting past the anger, is very destructive. It may not result in death of the body, but it definitely kills the spirit... the soul."

"And what is it that angers you, Mrs. Hart?"

Unwilling to admit that his arrogant mocking made her angry, she denied the allegation. He locked his gaze on her eyes. "I can see it in the very way you sit there. So is it I who have made you angry, or is there a deeper cause?"

She adamantly reiterated, "I am *not* angry."

With a sardonic grin, he tossed the book onto the table, then leaned back in the loveseat. Steepling his hands, he tapped his lips with the tips of the index fingers and stared at her.

The gesture was the same quirk Ted had when he was stressed or very deep in thought. She wondered if it was a holdover from his past life as Andrew or if Andrew did it because of Ted. Dispensing with the thought, she was determined to turn the table on him and asked, "What are you angry about?"

His eyes narrowed and his jaw tightened. "My anger is of no consequence."

"So you are angry." Remembering the man's grief from Ted's dream, she asked, "What was her name?"

She said nothing more, but he saw the compassion, the understanding. Hesitating, he took a stuttering breath. "Catherine." He paused. "My wife."

Silently, Andrew got up and crossed the room. He turned toward her and leaned against the corner of the mahogany desk but stared at the floor.

Ann moved around the furniture and leaned against the back of the chair closest to him. Quietly she asked, "What do you miss most?"

His eyes met hers. "Her love," he said matter-of-factly. "She was the very essence of my soul."

Neither said anything for a space of time until he asked, "And you, what do you miss?"

She sighed. "Many small things." She looked at him. "But like Catherine, they showed his love."

A sad smile crossed his face. "I had no idea that it was possible to be so completely happy." He looked at her. "So many of my friends had married for monetary gain or to consolidate property and family fortunes that I had forsaken ever finding love in marriage. Cathy changed that."

With the desk acting as support for him, he stayed there for several minutes, arms crossed, watching Ann, who was staring at the floor. He took the few steps that separated them and with his hand under her chin gently lifted her face to him. She looked up into his tear-filled eyes as he leaned close to her. She was sure he was going to kiss her. Instead he whispered, "He was a very lucky man." His hand dropped to his side, and he returned to the loveseat.

Ann didn't move, but after a few minutes, Andrew asked, "Mrs. Hart?"

She was waiting for the heat of her embarrassment to subside. She had wanted him to kiss her. She blew out a deep breath, humiliated that he apparently didn't want to kiss her. Steeling herself, she went back to her chair. She could feel his eyes on her, but she was unable to meet his gaze.

"Your anger is at his loss."

She really didn't want to discuss her personal life with him. Her curt response was, "I suppose."

Her tone and demeanor made him ask, "Something has changed. Have I offended you in some way?"

The question reminded her that she was supposed to be helping Ted, and being overly sensitive with his past life was not the way to handle things. She looked up and apologized. "I am too emotional of late." Then shifted her eyes away from him.

An understanding smile curved his lips. "Like my Catherine, you have a gentle heart." He leaned his head back and closed his eyes.

She watched for his breathing to go from deep exhalations to regular breath sounds, but it didn't, and suddenly Ted started to sob, sobs that led to heartfelt cries of anguish. *Was this Andrew distraught over the loss of his wife and child or was Ted in such distress?* The cries continued. Ann finally asked, "Ted?"

Gasping slightly, he said, "Yes."

"Try to take a deep breath."

His attempt only caused short bursts of air to escape his lungs.

"Where are you?"

"Hospital."

"Why?"

Through sobs, he told her, "Josh is dying."

"I'm so sorry," was the only thing she could think of to say. Reliving the worst time in his life, Ted's sobs turned to gut-wrenching cries.

Her instinct was to gather him in her arms to calm him, but her own natural reserve stopped her from doing it. Instead, she stood behind him and gently laid her hands on his shoulders. His sorrow-wracked body quivered under her hands. Her instincts finally got the better of her. Without further thought, she bent down and wrapped her arms around his neck. After a few minutes, he laid his right hand on top of her crossed arms.

"Thank you."

She released him and stepped away from the chair. "For what?"

He stood up and looked at her. "I'm not sure. All I remember is feeling extremely disturbed almost frantic, and you calmed me." Rubbing his eyes, and releasing a deep breath, he said, "I'm sorry."

"No need to apologize. Do you remember the session?"

"Most of it, but I have no idea why I feel like I've been crying for a long time."

"I was getting ready to bring you back, when suddenly you started to cry. You said you were in a hospital and Josh was dying."

"I'm sorry you had to deal with that. Thank you for helping me through it."

Suddenly embarrassed by the way she helped him through it, she hurriedly explained, "I've found that sometimes physical contact helps to calm people." She rushed on, saying, "I think it's because as children we're comforted by our mothers who use hugs and kisses. I believe that is why people respond to touch rather than to words. You're not really listening when you're agitated, so a calm touch gets through the disturbance when speaking doesn't." She didn't want to stop talking because she was afraid of what he would say, but she really didn't have anything else to add so now tried to relax.

Slightly startled by her rapid-fire explanation, Ted tried to ease her obvious embarrassment. "Whatever the reason, it seems to have worked, so thank you again."

His gracious appreciation in light of her outburst made Ann flush pink.

He stood up. "Why don't you let me take you to lunch? We'll have a nice leisurely meal and make sure we only talk about things"—he gestured around the room—"entirely unrelated to this. We can walk if it's not too hot for you." His face lit with a strange little smile.

"What?"

"I was just remembering that Sunday afternoon we went to a play at the Music Center and you decided to walk into the fountain because it was so hot. You were all dressed up in that lavender dress and straw hat, the one you called a picture hat." His smile broadened. "It had a ribbon that matched your dress, as I recall."

Ann giggled. He had actually enjoyed the fact that she'd done it and hadn't been embarrassed at all. That was when she started falling in love with him.

Chapter Thirty-Four

They left her office, and Ted gently but firmly wrapped her arm around his own, holding it tightly to his body. She peeked at him sidewise but didn't pull away.

It was comfortable walking with Ted's arm entwined with hers. She was still processing the fact that he remembered not only the incident in the Music Center fountain, but what she'd been wearing. She looked up at him out of the corner of her eyes and sighed. It felt... safe walking beside him. *Heresy,* her feminist self said, but her emotional self couldn't help it. Part of her wanted to hold on to him tighter, and part of her wanted to drop his arm. How silly could she be? He was only a man, not a safe harbor. She pulled her arm free and answered his questioning look with, "It's too hot."

Disappointed by the sudden movement, Ted just nodded.

They continued to walk, but after a block and a half, he stopped.

Ann had taken a few more steps before she realized it. She turned back to him. "What's up?"

Looking at a theater lobby card of Barbra Streisand surrounded by flowers he said, "Do you remember this? We saw it at that revival house. It was the film's thirtieth anniversary or something."

"Of course I remember."

"Are you still a Streisand freak?"

"I don't consider it freakish. But yes, I still like Streisand."

"We laughed for days at the clothes and makeup. Wait a minute. As I recall, you actually liked the clothes."

Ann smiled playfully. "Yeah," and with an exaggerated sigh added, "and Jack Nicholson was so cute."

Ted's eyes crinkled. "If you like that type."

She laughed out loud. "I can't believe you're still jealous of him."

He insisted, "I'm not jealous."

"Right." She turned and continued walking. It only took a few steps for him to catch up.

Lunch was relaxed and leisurely. True to his word, nothing was said regarding the session or its aftermath.

They talked about movies, music, food, ordinary things. There was no need to try to make a good impression or worry about making a bad one. It was comfortable.

Ann suggested they share dessert, but Ted wanted rhubarb pie, and the thought almost made her gag. She ate all the apples and most of the crust of a piece of apple pie à la mode. As she scooped up the last bit of fruit swimming in the melted vanilla ice cream, Ted brought up the strange coincidence of *On a Clear Day You Can See Forever* playing at the local theatre.

"Not so much because we saw it together years ago, but because it's about reincarnation. Remember how we laughed about that? Doesn't seem so funny anymore, does it?"

"No, it doesn't."

They left the restaurant, once again arm in arm, but this time it was her idea. It felt natural, having her at his side, and he began to wonder if a second chance was a possibility. Perhaps he would explore the idea after all this reincarnation stuff was sorted out. He was grateful to whatever power was responsible that he no longer saw the anger with which she greeted him the first few times they met.

As they approached her office, she said, "Are we doing this again tomorrow?"

"Having lunch?"

She sighed. "Yes, having lunch." She shook her head.

He smiled down at her. "I'm tied up the next couple of days. Have a few faculty meetings and grad-student-advisor meetings. We're all getting ready for next semester."

"So you'll call when you have the time."

"Actually, I was thinking maybe we could do another session now if you don't have patients."

"Really? This morning was so emotional. Are you sure you're ready?"

"As ready as I'll ever be."

"Okay. I don't have patients until this evening. I was just going to ride."

"Ride?"

"Bicycle."

He nodded as he held the door of her building open for her. Inside her office, Ann put her purse in the credenza. She couldn't help but smile at the little fountain. It was such a thoughtful gift that it brought back memories of their life together. He had always been thoughtful, which was why when Ellie told her she'd seen him with someone else Ann didn't believe it. He would never have done anything to hurt her like that. She'd been sure of it until she'd seen for herself. She swallowed to stop the tightening in her throat. No point dwelling on the past. She turned and saw that he'd lit the candle under the diffuser and started the water boiling for tea. He turned and smiled at her.

As she approached the conversation area, she asked, "Why did you get divorced?"

A bit surprised at the question since she'd never shown any interest in what he'd been doing since their breakup, he paused before answering. "Why does anyone get divorced? Neither of us cared enough to work at it."

"As a family counselor I've noticed that, generally speaking, the mother gets custody. Why did you?"

"Melinda's job kept her working very long hours, and she did a lot of traveling."

"But you used to travel a lot too."

He liked that she knew that. "Yes, but I didn't really have to. I started making sure it was never more than a few days, and since my folks are here, the children were always with family. She'd already been offered the position in Chicago, and it meant she'd be traveling even more. We decided it would be best if the kids didn't have to leave school and friends, and she didn't have to try to make arrangements in a strange city to take care of them."

"So, it was truly a joint decision?"

"Yes. We agreed to it before we went to the lawyer."

"Well, you've done a wonderful job."

He chuckled. "Thanks. Just wish it didn't feel like she's rearing me." He turned to make the tea then brought the brew to the table and sat on the loveseat. Ann was already in one of the Queen Anne chairs. The talk moved to small, mundane things until Ted set his mug down and leaned back against the loveseat and closed his eyes. He pretty much did the hypnosis himself now, so Ann watched as his breathing became deep and slow. A small smile curved his lip, and for a moment he looked just like Sara Jane. It made Ann wonder what their children would have looked like... if they'd had any.

Her mind thus occupied, she missed Andrew's entrance. His movements drew her attention as he leisurely draped himself on the loveseat.

"So... how have you found the voyage thus far, Mrs. Hart?"

Tilting her head slightly, she said, "It's been"—she crinkled her nose—"uncomfortable."

"Not a seaman, then?"

"I suppose not."

Of course, it wasn't the sea that caused the discomfort. And this time Ann intended to take control at the beginning. She started by requesting, "Tell me about Cathy."

She saw the dark cloud come into his eyes once again.

"What do you want to know?"

"What was it that made you so blissfully happy?"

"She loved me."

"That's it? She loved you?"

He looked askance at her. "Certainly you know, Mrs. Hart, that unconditional love is all it takes."

He appeared lost in his thoughts, and after a few minutes Ann cleared her throat.

He looked at her. "I would like to believe that I loved her enough to make her happy as well."

His eyes told of his absolute devotion and heart-wrenching loss. "I am in no doubt that you did." She ran her thumbnail over her lips and then lightly bit it. "Maybe you loved her too well."

A sad smile accompanied his response. "Is it possible to love too well?"

"Your love for her has kept you perpetually unhappy. Since she made you so happy when she was alive, do you think she would want you to be so miserable?"

"Perhaps not, but replacing true love is not easily done."

"Particularly if you are not open to the possibility."

With some disdain in his tone, he said, "You begin to sound like my family."

"How is that?"

Without looking at her, Andrew told her how much he enjoyed the solitude of life in Antigua, away from the pitying eyes of his friends and family. He explained how his mother and sisters paraded an almost constant stream of *eligible* women for him. The activity made his visits to Scotland trying. Even his father joined in the effort, telling him it was time to live up to his responsibility and take a wife. When he told his father he was not ready to marry again, that his grief was still too deep, his father accused him of weakness, exclaiming that a man pulls himself up and does what is expected.

Andrew rubbed his eyes dry. "My father is angered that I do not hide my tears; he considers it proof of my weakness."

Gently, Ann offered, "Tears are not a sign of weakness but of great power. Tears are a sign of overwhelming grief and overpowering love."

He met her gaze; he saw no pity, only compassion. With a sad smile, he said, "Thank you." He took a deep breath. "Cathy was far more intelligent than I. In fact, I never understood why she loved me, but she did."

Ann had to stop herself from smiling at his sincere self-deprecation.

He continued. "It was her gentle soul that drew me to her. I could not help but love her." A small smile curved his lip. "And she was amazingly generous." Almost to himself he repeated, "So generous." He came out of the slight reverie. "My father thought her naïve because she preferred to see only the good in people. It may have been naiveté, but if we were all like Catherine the world would be a better place." He stopped himself from crying again.

He got up and sat in the chair next to Ann and leaned his forearms on his knees. "You are American, are you not?"

Taken aback by the seemingly out of context question, she hesitantly said, "Yes, I am."

"Do you not believe that everyone is equal? No classes?" Ann agreed that the Declaration of Independence did say that.

"Cathy strongly concurred with your declaration."

"But you don't." It was a statement.

"Frankly, I had never given it much thought, but my Catherine was very persuasive."

"And your slaves?"

The cynicism in the question reminded him of her violent reaction to his admission of being a slaveholder, so he hesitated before saying, "Cathy was as vehemently antislavery as are you. Because of how she felt, I had refused the stewardship of the plantation, thinking that she would not want to live there with slaves, but she wanted me to take it. She told me that we could only change things if we were there."

He smiled at the memory and continued the story by telling Ann that the first year they were in Antigua, Cathy insisted he build a school on the plantation, explaining that his wife believed all people deserved an education—girls, boys, rich, poor, servant, and slave. She believed ignorance deprived people of the opportunities everyone deserved. Catherine did not believe that society purposely kept the poor ignorant in order to maintain class distinction, but she believed that ignorance created the separation of classes. He added that she also believed that children should not be put to work, so the school was for all the children on the plantation.

"I know that you consider me a despicable villain, and I may be. But the truth is that I believe it will not be long before the institution of slavery is outlawed. More importantly, I also believe that uneducated, untrained people will be of no earthly value to themselves or anyone else if, as free men and women, they are unable to function in society. To that end, the adults are also given the option of education at Cathy's school. The servants and slaves are taught to read and write, and many are taught trades that will allow them to be independent when the time comes." He pulled on his earlobe. "All because of my Catherine's generous heart."

"You have servants and slaves?"

"Only the field hands are slaves. All others working on the plantation are servants." He paused a moment, attempting to gauge her reaction, then added, "Paid servants. Cathy refused to have slaves in or around the house."

He then told her of the hospital he built in his wife's honor and the doctor who lived on the plantation and took care of everyone there—slave, servant, and master.

Staggered by the information, Ann could think of nothing to say that would not sound condescending. Even in her head, everything she could think to say sounded rude. It was an effort not to smile at his reference to himself as master, but she was prepared to forgive him that small slip, although she was sure he didn't think of it as a slip. Still, for the giant steps he'd taken to fulfill his wife's dreams, she was speechless.

Andrew looked at Ann, and she saw weariness. He nodded and leaned back in the chair. A few minutes later, Ted sat up.

He glanced over at Ann. "Quite a story."

"I'll say."

"Well, I've taken up most of your day, and I'm sure you've got stuff to do, so I'll be on my way." He got up and started to leave.

"Ted."

He turned back to her.

"Would you like to come over for dinner tonight?"

"I'd love to, but I can't."

"Got a hot date, huh?" she teased.

"As a matter of fact, I do." He paused for effect, delighted that she seemed a bit disappointed. "With Sara Jane. She came back today. Mom picked her up from the airport, so she's waiting at home for me."

Ann couldn't hide the relief, but tried to cover it by rushing to say, "I thought she was only going to be gone three days, so I assumed she was back already."

"She was only in Chicago for three days, but a friend of hers moved to Denver last year, so she stopped to visit for a few days."

"Well, tell her hello for me. See you in a couple of days, then?"

"Yes."

Chapter Thirty-Five

"Sweet pea, I'm home, and I've got dinner."

Sara Jane came running from the back of the house and threw her arms around her father's neck, forcing him to juggle the pizza and salad in one hand as he wrapped his now-free arm around her.

He squeezed her and kissed the top of her head. "I missed you so much."

"Me too. Me too." Sara hugged her father so tightly he finally said, "Hey, kid, I can't breathe."

She released him. "Sorry, I just really missed you."

"Let's get this stuff in the kitchen. You can tell me all about the trip over dinner."

"Let's eat by the pool."

"You got it."

As they made their way to the kitchen, Sara Jane explained, "Mom's place has a balcony, but it's really narrow and cramped feeling. Alicia's folks' house has a nice yard, but she wanted to go out every night. Relaxing by the pool with you will be heaven."

"I'm guessing you won't feel that way forever, so I'm going to take full advantage of it now."

After hearing about the shopping in Chicago and the sleepless nights and partying in Denver, Sara Jane and Ted quietly cleared the table, then Sara made her father a latte.

Not wanting the evening to end just yet, Ted suggested a movie.

"Do you have one in mind?"

"How about *On A Clear Day You Can See Forever*?"

"I thought you hated that movie."

"No, it just had bad memories attached to it."

"It doesn't anymore?"

"No."

"Why?"

"Not really important, but the bad memories have been replaced by better ones."

"Great. You know I love Streisand."

He shook his head. "Yeah, I know."

They sat on the couch, Sara nestled against her father's shoulder, his arm around her. As the FBI warning played, Sara asked her father a question. "Why this sudden desire to see a Streisand movie?"

"Why do you ask?"

"Well, I was wondering if it had something to do with Ann?"

Once again surprised by his daughter's insight, Ted admitted, "Yes, it does have to do with Ann. When we were together, we saw it in a revival house because she's a Streisand freak too."

"Hey! We aren't freaks."

Ted laughed. "Yeah, she said that too. Anyway, we had lunch today, and the movie is going to be playing at a theater near her office. We stopped and looked at the poster and were able to laugh about it, so I don't think seeing it will bother me anymore."

"Oh." Streisand began to sing, and the pair grew quiet.

As the psychedelic end credits began to roll, Sara Jane sat up. "Can I ask a personal question, Dad?"

"Can I stop you?"

"Mom and I talked more this time than we ever did before."

"That's good. I'm glad."

"One of the things we talked about was why you guys got divorced."

"And you don't hate me. That's a good thing."

"Why would I hate you?"

"I doubt your mother had very many nice things to say."

"Actually, she told me that you never really loved each other. That she was being pushed into marriage by her family, and you were on the rebound. She said that for some reason that neither of you ever really understood, it seemed like a good idea at the time. Mom said that by the time you guys decided it was a mistake she was already pregnant with Josh, so you stayed together. Then while you were trying to work things out, she got pregnant with me. But the bottom line was that you both knew it was never right."

"Yeah, that's pretty much what happened. So, what's your question?"

"Were you on the rebound from Ann?"

"I guess I should have seen that coming." He got up and said he needed another cup of coffee if he was going to get into it. Sara Jane followed him into the kitchen. "You want me to make you another latte?"

"Sure, why not?" He sat at the kitchen table as his very grown-up daughter made espresso and steamed the milk. She made herself a hot chocolate in spite of the hot summer night.

Giving him the latte and sitting down with her own mug of chocolate, Sara Jane asked, "So you and Ann broke up just before you married Mom?"

"Yeah."

"Why? I can tell when you guys are together that you still have feelings for each other even after this long. So why did you break up?"

He sat quietly for a while, afraid his beloved daughter would think less of him if he told her the truth.

She prodded him again.

"A few weeks before our wedding, a friend of hers claimed to have seen me on a date with another woman. She was mistaken, since I wasn't on a date with anyone else. But a couple of weeks later, Ann thinks she saw me with someone. When I denied it, she called me a liar, and threw her engagement ring at me. It was the last time I saw or talked with her until after the earthquake when I ran into her at the Red Cross Center." He swallowed the lump in his throat. "So there you have it, the sordid tale of our breakup."

"Did you?"

"Did I what?"

"Did you cheat on her?"

"No, I didn't, and I never would have, but she didn't trust me. I really believed that she was my soul mate. From the moment I met her, I never wanted to be with anyone else."

"I'm really sorry, Dad."

"Yeah, well, I made the mistake of not dealing with it and moving on, like she did. Instead, I married your mother less than six months after the breakup, which wasn't fair to either of us or to you and Josh." A long silence was broken by Ted quietly saying, "I really loved her and thought we would spend our lives together." He glanced up at Sara Jane and with a sad smile said, "We planned on having four children."

"I wonder why she never had kids."

"I don't know." Suddenly he got up. "Come on, I want to show you something." He and Sara Jane went into his bedroom. He'd finished decorating the room while she was away, so this was her first time seeing it. She smiled. The room was very similar to Ann's, but she was pretty sure her father had never seen Ann's bedroom. The antique bedstead was some dark wood, walnut probably, and the side tables were the same kind of wood but didn't match the bed. She was pretty sure they were all antiques. One of the nightstands had a marble top. There were two barrister bookcases filled with his book collection. Ted went to the highboy dresser that was also old and opened the small cupboard in the middle of the chest that originally was used for the storage of collars and studs. He opened a small box that said Big Bear on it and took something out. He turned to Sara Jane holding out a diamond ring. She took it. "This is the one you gave to Ann?"

"Yes."

"You've kept it all these years." It was a statement not a question. "Didn't that bother Mom, that you had someone else's engagement ring in your jewelry box?"

"I'm not proud to say this, but the truth is I didn't care. I wanted to keep it; it was as simple as that."

"No wonder Mom thought you never got over her." Still holding the ring, Sara Jane looked up at her father, and asked quietly, "Do you still love her?"

"I don't know. I certainly think I could fall in love with her again, but I'm pretty sure she isn't interested in rekindling things."

Sara Jane returned the ring and then hugged her father. "Too bad. You guys make a great couple." She yawned. "I think I'll call it a night." She kissed his cheek.

He did the same. "Good night, sweetie. Great to have you back."

"It's great to be back."

Ted sat on the bed and stared at the ring. They spent weeks looking in antique and jewelry stores until they found just the right one. It was new but looked vintage. The little-over-one-carat diamond was mounted in a platinum basket setting with smaller diamonds set in rose gold on either side. The shank of the ring was yellow gold. He held it up to the light. It was still beautiful. He closed his hand around it, making no attempt to stop the tears.

Chapter Thirty-Six

Ellie walked in without knocking. "Annie!" When she got no response, she went directly to the patio door, assuming her friend was outside. Ann was sitting on the pool deck with her feet in the water.

Ellie put her purse and the bag of hamburgers and fries on the table and kicked off her shoes. Pouring herself a glass of wine, she joined Ann at the pool's edge.

"So what's up? You sounded pretty stressed out on the phone."

"Oh, Ellie, I'm a mess."

"Why? What's happened?"

Ann took a sip of her wine, then said, "I don't know where to start." Taking a gulp of her wine this time, she continued. "I betrayed Alex, Andrew has me completely bewildered, and I think I may be falling in love with Ted."

"Wow!" They sat quietly for a few minutes. "Do you want to eat while the burgers are hot, or you want to get into it?"

Staring at the water, Ann said, "I don't know."

Ellie got up and brought the burgers and fries to the pool, then sat down again. "Okay, start at the beginning."

"I don't know what the beginning is."

"Okay, let's start with how you betrayed Alex."

She sighed. "Andrew."

When Ann said nothing else, Ellie said, "Yeah, I'm going to need more than that." When she still didn't get a response, she asked, "Andrew is Ted's past life, right?"

Ann mumbled, "Yes."

"He has you bewildered? How? Why?"

She took a deep breath. "He told me about his wife. He loved her so much. He's so sweet when he talks about her. I mean, her death devastated him. Then he turns into a... a... a libertine, which seems completely out of character for him."

"Libertine? Where to you get these words?"

"He's a cad, a bounder... a seducer of women."

"He seduced you?"

"He tried. At least I think that was what he was doing."

"Boy, you've got to get out more if you don't even know when someone's trying to seduce you."

"Maybe. But today he had the chance and didn't."

"Doesn't that mean he isn't a libertine?"

"I guess." She sighed. "But I wanted him to."

"To seduce you?"

"Yes. Doesn't that mean I'm betraying Alex?"

Trying to set it straight in her mind, Ellie repeated the explanation. "You feel like you're betraying Alex because you want Andrew to seduce you?"

"Yes."

"Honey, Alex is dead. I know it's only been a couple of weeks since we found out for sure, but the truth is we've known a long time. You can't betray him when he's not here anymore."

"Then why do I feel guilty?"

"I don't know. I don't think you should." Ellie popped a french fry in her mouth then asked, "So what's going on with Ted?"

"I invited him to dinner tonight, but he said he had a hot date. I feel like an idiot admitting this, but I was jealous until he said the date was with his daughter."

"Just so I understand this completely, Andrew is really Ted, right?"

"No."

"No? I thought Andrew was just a past life."

"Yeah, but they're not the same. I can tell the difference just looking at them... him."

"And you're sure Ted isn't the one trying to seduce you?"

"Yes. It's definitely Andrew." She almost snorted. "At least I thought it was, but it seems neither of them are particularly interested in seducing me. I guess it's just my imagination."

"Or wishful thinking," Ellie suggested.

Ann sighed. "Maybe, except Ted hasn't done anything..."

"You mean anything except buy a house a block away from you, right?"

"That was just a coincidence. They found the house before they knew I lived here."

"Uh-huh."

"Why do you question it?"

"Because Ted never stopped loving you, and frankly, I don't think you ever stopped loving him."

"That's ridiculous. I loved Alex."

"I know you did. And if we hadn't lost him, the two of you would have been happy for the rest of your lives." Ellie wondered if she really should tell Ann what she thought. She decided to preface it. "You believe friends should tell each other the truth, don't you?"

Ann looked over at her best friend. "Of course."

Ellie still hesitated a bit, but then began. "I do know that you loved Alex." Ann started to interrupt, but Ellie stopped her. "I know you still do. But it wasn't, isn't, the same kind of love that you and Ted had. You thought you'd found your soul mate in Ted, so when it ended you were devastated, crushed by his betrayal."

"What's your point?"

"I'm getting there. It took you a long time to get past it, but you did, and you fell in love with my brother, which was great. But I think, while you got past the end of your relationship with Ted, you never really got over him. When Alex died, it was as though you had to prove to the world how much you loved him by not accepting his death. But the truth is that no one else ever questioned it. I think you're trying to convince yourself to feel guilty because you think that you didn't love Alex as much as you loved Ted." Ellie stopped and looked at Ann whose face was streaked with tears. "But you're wrong. You loved them both equally. You just loved them differently."

Neither said anything for a few minutes, then Ellie finally added, "I guess the real question is do you want to have a relationship with Ted again or not?"

Sniffing back the tears, she said, "I don't know. I keep coming back to his betrayal twenty years ago, and I'm pretty sure I don't. But then we'll do something as simple as having lunch, and I want to keep seeing him. I don't know what to do."

"Frankly, it sounds to me like you're finally coming to terms with all of it, and I think that's a good thing."

"Maybe, but then shouldn't I feel better?"

Ellie patted her on the back. "You need to eat."

After finishing dinner and throwing away the uneaten french fries and paper bags, the two ladies went inside and made tea to have with the lemon pound cake Ann made that afternoon. In the living room, Ellie broached a new subject. "I have a theory about what's going on with Alex's computer."

"Really?"

"Yeah, and I think Alex is doing it. The websites were so you would be ready when you needed to help Ted. And the word *forgive* on the screen saver is a message to you to forgive him. I think Alex wants you to be happy, and he thinks Ted will make you happy. What did you tell him about Ted?"

"It wasn't a subject we discussed. He knew I was engaged to Ted, and he knew I broke it off because Ted cheated, but that's pretty much it. I'm guessing you told him a lot more than I did."

"Well, then he knows the whole story." A sly smile curved her lips. "Annie, he loved you. He wants you to be happy. I think it's as simple as that."

"You think that the ghost of my late husband is pushing me into the arms of an ex-fiancé experiencing... whatever it is he's experiencing... and it's simple? You really are nuts."

"Maybe so, but I'm right. You'll see."

Chapter Thirty-Seven

Thursday, July 10

The glass rattled slightly in the frame when Ted's last graduate student closed the door to his office as she left. He dropped his glasses onto the desk, leaned back in his chair, and closed his eyes. He loved teaching, but the tedious preparations were wearing. It seemed as though everything that was discussed at the various meetings was repeated over and over again. He supposed it was necessary, but he was certainly glad it was over.

He couldn't help but smile at the memory of Ann, "Toni," running through the fountain in front of the Dorothy Chandler Pavilion. She'd been like a kid running through the sprinklers, giggling with the pure joy of it. He wondered if losing her husband had taken that joy away. Ever since the first day he'd seen her again, there was a darkness in her eyes that he could tell had nothing to do with her anger toward him. He hated to admit it, even to himself, but the idea that someone had replaced him in her heart made him jealous. Still, he wondered if there was a way to help her overcome the loss. Would she take his help? He sat up. He needed to call her.

The phone rang five times, and as he prepared a message to leave on her voice mail, she answered.

"Hi. I didn't think you were there."

"Why did you call if you didn't think I'd be here?"

"I only thought it because... oh, never mind. I've finally gotten through all the stuff here at school and wanted to set a time to see you again. Is tomorrow afternoon good?"

"It would have been a few minutes ago. I moved a today appointment to tomorrow, and it will probably take most of the afternoon."

They were both quiet until he finally said, "Does that mean you're available now?"

She paused. "Yes, I guess it does."

"Is it too out there to say I can be there in half an hour?"

"Out where?"

He chuckled. "Wherever there is." He waited for a response. "You didn't answer."

"Answer what?"

"Whether I can come over now."

"You didn't ask."

"I know. Say what I mean and mean what I say. So I'm asking now."

"Sure, why not?"

"I'll see you in about a half hour then."

"Okay."

It was a strange knock, but Ann responded with, "Come in," anyway.

He kicked the door again. "I can't."

Ann jumped up and ran to the door, saying as she opened it, "Why can't you?" She looked at him. "Oh."

Ted stood in the doorway with two ice cream cones and held one out to her. "Here, I brought you an afternoon treat. I trust you still like burgundy cherry." Ann took the cone, and Ted asked, "Can I come in?"

"Of course." She stepped aside. Looking at the ice cream and then at Ted, she said, "I didn't think they made burgundy cherry anymore."

He looked at her with squinty eyes. "They call it cherries jubilee now. Can't you just say thank you?"

She looked surprised. "Yes, yes. Thank you. You took me by surprise, that's all."

"Eat it before it melts."

Ted went to the loveseat and sat down. She closed and locked the door, then sat in one of the chairs across from him. "I haven't had an ice cream cone in a long time. I never think about it when I'm out, only when I'm home and generally don't feel like going out just to get one. It tastes really good. Thank you."

His only response was a slight smile. He popped the end of the cone into his mouth.

"You ate that fast."

"Had a head start."

As she finished off her own cone, she asked, "What made you do it?"

"It?" *Was that suspicion he heard?* "The ice cream?"

"Yeah."

Defensively, he said, "I parked a couple of blocks away, and I saw a kid come out of an ice cream shop with cherry ice cream and remembered that it was your favorite. That's all there is to it."

"I'm sorry. I didn't mean anything by it."

"Yes, you did. You assume I have ulterior motives for everything I do."

"No, I don't."

They were both quiet, each wondering if they were being overly sensitive or if the other wasn't being honest.

He broke the silence.

"Would you be more comfortable if we didn't continue this?"

"Why would you ask that?"

Exasperated, he said, "Ann, please just answer the question. I know you started this because Jamie asked you to do it."

"But I'm doing it for Sara." She paused a moment. "I'm sorry, Ted. It isn't that I think you have ulterior motives. It's just that..." She added almost apologetically, "I have trust issues, so I guess I do tend to get a bit suspicious."

She seemed to be uncomfortable saying it, and he wondered if it was because she was starting to believe him about their past or if she was forgiving him. Perhaps she was trying to decide. Whatever it was, he opted not to push it. "Shall we begin, then?"

She almost whispered, "Yes."

Completely lost in her own jumbled thoughts, Andrew startled her. "How are you this afternoon, Mrs. Hart?"

She tried to cover her surprise by rushing to say, "Fine, thank you." When he said nothing else, she offered tea. He accepted. She went to the antique sideboard and filled the pot and set it to boil. She sat on the loveseat.

"How did Cathy die?"

The darkness she saw in his eyes went well beyond grief or sadness. "I killed her."

"I don't understand."

"Her death was my fault." He covered his face with his hands. "I killed my very soul."

His confession was heart wrenching, but she was sure Ted's dream showed that Cathy went into early labor and gave birth to a stillborn child and then died in his arms a few days later, probably from some hideous infection. "What happened?"

"She died after giving birth to my son."

"Her death was *not* your fault."

"It was. The priest said that we were two individuals who, by exchanging vows, became one. I wanted to truly make us one; I wanted to ignite the fire in her that burned in me." A sad smile accompanied the next statement. "We even talked of how the bonfire of our love would light the world." He looked away. "But that fire is what killed her. I killed her."

Ann got goose bumps, suddenly realizing that he believed his love was responsible for Cathy's death. No wonder he never remarried; he was afraid it would happen again. Not an unreasonable fear in 1805.

She got up and sat on the table in front of him. After brushing the hair off his forehead, she took his hands in hers. "Your love did not kill her."

"You are wrong." He sat upright, his back straight. "She died in my arms after my son was born."

"He was her son too," she said quietly. A quizzical look met her statement. "But having the baby isn't why she died, Andrew."

His head jerked up, and he looked at her. She didn't understand the surprise she saw there, but since he said nothing, she continued. "A long time ago a Dutch scientist discovered bacteria, tiny animals that can only be seen with microscopes. Some people today believe those bacteria cause diseases and infections. I suspect a bacteria was the true cause."

"That kind of sickness could be why they died?"

"It is likely the reason Cathy died. The baby may not have been strong enough."

"She was so small and delicate, I was sure that the strain had been too much for her."

"Divine providence created women to bear children. It is completely natural; in and of itself, giving birth is not fatal."

"She should not have been on the ship with me." His eyes filled with tears. "But she desperately wanted to go, and I could refuse her nothing."

Ann squeezed his hands. "If she had stayed in Scotland, you wouldn't have been together. She would have died alone. I'm sure in your arms is the way she wanted it."

Andrew rested his head on their joined hands. He was crying, his body quivering. Finally, he let out a shuddering breath and sat up. The release seemed to help.

Ann smiled at him and started to get up, but he held on to her hands, squeezing them just enough to stop her movement. She swallowed hard. "What is it, Andrew?"

The same surprise she saw earlier filled his eyes. "I am unused to strangers calling me by my given name." He let her go.

She stepped away from him, reminding herself that even in the novels of the era, married couples referred to each other as Mr. and Mrs., using given names only in private. She apologized profusely and claimed the intimacy of the moment had caused her to forget herself.

He nodded his acceptance of her explanation, then leaned back into the corner of the loveseat and closed his eyes.

Ann sat in the armchair again. How many other mistakes would she make before they learned what they needed to know about him? She watched as he appeared to sleep. Expecting Ted would be returning, Ann went to the sideboard to brew the tea. As she waited for the water to boil again, she glanced over her shoulder. His eyes were still closed. Ted was having trouble sleeping, so he was probably taking a catnap. The water was boiling, and she turned back to her task.

Quietly, he sat up. If Ann had seen the look in his eyes, she would have blushed bright red. As it was, she didn't even hear as he approached so was surprised when she turned around to find him directly behind her. She attempted to hand him a steaming mug, but he ignored her outstretched hand and stood as close as he could get, making her back up until her hips touched the sideboard. Still holding both hot mugs, she was trapped. He was so close she couldn't even turn to put the mugs down.

Andrew reached up and brushed the hair off of her shoulder. Ann drew back, but with nowhere to go he easily stopped the movement by gently resting his hand on the nape of her neck and drawing her to him. She stiffened at his touch. He tilted his head and gazed into her eyes; they spoke of longing stirred by fear. He could not discern the cause, but it mattered not. Caressing her softly, he ran his fingertips around her neck and up to her chin. She closed her eyes and lifted her face to accept his kiss. Cradling her face in his hand and leaning even closer, he breathed, "Thou art as wise as thou art beautiful." She opened her eyes. His smile tightened her stomach. He took the mug from her hand.

Ann stood where he left her, willing herself to stop shaking, trying to regain her bearings even as he casually returned to the chair.

This time, she was sure he was going to kiss her. Why didn't he? She was sorely disappointed. *God, what was she thinking?* She looked over at him. He was watching her, and she realized that she couldn't stand there forever, so she sat across from him at the opposite end of the loveseat. It was as far away from him as she could get without going to an entirely different part of the room.

After taking a sip of tea, Andrew said of the bone china mug, "This is a cunning vessel."

Ann, still a bit discombobulated, had no idea how to respond. His gentle smile slightly eased her anxiety. Quietly, he finished his tea, then leaned back and closed his eyes.

When he'd been quiet for several minutes, she looked over at him. "Ted?"

"Yes."

Suddenly embarrassed by her reaction to Andrew, she went back to her desk. There, in the safety of her pink leather chair, she proceeded to bring him back with the reverse count.

Just as she said one, Ted opened his eyes. Finding her gone, he looked around. She was diligently avoiding looking at him. He rose and strode to the desk, standing next to the chair, looking down at her.

"Why do you keep running away from me?"

"I don't."

"Of course you do."

Unable to meet his eyes, she asked, "So do you want to make an appointment for later in the week?"

Had he sensed that she wanted Andrew to kiss her? The question was lost when the university fight song began to play on Ted's cell phone.

As he removed it from his pocket he apologized. "I had it off during the session. I just turned it back on." Into the phone, he said, "Hey Jamie, what's up?"

His startled reply made her look up at him. "Oh, my God."

His eyes filled with terror, and he turned toward the door. Ann jumped to her feet and went after him, "What happened?"

"Sara Jane was in an accident." He fumbled with the locks on the door. "God, let me out of here." Quickly she unlocked and opened the door. He darted out.

Chapter Thirty-Eight

The automatic emergency room doors slid open, but very slowly. *What idiot designed this place?* When there were about six inches between the doors, Ted forced one of them open and rushed into the hospital. At the desk, he demanded to see his daughter. The nurse tried to calm him.

"Please, Mr. McConaughy..."

"Doctor."

"Oh, sorry, Dr. McConaughy. Sara is in radiology."

"Why? What are her injuries?"

"It's best if you talk with the doctor."

"Fine, get him."

"Her."

"Whatever." When she excused herself to answer the phone, he turned away, trying to gather himself as fear gripped his very being.

After only a few moments of waiting for the emergency room doctor, he left in search of radiology. The signs led him down two hallways and through another pair of automatic doors that also seemed to take forever to open. He burst through and demanded to see his daughter. Sara Jane was sitting on a gurney, waiting patiently, her arm propped on a pillow. She saw her father barge through the door.

"Daddy!"

"Baby!" He grabbed the hand of her uninjured arm. "Are you all right?"

"It was really scary, but I'm okay now. I broke my arm, but it could have been a lot worse. Jenny's car is a mess."

"Well, I'm not too concerned about Jenny's car. You scared the hell out of me."

"Sorry. The other car ran the light."

A radiology technician came to the head of the gurney. "Okay, it's your turn." He turned to Ted. "She'll be going to her room after this."

"She has a room?"

"She's being admitted. We're just waiting to hear what room."

"Do you want me to come with you?"

"No, I'm fine. I'm all right."

"Are you sure?"

"Yes." He kissed her forehead and released her hand, then watched as she was wheeled away, his heart in his throat.

He stood outside the automated doors of radiology and took several deep breaths. He still wanted to talk with the ER doctor so wound his way through the halls to the emergency room lobby. The nurse told him that Dr. Linehan was with a patient but would be out to talk with him as soon as she was finished. Reluctantly, he took a seat, trying desperately to stay calm and not run screaming through the halls of the hospital. Thinking of all the things that could go wrong, he was startled by someone saying his name.

"Ann. What are you doing here?"

She offered him a paper cup. "Figured you could use a cup of tea."

Slowly, he took the cup. She answered the question on his face. "I called Jamie to find out what happened. Since you were my last appointment, I decided to come. Do you mind?"

"God, no, I don't mind."

"Good. This isn't the kind of thing you should do alone. How is she?"

"She says all she has is a broken arm, but I haven't talked with the doctor yet."

Ann looked around. "Where's Jamie?"

"On campus, I think. Why?"

"He was here when I talked with him."

"I saw him after I saw her and told him he didn't have to stay, and since he had a meeting, he left."

As he finished the statement, an attractive young woman approached. "Mr. and Mrs. McConaughy?" They turned to meet her. Ann's first reaction was to tell the doctor that she wasn't his wife, but it seemed a silly, unnecessary detail at the moment. Ted's only thought was that she didn't look much older than Sara Jane. Her cheerful smile and bouncy demeanor did nothing to instill his confidence.

"I'm Jennifer Linehan, the emergency room doctor. I examined Sara when they brought her in. The car she was in was T-boned on the right side. Fortunately, she was in the middle of the backseat, so while she does have a broken right arm which will probably need surgery, I believe that is the extent of her injuries. However, I've called in an orthopedic surgeon and have ordered a CT scan of her head."

Before she could say anything else, Ted demanded, "Why?"

Ann gently took his hand and squeezed it. He took a deep breath and apologized for interrupting her.

"It's okay. I understand how upsetting this must be. Sara hit her head on the car frame. She doesn't seem to be affected by it, but I want to make sure"—she paused—"to be on the safe side. As soon as we know something, I'll let you know."

She turned to go, but Ann stopped her. "Doctor." The young woman turned back. "There were other people in the car. How are they?"

"There were two girls in the front seat, but the car was hit in the rear so Sara got the worst of it. The other girls have bumps and bruises. They were released."

"Oh, great!" Ted blurted out. "I always told her that the middle of the backseat was the safest place to be."

"And it is," the doctor said. "It's probably the reason her injuries aren't any worse than they are."

Ann could feel the tension in Ted's hand, so she squeezed it again. He took a deep breath and blew it out. "The radiology tech said she was being admitted. Do you know what room?"

"I'm sorry, I don't. You'll need to go to admitting for the paperwork, and they should be able to tell you."

Ann said, "Thank you. Will you please tell the orthopedic surgeon we'd like to talk with him after he sees Sara?"

"Yes, I will, Mrs. McConaughy." She nodded to Ted and returned to the emergency room.

Ted squeezed Ann's hand. "Thank you for reining me in."

"I came to help, so I'm glad I could."

Ted heaved a deep sigh of relief and sat down. "I was afraid it was happening all over again."

"It occurred to me too."

"Is that the real reason you came?"

"I came because I'm concerned about you and Sara, and I didn't think you needed to be doing this alone."

Ted leaned over and kissed her cheek. "Thank you... Mrs. McConaughy." Ann smiled at him.

Holding the tea Ann brought him, he leaned his head back and closed his eyes in a concerted effort to keep himself together. Knowing that Sara Jane would be all right didn't stop the flood of memories of Josh's accident. The images of his young son lying on the gurney, so small and helpless, were seared into his memory. But what he remembered most was how still his boy was. He didn't move. He couldn't move. He never moved again. Ted rubbed his eyes dry and sat up. He glanced at Ann and was grateful that her sweet and generous heart had brought her here. This was going to be much easier with her at his side.

She looked over at him and saw the tears. "Are you okay? Is there something I can do?"

He smiled at her. "I'm fine. Your being here is all you need to do."

She returned his smile. "Did you call Melinda?"

"Not yet. Figured I'd find out what's going on first."

Taking a deep breath and inhaling the spicy aroma of the tea, he wondered what it meant that she remembered such a small, mundane detail of their past like the kind of tea he drank. He sighed, breathing in the fragrance and the memories they kindled.

"Why did the hospital call Jamie instead of you?"

"He's listed as the second emergency number on her identification, and I didn't answer my phone since it was turned off."

"Not her mother?"

"When I was still traveling, I wanted the kids to have someone local they could call. I was just going to use my folks, but the kids wanted Jamie. He was on his way here when he got hold of me."

Wanting to help him think about something else, Ann said, "Sara told me about your family tradition of watching the Westminster Dog Show."

He turned and smiled at her. "Melinda hated it, but I've been hooked ever since you got me to watch it with you."

"So are you going to get a dog now that you have the house?"

"She told you that, huh?"

"Yep."

"I haven't thought about it, and she hasn't said anything."

The conversation ended when a large man approached them from across the lobby.

With a nod of his head, he greeted them. "Mr. and Mrs. McConaughy? I'm Charles Bechtol, the orthopedic surgeon." He shook hands with both of them. "I've seen Sara. Dr. Linehan was right; there is a comminuted fracture of her right ulna. It isn't as bad as it might be, and I'm confident that, with a couple of small plates and screws, she'll be fine." He paused to allow them to ask questions. When none were forthcoming, he continued.

"Now she's waiting for the CT scan, so I asked the neurosurgeon to take a look at her. He agrees with Dr. Linehan that a brain injury is unlikely but will withhold comment until after the scan. He did tell me that he thinks she just got a nasty bump, which she reminded all of us was what she had told everyone when she came in."

"Sounds like Sara Jane," Ted nervously admitted.

"You've got a very strong and brave young woman there."

Ted thanked him.

Ann asked, "Will you do the surgery today?"

"Yes. I think we should do it as soon as possible."

She smiled. "Thank you, doctor." He turned and walked away.

Ted said, "Thanks for asking that. I didn't even think about it." He heaved a deep sigh. "I really appreciate you being here." Then he added, "But you don't have to stay."

"I know." She reached over and clasped his hand.

Ann stood in the doorway of the hospital room and watched father and daughter. The mischievous side of Ted that could and often did irritate her was contrasted with this loving and devoted father—something she had always imagined but never expected to witness. She could see fear and relief in his body language as he gently brushed the hair off of Sara's forehead. She could tell he wanted desperately to grab her and hold on to her for dear life but at the same time was terrified that he might hurt her.

She was brought out of her reverie by Sara Jane. "Ann!"

Ann walked to the end of the bed and lightly pinched Sara's toe under the blanket. "Hi, sweetie pie. How are you feeling?"

"I've been better, but according to the doctors, it could have been a lot worse. So, I'm glad of that."

"So am I. Have they said when the surgery will be?"

"Tonight sometime. They're scheduling it right now. I told them it could wait until tomorrow—I didn't want people to have to work late because of me—but the doctor said he doesn't want to risk a bone fragment or ragged end damaging a nerve."

"You don't have to worry about people working late, honey. I'm pretty sure they have an evening shift in the OR, so the staff is here whether they're operating or not."

"Oh." Her eyes fluttered. "They gave me something for pain, and I'm having a terrible time staying awake."

Ann offered, "Don't try to stay awake. The more rested you are, the faster you'll heal."

Ted looked over his shoulder at her and smiled as Sara Jane drifted off into a morphine-induced slumber. He leaned over and kissed her forehead, then escorted Ann out of the room.

"Thank you again for coming. She really liked that you were here."

Ann smiled.

The chair in Sara Jane's room wasn't the most comfortable, but Ted still drifted off, waiting for his daughter to wake from the anesthesia and pain medications.

When she opened her eyes, she was surprised to see him sitting there. She hadn't seen him since she was a little girl. "Mr. M, what are you doing here?"

"I came to see you." He moved the chair closer to the bed and gently patted her hand. "You are injured."

"I was in an accident."

"Will you recover?"

"Oh, yes. It's nothing really." She smiled. "I haven't seen you in such a long time."

"There was no need."

"But I've missed you."

"And I, you. I am glad you are doing well. However, I see an unease that is not caused by the accident. Are you sure there is nothing else causing you distress?"

"I'm fine." The drugs were making her mind fuzzy. "But Dad. He's..." Her eyes fluttered. "He's..." Her words stalled.

Mr. M squeezed her hand. "Do not distress yourself, my dear. All will be well."

Sara Jane's eyes closed, and her head rolled to the side. A small, dreamy smile ended the visit.

Mr. M kissed her forehead.

Chapter Thirty-Nine

Monday, July 14

Ann's smile when she greeted him at the door lightened his heart. She looked stunning. Her cheeks were rosy, her eyes sparkled, and her beautiful hair fell softly around her shoulders. He sighed as his eyes followed the mahogany tresses where they stopped against the soft skin just above her cleavage, which was accentuated by the dress she wore. The high waist exaggerated the enticing swell of her breasts. He couldn't seem to take his eyes off of her.

Her smile turned playful although unseen by Ted. "Easter eggs," she said cheerfully.

Ted's eyes went immediately to her face, and his quizzical look was answered with, "The design in the fabric is Easter eggs. I made the dress a few years ago for Easter, but I love the colors."

Her smile made him blush a deep red, suddenly aware that she'd caught him staring at her breasts. The foolish, adolescent action made him feel like an idiot.

She stepped back, holding the door open. "Come in." Her eyes twinkled with humor.

"I'm sorry," he offered as he crossed the threshold into her house.

Her telling smile didn't stop her from asking, "For what?"

The red once again rose in his cheeks. "My eyes wandered away... from your lovely face."

"Did they?" It was a bit fun that he was the one embarrassed this time.

"You're just going to let me swing at the end of the rope I'm hanging from, aren't you?"

She giggled. "No. It did remind me of all the times you claimed that my face was what attracted you when we first met. I noticed more than once that your eyes appeared to be focused a bit south of my face."

"You never said anything about it before."

"It didn't bother me. It doesn't bother me."

"You don't consider it sexist?"

"No. We are sexual creatures, and are attracted to what arouses us sexually." She stood on tiptoe and whispered in his ear, "I've always thought you have a great ass." She turned and almost skipped into the kitchen, hopefully fast enough to stop him from commenting. But she needn't worry. Ted was tongue-tied, stunned by the admission.

From the kitchen, she asked if he wanted coffee or tea or something else entirely. Still a bit dazed, he made his way to the kitchen door. Her playful greeting reminded him of the girl he'd planned to marry but hadn't seen in years. Seeing her busy in the kitchen, cheerful and confident, was heartwarming and heart wrenching at the same time. When they lived together, he would sometimes watch surreptitiously while she cooked and baked, singing and dancing, assuming she was entirely alone. He smiled at the cherished private memory, for had she known, she would have been horribly embarrassed.

The memories were cut short when she glanced at him over her shoulder. "So is it coffee or tea?"

"Coffee's good."

She picked up a tray with a carafe, mugs, cream, sugar, and freshly made coffee cake. She turned to him. "Open the sliding door for me, please."

Silently, he did, closing it after they were both out. Ann set the tray on the patio table and sat down. Ted followed suit.

Opting not to carry on with their previous conversation, Ted said, "Thank you for seeing me here. I want to be close in case Sara Jane needs me. Not that your office is so far, but I can literally run home from here."

"I understand. How is the invalid doing?"

"She's fine. I suspect she's in more pain than she admits. She's been very stoic about it. She insists she's fine—I don't need to wait on her, she's not an invalid, and she can take care of herself. She keeps saying, 'It's all good, Dad.'" He smiled. "What're you going to do?"

"So she takes after her father."

"I'm not at all stoic."

"No, but you think you ought to be able to handle everything by yourself."

"Point taken."

"She really loved that you made dinner for us the night she came home. She instructed me to thank you again."

"Tell her she's more than welcome. Sometimes comfort food is the best medicine."

"Well, she wants the prescription for the chocolate cake. She said it was the best one she'd ever had."

"It's my grandmother's recipe, dense and very chocolaty."

"The fudge frosting certainly added to it."

"I'm glad you both enjoyed it."

After leisurely sipping the hot coffee and sampling the cinnamon coffee cake, Ted ventured, "Andrew seems to take notice of his surroundings. How do you plan to explain the change in location?"

"He thinks my office is the ship's library, so I figured I'd just say it was the ship's salon if he asks." She thought a moment. "I don't even know if ships had salons then. Maybe I should just say it's the sitting room of my stateroom."

"Might be risky letting him into your stateroom."

"It's not really my stateroom."

"He doesn't know that, and he might see it as an invitation."

"An invitation?"

"To... to... take advantage."

"Yes, he might. But he can't take advantage unless I want him to, and since I don't want him to, it's not a problem."

"Oh, good."

Ted reached down and scratched Gigi's head; the large dog lay between the chairs he and Ann were sitting in. "And Gigi?"

"I'll put her in her run before we go in. I'm pretty sure people didn't travel with pets in those days."

"This coffee cake is wonderful. Sara Jane would love it."

"You can take the rest of it with you if you'd like."

"I'd like."

They sat quietly for a while, then Ted broke the silence. "May I ask an extremely personal question?"

She was slightly taken aback by the request. They had judiciously avoided much in the way of personal discussions, and she couldn't imagine what it would be. "You can ask. Won't promise I'll answer."

"Fair enough." He took a swig of coffee and refilled his mug from the thermos carafe. "Did Alex not want to have children?"

That was definitely not something that had crossed her mind when possible questions started whirling around in her head.

"I have to admit that I'm not entirely sure. He said he did, and we tried, but I always had the feeling that he was quite happy not having children at all."

"I can understand that. He wanted you all to himself. Smart man." He felt the pain he knew not having children must have caused her so wasn't about to delve any further into it.

Before he said anything else, she offered, "You know I wanted children, and they couldn't find anything wrong with either of us, so we discussed fertility treatments. But some part of me felt that, if nothing was wrong but we weren't getting pregnant, it was because we weren't supposed to have children. We finally decided that, for whatever reason, God had other plans for us. It made me angry for a while, and I still get sad sometimes, but there's no point dwelling on it."

He couldn't imagine why God wouldn't have wanted her to be a parent. He knew from the moment he met her that she would be an amazing mother. Saddened, and unable to think of a response, Ted got up and wandered toward the pool, stopping at the miniature cottage.

He turned to her. "What's with the dollhouse?"

She got up and stood next to him. "It's a fairy house. Alex saw it in a shop window and stopped to look at it. The woman in the shop said that all gardens have fairies. If you're good to them, you and your house will always be protected, so he bought the house for them. Grace, Jamie's daughter, made all the tiny stuff inside."

He bent down and peered into the miniature window. "Grace is very talented." He stood up. "That fairy story is nice. Have the fairies protected you?"

"After the earthquake, it seemed so, but we put the house into the garden the day Alex disappeared, so they weren't doing much protecting that day."

"Maybe fairies hate moving as much as I do and just hadn't moved in yet." He smiled.

"Could be. I don't suppose anybody likes to move, even fairies."

"Shall we go inside and do this?"

Ann took Gigi to her run while Ted carried the coffee things back to the kitchen. Before joining Ted in the living room, Ann refilled their coffee cups and picked up a small basket of strawberries that was on the tray.

Chapter Forty

Ann glanced at Ted through the steam rising from the freshly brewed coffee. Her stomach did flip-flops when Andrew's midnight-blue eyes looked back at her, reaching into her very soul. Hurriedly, she set the tray down and sat down rather too hard in her chair, making it jump slightly.

She took a short but deep breath. "Good morning."

Andrew nodded in response, his face filled with a mischievousness that put her on edge, but she said nothing. Nervously, Ann ran her hands through her hair, propped one elbow on the arm of the mission chair, and rested her head on her hand in as nonchalant a manner as possible.

"See how she leans her cheek upon her hand! O that I were a glove upon that hand that I might touch that cheek!"

Quickly dropping her hands to her lap, Ann asked, "Excuse me?"

Playfully, he said, "She speaks. O, speak again, bright angel! For thou art as glorious to this night, being o'er my head as is a winged messenger of heaven."

Her inability to respond gave him the opening he wanted. The teasing look left his eyes, he leaned forward a bit. "You look most becoming today, Mrs. Hart."

Unable to stop the blush that accompanied her "Thank you." Ann turned her head away.

Andrew took a strawberry from the server that included whipped cream and sugar. After eating one of the sugar-drenched berries, he leaned back in the mission chair and rested his elbows on the oak arms. Steepling his fingers, he lightly tapped the tips of all his digits against each other.

Ann kept her eyes downcast, her hands tightly clasped in her lap. He was different today, and it made her nervous. She stiffened slightly at the sound of his chair creaking and didn't look up even when she felt him standing next to her.

Without a word, he lifted her face with his left hand. With a strawberry held gently between the thumb and forefinger of his right hand, he caressed her lips with the fruit. She couldn't help but lick her lips. The roguish smile curved his lips as he popped the berry into his own mouth. Afraid of what she saw in his eyes, she whimpered and jumped up.

Standing at the fireplace with her back to him, she took several deep breaths, the last of which caught when she felt him behind her, causing her legs to go weak. Afraid she might fall against him, she stiffened her back. Unmoved by her actions and stance, he pulled aside her hair and kissed her neck, stroking both of her arms with a gentle but firm hand. Instinctively, she rolled her head back, and he kissed the front of her neck. Realizing suddenly what he was doing (what she was doing) she bolted sideways and returned to her chair. He stood at the fireplace and watched her.

He knew she wanted him to kiss her, but something had stopped her, stopping him in the process. Convinced that Mr. Hart's ghost was the cause of her reluctance, he now resolved to overcome the specter.

She sat, staring past him into the empty fireplace, afraid to look at him, her heart fluttering in her chest. She was finding it harder and harder to resist him... to stop herself. Her heart sped up, imagining his arms around her. God, what was wrong with her?

Returning to the chair, he reached across the small table separating them and took her hand, then gently stroked the palm and the inside of her wrist with a very light touch.

"Was he a gentleman?"

She pulled away and put her hand to her mouth. "Who?"

"Mr. Hart."

"Why do you want to know?"

Expecting a simple yes, he leaned back in the chair. He wondered at her reaction, but when she still said nothing, he asked, "Why do you hesitate telling me? Was he a cad, a cruel bounder?"

Startled by the suggestion, she insisted, "God, no! He was a *true* gentleman."

"Yes, well I did assume he was."

Flashing on novels of the period, she realized he meant a man born of high social standing, so gently corrected the impression. "I didn't mean a gentleman in the way you do, although he was. I meant he was a gentle man—sweet, kind, with a gentle heart. Everyone loved him."

"Even women?" he teased.

She smiled and took a breath. "Especially women."

She could read the look on his face; she responded as though he'd asked the question. "He chose me." To his surprise she continued. "Like Cathy, he was intelligent, very intelligent. I loved that about him." She loved his body too but opted not to say it.

A sadness came over her, and tears filled her eyes. He reached over and touched her hand. She withdrew it and rubbed her eyes. "I miss being able to talk with him."

"Will you ever love again?"

"I don't know. Sometimes it doesn't feel possible."

Determining that she had reached her limit as regarded discussions of her late husband, he asked, "Where in America do you live?"

Taken aback by the sudden change in subject, she had to think quickly. California wasn't a state in 1805, but New York City had been around since the seventeenth century, so that was the answer she gave.

"You live there with your parents?"

"I live in the home Alex and I shared."

"Have you siblings?"

"I have one brother, Tom. You?"

"Two sisters and two brothers."

She remembered him saying that he was the eldest son, so in an attempt to keep the conversation safe, she asked, "What do your brothers do?"

"Do?"

"For a living."

He looked at her strangely, the question still hanging in the air.

"Are they lawyers, doctors, what?" she clarified, forgetting that wealthy, Regency gentlemen didn't work for a living.

"One is an officer in the Royal Navy." In a slightly derogatory tone, he said, "the youngest has taken orders."

"A priest?" she asked.

He shrugged his indifference.

"Is it the clergy you don't believe in or God?"

His disdain was palpable. She wasn't sure whether the disdain was for the brother or the calling. She watched him for a few minutes, but he would not meet her gaze.

"You blame God for taking Cathy, don't you?"

His voice rose as she had never heard before. "If God is merciful, then why did he take her? He destroyed my family and left me alone. There was no mercy in it, only misery."

He brought the discussion to an end by rising and stepping to the fireplace. He took several deep breaths. After a few minutes, he reached up and lightly touched the glass of a picture frame sitting on the mantel. "I have never seen a portrait so lifelike."

She got up and stood next to him. "It's Alex."

He turned and looked down at her. "So neither of us will ever love again."

The twinkle in his eye and the sly grin that she had not seen since the very beginning of the meeting were back. Her stomach jumped. But before she could move, he cupped her face in his hands, gently but still preventing her movement, and bent to kiss her. She leaned away. He slid one hand around her neck and drew her to him. This time she gave no resistance and returned his deep and passionate kiss with pleasure. He pulled her into his arms, kissing her neck, her eyes, kissing her full on the mouth again, holding her as though he would never let her go, and for the moment, she didn't want him to let her go.

But then she came to her senses and broke free. She excused herself and rushed to the kitchen. At the table, she buried her face in her hands. What was she doing? What had she been thinking? The problem was that she reacted emotionally, with no thought at all. After a few minutes, she had collected herself enough to return to the living room even though she had no idea what she would say to him.

Chapter Forty-One

Ted found himself standing on the hearth, alone. He looked around the room. Ann was gone. His first reaction was to call her name, but what would he say to her? He was leaning against the used brick of the fireplace when something caught his eye. Next to the picture of her husband was a small silver cigar lighter. A Victorian piece he and Toni (*Ann*) found in a small shop in Virginia City, Nevada. What did it mean that she still had it *and* displayed it? He reached up and gently touched his lips. Was that kiss intended for him... or Andrew?

The drapes she had closed before the session were now open, exposing the backyard. Ted stood at the sliding glass door, looking out on the pool and waterfall.

He turned at the sound of her approach.

Part of her breathed a sigh of relief that she didn't have to confront Andrew, but the other part was afraid of what Ted would say. His eyes didn't leave her as she came and stood next to him. Although she didn't look at him, she knew she had to deal with what had happened and saw no percentage in trying to delay or ignore it.

"A penny for your thoughts."

His eyes turned back to the outside landscape. A sadness crept into his voice that she could not deny. "You kissed him."

Defensively, she said, "He kissed me."

"I didn't sense a lot of resistance."

Embarrassed by the truth, Ann became unreasonably angry. "Well, it's none of your business."

A sardonic laugh burst from him. "How is it not my business?"

Heatedly, she replied, "So, it was a mistake that will never happen again." She turned away, fully intending to return to the kitchen or anywhere to get away from him. As she took the first step, he grabbed her arm.

"Running away again?"

Pulling her arm free of his gentle grip, she whirled around. "I'm not running away."

"Where were you going?"

Flustered, she stumbled over the words. "I was, I mean, I..." Finally, she said, "I need to go to the bathroom."

With a condescending smile, he said, "Convenient."

She turned again and hurried off, but before she was out of the room, he added, "I'm not going anywhere." She looked over her shoulder at him. *Oh, God.*

She leaned against the powder room door. *Now what?* She couldn't stay in the bathroom forever. She steeled herself and returned to the living room. Silently, she hoped he'd left, but there he was, having refreshed their coffees during her absence and now sitting in the leather-and-oak chair near the fireplace, Gigi at his feet.

"Why did you bring Gigi in?"

"I wanted to. Is it a problem?"

Sheepishly, she said no.

Ted reached down and scratched the dog's head, then leaned back in the chair and, in a gesture reminiscent of Andrew, steepled his hands. He watched her as he tapped the tips of his index fingers lightly together. "Tell me why you're angry at me."

"I'm not angry."

"Ann, as you've said to me more than once, I know you. Besides, you're not exactly hiding it."

She really wasn't angry. She just didn't know how to deal with the situation she had created. She took a deep breath. "I'm more embarrassed than anything else."

"Embarrassed? Why?"

"Because I let it happen."

"You didn't let it happen, you wanted it to happen."

She sighed. "I'd like to say 'no I didn't,' but part of me did, and I enjoyed it. I felt alive for the first time in a very long time."

She wasn't sure if it was anger or sadness she saw when he asked, "And Andrew did that for you?"

In spite of the mortification she felt, she nodded in the affirmative.

"Here's a man you called a villain, a bounder, a cad, but you welcomed his advances, and you wanted him to kiss you and admit that you enjoyed it when he did. But me, you keep at arm's length or run away."

She could not deny the truth. "I know, but I just can't get past your betrayal. I know that after all this time it's just wounded pride, and I need to let it go, but I can't seem to do it."

He wasn't sure what he thought she was going to say, but that wasn't it. There was no point denying the betrayal. She didn't believe his denial twenty years ago, and she certainly wouldn't believe it now. It made him angry that he could do nothing to change her mind. He stood up.

"Perhaps we should end this now."

"What do you mean?"

"It may be best that I not come back. No more sessions."

"What about Andrew?" Ted's raised eyebrow said more than she needed to hear. "I mean we haven't locked his door."

"I can do it without you. Besides, I have the distinct impression that you don't really want to lock him away."

"Why do you think that?"

"Ann, I assumed you had already figured out that I only kept this up because you seemed to want to, and I took that as a sign that you wanted to see me. *Me*, not Andrew. But you've made it clear that's not the case."

He stood looking down at her and couldn't help himself. "I never cheated on you! EVER! I don't care what you think you saw." Without waiting for a response, he strode to the door.

Ann jumped up and went after him. "Ted, please. I don't want..." She didn't finish the sentence.

He turned back to her. "You don't want what?"

She wasn't sure what she wanted or didn't want, and she couldn't stand seeing the pain and fury in his eyes. She looked away and said nothing. He nodded and went to the door. She stood next to him as he reached for the doorknob but could not meet his gaze when he turned back to her. Gently, he lifted her chin, forcing her to look directly into his eyes. The fury had been taken over entirely by the pain, and tears filled his eyes almost to brimming. Still holding her chin in his hand, he bent down and whispered, "Good night, good night, parting is such sweet sorrow." He dropped his hand and swallowed hard. "Good-bye, Toni."

She sat down on the parson's bench as the door closed behind him. *Good-bye.* Did that mean she would never see him again? The day had started out so well but now had crashed down on her. Tears slipped down her cheeks.

Chapter Forty-Two

Saturday, August 2

The flag fluttered in the remnants of the Santa Ana winds that had kicked up the day before. She'd lowered it to half-staff the day after Bill Wyman came by to tell her that they'd found Alex—well, his remains. Now they were going to bury him, and it would finally and really be over. Ann watched the flag without seeing it. She was in a daze. She'd turned down all the offers to accompany her to the cemetery but now questioned the wisdom of that decision. She forced herself to snap out of it.

Luckily, the 405 freeway was fairly clear, it being a Saturday morning. She'd chosen an early hour so it wouldn't be too hot. She drove through the open cemetery gates and parked. The rows and rows of white marble gravestones brought tears to her eyes.

Alex's service would be held in the pergola, a crescent-shaped building of used brick with arches connecting the brick-and-wood colonnades. The arched insets along the only solid wall were filled with brass memorial plaques. The cemetery staff had set up folding chairs between the wall and colonnades. She'd come early to check on the arrangements. Since everything seemed to be in order, she went in search of two graves.

Her grandparents were buried here. Grandpa had fought in the Pacific theater during World War II and had been given a full military funeral with Marine honor guard, folded flag, twenty-one-gun salute, and "Taps." She'd been twenty-seven at the time and "Taps" had been the hardest part of the ceremony. The mournful sound still made her temples throb and eyes tear up. Grandma died two years before he did, and their ashes were buried in the same grave. Ann's great-grandmother had joined the Army Air Corp during the Second World War which she spent in Tonopah, Nevada making parachutes. So she was here too.

Sweet peas were her grandmother's favorite flower, but they had long since bloomed out this year. So Ann had picked Shasta daisies from her own garden for Grandma's grave. She mixed the daisies with bachelor's buttons because Grandpa had loved the color of the little blue cornflowers. The small nosegay covered the brass plaque that marked their final resting place.

She'd gathered six partially opened rosebuds to put on her great-grandmother's grave. Amo had preferred gardenias to all other flowers, but Ann disliked the strong fragrance of them so had none in her garden. Roses would have to do. As she laid them down in the grass, she looked at the flat landscape of this part of the cemetery—no marble headstones, only countersunk bronze markers so the lawn mower was unobstructed. It reminded her that Alex was getting one of the last burial sites and would have a marble headstone. Soon he would be part of the sea of white.

The physical exertion of walking the hills and roads of the cemetery made her feel a bit less dazed, and she breathed deeply as people started to arrive.

The service ended with a young Marine in dress blues bending down to hand her the flag. The mournful sound of "Taps" was ringing in her ears as the young man said, "On behalf of the President of the United States, the Commandant of the Marine Corps, and a grateful nation, please accept this flag as a symbol of our appreciation for your loved one's service to Country and Corps." He stood up, but all Ann saw was the red stripe on his blue pants. She stared at the ground as the group of seven Marines marched along the side of the pergola and away. She'd decided against a graveside service because of the summer heat. As the Marines marched away from the building, people started to get up and move around. All Alex's flying buddies stopped to say something to her, his parents, and Ellie, his sister. Several people from his work stopped as well. Most of them would be coming to the house for a wake.

Ann's father and Uncle Jamie walked her to her car, and her father insisted on driving her home. Her initial reaction was that it wasn't necessary, but the truth was that she wasn't focusing very well, and it would probably be better not to drive. Uncle Jamie took her arm and led her around the car and opened the passenger door. She started to get in when Jamie waved to someone. She glanced around to see who it was and was surprised to see Ted and Sara. Sara waved at her, Ann waved back, and Ted nodded in acknowledgement. She slipped into the car.

Jamie closed the door, and through the window she said, "I didn't expect to see them here."

Her uncle smiled. "They're friends."

"Not Alex's."

"They're friends of yours, and funerals are for the living, not the dead. You really do need to control your suspicions, honey. Not everything Ted does is meant to hurt you."

Apologetically, she said, "I know."

Jamie leaned through the window and kissed her cheek. "See you at the house."

She leaned her head back and closed her eyes. Ann's father patted her knee and pulled out of the parking lot.

When Ted passed Ann's street and turned down their own, Sara Jane said, "Aren't we going to Ann's?"

"No."

"Why?"

"I don't want to go, but I'll drop you off if you'd like."

"Why you don't you want to go?"

"Honey, I just don't, and I'm pretty sure she doesn't want me there."

"Why?"

As he got out of the car, he said, "It doesn't matter." He went around the car and opened the passenger door.

Knowing it would take major maneuvering to get anything out of him, Sara Jane said nothing else... for the moment.

Assuming he dodged a bullet when his daughter asked about Ann, Ted suggested they watch a movie in the cool of the air-conditioning on this hot August day. His daughter, however, had a very different idea about how they should spend the afternoon. She sat down in the chair opposite him, resting her cast on the arm of the chair.

"All right, Dad. What's going on?"

"With what?"

"Please stop treating me like a baby. I know you haven't seen Ann for a couple of weeks. You haven't said anything about the situation, the past lives, whatever it was that was going on. But you've been weird, which means either it's still happening or something is seriously wrong. So what's going on?"

"Oh, babe, it's complicated."

Irritated she shot back, "More complicated than two past lives invading your dreams?" Sipping his Coke, he made no response. "You said you aren't going to see Ann anymore, so does that mean you finished your sessions with her?"

He really didn't want to get into it but saw no way out. She'd badger him until he told her. "I won't be going back. Let's just leave it at that."

"Does that mean that the whole past-life stuff is fixed? No more dreams? Or did you guys just have a fight?"

"No. No fight, but like I said, she doesn't want to see me, so I'm obliging her."

"Why did she suddenly decide she didn't want to see you?"

"Sara, please don't do this."

"Will you at least tell me if all the dreams and blackouts and stuff are over? Are you okay now?"

"There's no way to know for sure. If it never happens again, then it's over."

"Are you still having dreams?"

He hesitated. "Kind of."

"What's that mean?"

"The witch trial dream has stopped entirely."

"Because you locked the door?"

"Maybe."

"So did you lock the other door too?"

"That's the plan."

"So no."

Ted shrugged.

"Is the other dream still really emotional?"

"It gets to me sometimes."

She could tell by the way he said it that it was still devastating him, which made his refusal to tell her why he wouldn't see Ann much more upsetting.

Ted saw the concern on his daughter's face and debated with himself about telling her everything but opted against it. Still feeling some of the frustration that his last session with Ann had created, he got up. "Sara Jane, this is really something I don't want to talk about. Ann said she can't trust me, and there's nothing I can do to change her mind, and without trust the hypnosis won't work. So we decided I'd complete the process by myself." He kissed her cheek and went to his bedroom.

Frustrated by her father's evasion but unsure what, if anything, she could do about it, Sara Jane changed out of her funeral clothes. The pink-and-white gingham sundress she put on was light and loose. Ever since she got home from the hospital, she'd found tight-fitting clothes and jewelry irritating.

She couldn't focus on reading but didn't know if it was the discomfort of the hot, itchy cast or her father's situation so decided television might be more of a distraction. Surfing the entire gamut of channels, she finally settled on one that sounded marginally interesting, a show about the use of forensic science by art historians. But the distraction didn't really work. By the time the show ended, she realized that if someone had asked her about it she wouldn't have been able to tell them anything.

She turned off the television and leaned her head back against the chair and closed her eyes. Her arm hurt. Sara Jane woke up from what turned out to be a forty-five-minute catnap. From the doorway of her father's bedroom, it appeared he was asleep. She decided not to disturb him.

Ann stared at the empty driveway as the last of her guests drove away. The flag still flew at half-staff. *How long are you supposed to wait before raising it again?* Inside the house, she listlessly changed her clothes and then found herself wandering around the house. It seemed so empty today, which was ludicrous. She'd been living alone in the house for more than six years. *Why today?* Alex had been gone so long that, while emotionally she kept trying to deny the truth all these years, the reality had always been ever present. Now it was final, no questions, no wondering. Alex was gone.

She'd left the folded flag on the parson's bench when she came in from the service and now took it in to the office. She stared at the silver *forgive* as it continued its seemingly endless motion on the monitor screen, something that added to the already-surreal feel of the day.

Was Alex doing this? They used to leave messages to each other that way. Sometimes it was "let's go out for breakfast" or simply "I love you." She just never knew. The memory of rushing to the office in the morning just to see what message he might have left after a late work night brought a sad smile to her face.

She sat down and called up the screen saver window and typed in her own message by adding "who" and a question mark, to the "forgive." She watched it for a moment as the new message, "forgive who?" moved on the screen. A self-derisive snort escaped her throat as she left the room. How silly was she to be leaving a message for a ghost?

The kitchen was immaculate. The women in the family had cleaned up everything, including putting away all the leftovers from the catered deli lunch. She appreciated the fact that they had done it, but it left her with nothing to do. She took her iPod and a glass of iced tea and went outside.

Chapter Forty-Three

Sitting on the edge of the pool close to the fairy house, Ann stared into the water, listening to the music. The speakers she found that looked like rocks sounded pretty good considering they had to compete with wind, trees, and birds as well as the occasional car and plane. She heard something and squinted trying to hear it but when she didn't hear it again decided it had been her imagination.

Sara Jane stepped off the porch. Ann's car was in the driveway, and she could hear music, so why wasn't she answering the door? Maybe she didn't want company. She could respect that, but she had to know what was going on with her father. Hopefully Ann would be willing to shed some light on the situation. As she walked toward the driveway, she realized the music was coming from the backyard. Maybe Ann didn't hear the doorbell. Reaching over the gate with her left hand, Sara unlatched it. Gigi heard the gate open and ran to greet Sara as she rounded the corner of the house.

Ann saw the flash of white out of the corner of her eye and followed the dog's movement. She got up. "Sara. Did you ring the doorbell?"

"Yes."

"Sorry. I wasn't sure I heard it. Come in. Do you want something to drink?"

"I'd love some iced tea, but I'll get it."

"Don't be silly. Sit down and elevate your arm. I'll be right back."

Ann came out and handed Sara a pretty frosted glass with red hearts scattered on it. The beads of moisture looked refreshing, and she accepted the drink with appreciation. Her hostess joined her under the sun umbrella.

"Why didn't you guys come to lunch?"

"Dad didn't want to."

"Oh."

"He said that you didn't want to see him, so he was obliging you was how he put it."

All Ann said was "Oh" again.

After a few minutes of silence, Sara said, "I know that what's happening between you and Dad is technically none of my business, as he's repeatedly told me, but it's affecting him which means it's affecting me, and I don't know what to do about it. He won't tell me why you stopped the sessions when he's still having the dreams and blackouts, but I have to know what's going on."

"He's still having the dreams and blackouts?"

"All he said about the blackouts was that if they don't happen again the sessions worked. He did say that he hasn't had the witch trial dream since you locked the door, but the other one is still really emotional."

"He said that?"

"No, but I could tell that it is." She shifted in the chair.

"Are you oaky?"

"My arm's bothering me today."

"Would you be more comfortable inside?"

"No, I'm fine. Back to Dad, he's getting almost reclusive. It took an act of Congress to get him to take me to the funeral. Of course, I think he assumed you wouldn't want him there. He's only left the house a couple of times because he had to go to school. He even turned down a dinner invitation from Grandma. It's scary to see him like this. It's almost like when we lost Josh. He's that out of it."

"I'm sorry to hear that."

"Why don't you want to see him anymore?"

"I never said I didn't want to see him. He said he thought it best that we not see each other. I accepted that it was what *he* wanted."

"He told me that you said you'd never be able to trust him, and without trust the hypnosis wouldn't work, so he didn't see any point in continuing the sessions."

"I never said I..." She stopped herself. She may not have said it in those words, but she had said it. Sara waited, and just before she started to say something, Ann said, "I'm sorry Sara. I don't know what you want me to do. He said he could handle closing the door on Andrew by himself, so he didn't need to see me anymore."

Sara queried, "Andrew?"

"Andrew Mcnaughton, the other past life."

Sara got up and walked to the edge of the pool and stared down into the water, deep in thought.

"Sara, is something wrong?"

"No. Do you mind if I put my feet in?"

"Of course not. In fact, I'll join you." As Ann sat down next to the teenager, she said, "Be careful not to get your cast wet."

Sara nodded.

Sara's legs made concentric circles in the water. "You know, when I was in Chicago, Mom and I talked about why she and Dad got divorced. She told me they never really loved each other. Her family was pushing her into marriage, and Dad was on the rebound. She also told me she knew from the beginning that he'd never gotten over the other girl."

Ann knew where the conversation was headed but said nothing.

"Dad told me why you guys broke up."

Surprised Ann said, "He did?"

"Yep." Sara stared into the water. After a few moments, she asked, "Did he tell you about the sleepwalking?"

"Yes. We were never able to determine if it was connected to the rest of it."

"I'm pretty sure it is."

"Really, why?"

"Can I tell you a story?"

"Sure. Would you like more tea?"

"No, thanks. I'm good." Sara held up her glass then took a sip.

"When I was in the hospital after the surgery, I woke up and had a visitor. He was sitting next to the bed, holding my hand. He told me that he'd come because I was injured but said he knew the injuries from the accident weren't the only reason I was in pain. He was right, of course. This whole past-life stuff with Dad has had me pretty freaked out. But then Mr. M was generally right about things like that.

"Mr. M was what I called him when I was eight. At the time, his name was hard for me to say. He started visiting me right after Josh died. He was really sweet and said he understood what I was experiencing because he had had losses in his life too. He told me that it would hurt for a long time, but one day I'd remember the happy times and not be sad.

"I only saw him a few times after Josh's funeral, but he really helped me. He made some of the nights, when I felt so alone, not so bad.

"It's funny. Until I saw him again at the hospital, I didn't realize I missed him."

"Who is this guy? Is he a friend of your father's?"

"No. He is my father."

"Excuse me?"

"When you said his name just now, it all came together. His name is Andrew Mcnaughton, but I had a hard time with it when I was little. He told me that ladies do not use a gentlemen's given name in conversation, and as he knew I was a lady—when I was eight that was a pretty cool thing to hear—Andrew was unacceptable. He said I could call him Mr. M to make it easier for me."

"You never told your father?"

"No. He never said anything, so I thought he wanted it to be our little secret."

"How is it you never said anything during all this current stuff?"

"I didn't connect it. Dad never mentioned names the few times he talked about the two lives. He just said that one was a judge at the witch trials and the other was a man from the nineteenth century. That was all he ever said about either of them. I had no idea.

And I'm pretty sure the sleepwalking is Mr. M too. When I saw him in the garden, I assumed it was Dad sneaking a smoke. But thinking about it now, there was something different in the way he moved and looked that wasn't like Dad. It was Mr. M, I'm sure of it. It even makes sense that it was him, don't you think?"

Stunned, Ann managed to say, "It does seem logical, I guess."

Sara reached up and ran her left hand under the sling strap at her neck. "This thing is really bothering me in the heat."

Ann got up and grabbed a camp pillow from the closest chaise lounge and returned to the pool's edge. "Let's take it off for now, and you can rest your arm on this." She placed the pillow on Sara's lap and then gently eased the sling from the teenager's neck. "How's that?"

"Much better, thanks. You know, you'd be a great mom. Did you know that everyone at the hospital thought you *were* my mother, that you and Dad were married?"

"Yes, I know," she said quietly.

"And Dad never told them you weren't married."

"Your welfare was far more important than what a few strangers thought."

"It was more than that. He was happy about it. In fact, the weeks before the accident, and even those two days I was in the hospital, I don't think I've ever seen him happier." She added quickly, "Once he knew I was okay."

Ann had no idea how to respond, so she didn't say anything. She simply nodded.

"I have kind of a strange question." She bit her lip before continuing. "Has it ever occurred to you that back then, when you and your friend saw Dad with someone else, it was really Mr. M... Andrew that you saw?"

Completely startled, Ann looked over at Sara. "No, it never did."

"Even now?"

"No, not even now."

Sara raised an eyebrow very much like her father. "I don't think it ever occurred to Dad either. So I was wondering, if it was Andrew you guys saw, was *Dad* cheating?"

"Oh my God." Why *hadn't* it occurred to her? She knew how Andrew was. Why hadn't something clicked? She even knew that Andrew and Hathorne made appearances when Ted lost time. The first time she met with Ted in her office, he admitted to having experienced blackouts while they were living together. Sara's theory definitely made sense. Twenty years ago, she had seen his short bursts of anger, forgetfulness, and drifting off as signs of stress and overwork, which was exactly what he had done, but she should have realized that something wasn't right.

Ann got up and started to pace. It really was possible that Ted had been completely unaware of what was happening. She looked at Sara, and her throat and chest tightened. She sat down at the table.

She was a physician, for God's sake. She should have seen it or at the very least suspected the possibility that something was wrong. Instead, she had allowed her wounded pride to get the better of her. Ann buried her face in her hands.

Sara got up from the edge of the pool and went to her friend, laying her hand on Ann's shoulder. "Are you all right? I'm sorry. I didn't mean to upset you."

Ann looked at the young woman, and into Ted's eyes. The tears she'd been fighting finally spilled onto her cheeks. Sara asked if there was anything she could do, but all Ann did was shake her head. The tears began in earnest, and in spite of forcing herself to gulp air, she could not stop crying.

Sara didn't know what to do. Ann just kept crying, and no matter what Sara said or suggested, she just shook her head. Ann was so upset that Sara couldn't just leave, but she didn't seem to be able to help. She finally rushed into the house and pulled out her cell phone.

"Dad, I'm at Ann's I just came by to see if she was okay, and she's a mess. She's crying so hard that she can't talk, and I don't know what to do. You have to come over here."

"I can't do that."

"Dad, she needs help now."

"Okay, honey. I'll take care of it."

Sara didn't know what that meant, but if her father said he'd take care of it, she was sure he would. She went outside with a damp washcloth and handed it to Ann, whose deep-seated sobs had gotten worse.

At home, Ted called Jamie and explained the situation. Jamie asked, "Why don't you go over there?"

"I can't. I just can't do it."

"Well, neither can I. Maura and I are on our way to the chancellor's house for dinner."

"I'll call her parents."

"They've got the grandkids. You go."

Ted ignored the suggestion. "I'll give Ellie a try then."

"Ellie's parents are in town, and they just buried their son and brother."

Ted was silent.

Jamie said, "Ann just buried her husband. She needs a friend, not relatives who lost him too." There was a long pause, and Ted could sense his friend's impatience. "Suck it up, Ted," he said brusquely, then disconnected the call.

Before Ted was able to put the phone down, Sara Jane called again. "Dad, she's almost hysterical. She's taking little tiny breaths, almost like she's hyperventilating. Please come and help!"

"All right, sweetie. I'll be there in a few minutes."

He ran most of the way. Sara Jane was in the front yard when he arrived. "She's in the back by the pool." He headed toward the gate but realized that his daughter wasn't with him. He turned, but she was still on the lawn in front of the house.

"Aren't you coming?"

"No, I'm tired. I'm going home to lie down."

"Are you sure you're all right?"

"I just need to rest." She turned and waved, relieved and exhausted. "Thanks, Dad."

He watched his little girl as she walked away. He reached up to unlatch the gate as the strains of "Nights in White Satin" drifted through the summer afternoon. He withdrew his hand and stood still in the hot sun. She was listening to *their* song from the Moody Blues album *Days of Future Passed*. He scoffed at the ironic title, considering what brought them back together. He continued to listen for a few minutes. What did it mean that she was listening to *their* music? What was he thinking? It means she likes it, nothing more. He went through the gate.

Ann was in a chair by the pool and, as Sara Jane had described, was sobbing. The only time he'd seen her like this was when she broke up with him. But this time she was crying over another man. How was he supposed to help with that? He seriously considered leaving when Gigi came running over to him. Ann looked up when the dog left her side. The shock he saw was genuine. He assumed Sara Jane had told her he was coming, but she obviously hadn't. He hurried to her.

She jumped up as he approached and through the tears asked, "What are you doing here?"

"Sara Jane was concerned about you and didn't feel she was helping, so she called me and asked me to come."

She sobbed and looked around. "Where is she?"

"She was tired. She went home."

Ann gulped air and released a shuddering breath. "You don't have to stay. I know you don't want to be here. I'm okay."

Seeing the tears streaming down her face wrenched his heart.

"Yeah, I can see that. Come on, sit down."

"I don't want to."

"Let's go in the house then."

She bit her lip and ran to the house, leaving the sliding glass door open as she went.

She wasn't in the kitchen or living room. Ted called out, "Ann." When he got no response, after a reasonable amount of time he tried, "Toni!"

Through the bathroom door, she said she'd be out in a minute. In the powder room, Ann leaned over the sink. Her eyes were red and her face puffy. She forced herself to take several deep breaths. The washcloth Sara had gotten her was still clutched in her hand. She rinsed it in cold water and held it on her face for a few moments then folded it and laid it on the back of her neck. Quickly, she ran a brush through her hair. Tucking a tissue into the bodice of her dress, she opened the door.

Standing in the living room, the tears barely under control, she said, "Thank you for coming. You don't have to stay."

He stretched his arm out to her. "Come over here and sit down."

She stood staring at him.

Firmly he said, "Ann, come over here." When she was finally able to make her feet move, she sat on the couch across from him.

Ted was surprised that she was so distraught. When she told him about Alex's friends finding the plane, she had been very calm and matter-of-fact about it. She was obviously affected by it but was very controlled, so this hysteria took him by surprise. Perhaps the funeral had made the finality of it far more real.

His sweet understanding smile hurt. She didn't deserve his kindness and comfort. She'd never even given him the chance to explain. All she'd done was hurl accusations at him, refusing to listen to anything he had to say. She had been so wrapped up in her own stuff, with school and wedding plans, that she had ignored the signs that something was wrong. Over the past few weeks, she had seen in his eyes that he really didn't know. He honestly believed that she had been mistaken about seeing him with someone else. *Oh, God! How had she let this happen?* Tears filled her eyes. Her stupid pride had ruined everything, then and now. She dropped her chin onto her chest and started to rock, unable to stop the sobs this time.

Ted moved to the sofa and put his arm around her shoulders. She leaned her head on him and cried.

"I know it hurts," he said. "The hurt never completely goes away, but it does get easier with time, trust me. They talk about closure, but I don't believe there is closure. Besides, you don't want to close the door on everything you had with Alex. He was an important part of your life. Eventually, the things that hurt now will turn into happy memories, and you'll be able to feel joy again."

She looked up at him, her face red with tears. He thought she was crying over Alex. How could she tell him she was crying over losing him? That she'd thrown it all away? That she was mourning the loss of what they could have had?

Ted saw the tissue peeking from her cleavage and gingerly pulled it free. "Your nose is running." He started to wipe it, but she took it.

"I'll do it." She slipped the tissue back into her bodice and looked into his eyes. Was that sadness or pity? What was he thinking? She didn't really care. She put her arms around his neck and pulled herself to eye level. She kissed him.

Startled, he pulled back and gently but firmly pushed her away.

"No."

"Why?"

The whine irritated him, but he tried not to sound like it. "You are emotionally distraught right now. I know you, and you'll regret it later. So no." He stood. "Maybe I should go."

"Wait, please. I'm sorry. I want to talk to you about something."

What could she possibly have to say? Still, he agreed but sat in the chair opposite her.

It took several minutes, but Ann was able to get control of her roiling emotions. "Sara said that you haven't been able to close the door on Andrew."

He wasn't particularly interested in talking about Andrew with Ann but conceded, "It just hasn't worked like I thought it would."

"Why don't we do another session, and perhaps we can close the door together. I feel like I've left you hanging, and that's not fair to you."

He didn't say anything but looked at her over the tops of his fingertips as he tapped his lips.

So she added, "Just one session to see if we can end it."

He wanted to refuse but supposed this wasn't the time to get into it. "Let me think about it."

Sheepishly, she said okay.

After a few minutes, he asked if she'd be all right if he left.

She didn't want him to leave but had no right to ask him to stay. It appeared that Sara hadn't said anything to him about her Andrew theory, and Ann certainly needed to get her emotions under control if she was going to do it. Besides, she needed time to absorb it, so she told him she'd be fine. He smiled as he got up, and silently they walked to the door together.

He turned to her and asked, "Are you sure you'll be all right?"

"Yes."

"If it gets too hard and you don't want to be alone, call me. I'm only a block away." He smiled.

She nodded.

"Thanks, I'll be okay."

She sat on the parson's bench after he left. At least he didn't say good-bye this time.

Chapter Forty-Four

Saturday, August 9

The woman in the mirror looked back at Ann. She'd changed her hairstyle three times and had changed clothes four, finally settling on her "at home" dress with dusty rose flowers. She'd accented the sleeves with satin ribbon and created a band at the high waist. She shook her hair loose from the upsweep she'd had it in and turned her head upside down to brush it through, then just used her fingers to fluff it. It actually looked pretty nice, clean and shiny, and the little bit of natural curl made it fall gracefully over her shoulders and down her back. Was she getting too old to wear her hair this way? She didn't care if she was. Her hair was still very pretty, and she intended to show it off to its best advantage. Her mother had always taught her that you accentuate the positive, and her hair was definitely one of her positives. She put the boar bristle brush down, tucked a tissue in her bodice, and took a deep breath.

Ann finished making her bed, shaking out the comforter and fluffing the pillows. She set the breast-cancer teddy bear on the bed leaning against the shams that matched the floral

comforter. She still loved stuffed animals, but the pink bear
was the only one she put on her bed. The stuffed creature
had special meaning. A few years ago a close friend had been
diagnosed with breast cancer, and during one of the early
hospital stays Ann had given Jody the soft, cuddly pink bear
with a ribbon on his foot. Jody had fought a valiant battle but
in the end had lost. Ron, Jody's husband, gave Ann the bear
because his wife had loved it so much and it had been such a
comfort to her. Ann liked remembering the strength her
friend had. Jody and Ann had talked about death as the end
grew near. One day Jody gave Ann an envelope and asked
her to wait to read it until after she was gone. Framed now, it
hung next to her bed.

"The boundaries which divide life and death are at best
shadowy and vague. Who shall say where the one ends and
the other begins?" It was a quote from Edgar Allan Poe. She
looked at it now and thought about Ted.

He was coming over today for the final session in an
attempt to close the door on Andrew. It had been a week
since she'd seen him, since the funeral. Every day she hoped
to hear from him and when she didn't was forced to think
about everything that had happened, which was probably a
good thing even though it was hard. In the hopes of getting
some sage advice, she talked with her Uncle Jamie and Aunt
Maura. Their advice was to talk it through with Ted. Ellie's
parents didn't go back to New York until Friday, so she
hadn't had the chance to tell her friend what had happened.
When she finally did, Ellie's advice was, not surprisingly, to
jump in with both feet and go for it. She wasn't even sure
what "it" was.

This morning she kept finding little things to do because
she couldn't seem to sit still. She was nervous, anxious,
scared, and giddy all at the same time. It had taken most of

the week for her to decide she needed to tell Ted about the "Andrew" theory if Sara hadn't done it herself, and based on the phone conversation she had with him, she assumed Sara had not. A very large part of her did not want to tell him, mostly because she was afraid of what his reaction might be. Would he just accept it? That was unlikely. Would he be angry at the injustice with which he had been treated? She saw that as a distinct possibility, perhaps because it would probably have been her reaction. Would he hate her? She hoped not, but based on their last meeting, she guessed that hating her might very well be the reaction. There was the slight chance that he would be relieved that she now believed him and they would then have a second chance, but she wasn't holding her breath. She had no clue what he might say or do. She was still trying to decide when she would tell him, right away or after the session, when the doorbell rang.

As soon as Ted pushed the doorbell button, he started to question the wisdom of coming here. Had Sara Jane not badgered him, he wouldn't have. His stomach hurt from the emotional turmoil and anxiety. If he'd been able to lock the garden gate on Andrew himself, he wouldn't be here. But try as he might, he had been unable to accomplish the self-hypnosis necessary. Jamie told him it was because subconsciously he wanted to do it with Ann and not alone, so it simply hadn't worked. If his friend was right, they would find out today. He knew the only reason he didn't want to see Ann was because he still loved her, and she obviously didn't feel the same way, so it hurt to be around her. He almost gasped when she opened the door and smiled at him. She was breathtaking.

Her greeting was warm and friendly. "I'm really glad you came."

"Well, thanks for seeing me again."

They stood looking at each other, neither saying anything else. Finally, she stepped aside and asked him to come in.

"How's Sara doing?"

"She's fine, although this stuff with me is upsetting her, so I'm hoping today will put an end to it."

Behind Ann's smile was a fear that it would put an end to her relationship, or possible relationship, with Ted as well.

"I have coffee, tea, iced tea, and lemonade. What's your poison?"

She was being so friendly that it was hard for him to retain the cool demeanor he had intended to use during their session. He couldn't help but smile at her. "Have you anything to go with coffee?"

"You know you're in the unofficial national bakery. So, of course, I do. Blueberry muffins, as a matter of fact."

"My favorite."

Her coy smile made his heart skip a beat. "I know."

As he followed her into the kitchen, he realized how difficult this session was going to be. He loved being with her. He loved the way she made him feel, whether she wanted to do it or not, which was why being here was ultimately so painful.

It took all her reserves not to throw her arms around him, but she had to do this right so kept her back to him as she steamed the milk. She had the tray with muffins and butter ready to go and then set the two cups of coffee on it.

"I thought we could have this outside since the sun doesn't hit the backyard until late afternoon."

He picked up the tray. "Sounds good."

Trying not to get into any heavy discussions that would put a pall over the meeting, Ann asked about school.

"I'm all set, but classes don't start for another couple of weeks."

"The time has gone so fast. It seems like the earthquake was a few days ago. But summer is almost over, and September is around the corner. Hard to believe that Halloween, Thanksgiving, and Christmas will be here soon."

Ted got quiet.

"Is something wrong?"

"Not really, but you mentioning Christmas reminded me that Melinda wants Sara Jane to go to New York with her this year, which means I'll be alone."

"What about your parents?"

"They're taking a cruise. Mom said I could join them, but I'd feel like a third wheel. Besides, Christmas while cruising the Greek Isles just doesn't seem right. Melinda actually invited me too, but her parents have never forgiven me for the divorce and Josh, so it would be really uncomfortable."

"They blame you for Josh too?"

"Too?"

"Sara told me that Melinda blames you because you didn't pick the boys up."

"I didn't realize she knew that."

"Melinda told her, but Sara said that she was glad you didn't because she thinks she would have lost both of you."

"I've wondered about that myself."

Returning the conversation to Christmas, Ann offered, "If you get too lonely you can always join us. The whole family will be at Mom and Dad's."

"I'm guessing that might be a bit uncomfortable too."

"I doubt it. Mom and Dad love you, and you know Maura and Jamie love you."

"They're not angry over how we ended?"

"They were, but they got past it. Actually, my mother thought I overreacted at the time, and they were disappointed that you and Sara didn't come to the wake last week because they really wanted to see you."

The inference being she hadn't, so he said only, "Thanks for the invitation. I'll think about it." Attempting to find a neutral subject, Ted commented on the relaxing atmosphere of Ann's backyard, specifically the wilderness garden.

"Thanks. That was the plan, a sort of retreat."

"Well, it works." After a few moments, he asked, "Have you ever seen the fairies?"

"No, but there have been a few times I was sure I saw movement inside the house. One evening I meticulously arranged everything inside, and the next morning a book that had been on the bookcase was on the table, the plate that had been on the table was in the sink, and a cup and saucer were next to the book. If the dishes had just been on the floor or something I would have assumed that a bird landed on the roof or Gigi's tail hit it or even a raccoon had been in the yard, but what I found can't be explained by any of that." She giggled. "It's always been my little mystery. Perhaps there really are fairies."

"Perhaps there are." The look on her face as she gazed at the little dollhouse made his chest tighten. He loved her too much to drag this out anymore. They needed to close the door and be done with it. "Shall we get on with it?" Her smile when she said sure made the knot in his chest tighter.

Chapter Forty-Five

He opened his eyes and looked directly into hers. Ann's stomach filled with butterflies. She didn't understand why she was so comfortable with Ted when Andrew made her feel a sense of danger mixed with excitement. Before she could voice a greeting, he spoke.

"I should apologize."

"For what?"

"My advances when last we met were... unseemly."

The butterflies receded enough to allow her to question the sincerity of his apology. "I have the impression that you don't really think you need to apologize. So why did you?"

"I suppose it was because of your reaction." He watched her for a moment, then added, "I do believe that you wanted me to kiss you, and only propriety stopped your enjoyment of it."

She started to protest, but it would be a lie so conceded, "You're right, I did want you to." She opted not to tell him that she enjoyed it immensely. She bit her thumbnail before asking, "Do you do that often?"

His look was a combination of guile and inquiry.

"Do you often make unseemly advances to women?"

He shrugged. "I like women."

"And I have no doubt that women like you."

He smiled broadly.

"Have there been a lot of women?"

He cocked his head. "I have had my share if that is your meaning."

"Did you before you married Catherine?"

"Did I what?"

"Have a lot of women."

Insulted at the inference, he insisted, "No!" The slyness and guile were gone. The gentle, loving man she liked returned.

"An..." She stopped, suddenly remembering. "Mr. Mcnaughton, I believe your womanizing is a ploy to prevent you from falling in love again. By having only short-term physical relationships, you don't have to make an emotional connection. If there's no emotional connection, you can't fall in love and risk losing again."

He looked down at his hands resting on his knees and almost whispered, "It is better this way."

"Don't you want someone to share your life, have children with, someone to love, and who will love you in return?"

He looked up. "Someone to die."

"You can't stop caring about people because you're afraid of losing them."

"You have."

"I know, but I've been wrong. You've been wrong."

"You can love someone other than Alex?"

"I believe I can." It was barely a moment before she added, "We, you and I, need to be grateful that we had Cathy and Alex in our lives, even if it was just for a short time. We were lucky enough to have had the opportunity to love them, and best of all, they loved us."

Andrew was unwilling to meet her gaze, not wanting to admit she was right.

When he did not respond, she continued.

"You need to open yourself to the possibility of falling in love again."

"I will never find another love like Cathy."

"Probably not, but you will find a different love, a new love." She lowered her eyes and voice. "Someday." He looked at her without comment, and Ann knew he wasn't convinced. "I know it doesn't seem possible, but it is. I firmly believe that."

"Because you have found a new love?" he asked, incredulous.

"New? No, not new." She sighed. "But there's the hope of another love. And I want that hope for you too."

She hadn't even finished the statement before he had risen, pulling her to her feet in a quick, smooth motion. Although he felt no resistance, the kiss was not as passionate as the previous one had been. In fact, he felt a certain resignation rather than anything more intimate.

Holding her in his arms he said, "Perhaps you are my new love."

Ann, her head still resting on his chest, giggled.

Andrew pulled back a little, and tilted her face to look at him. "You find that amusing?"

"You know very well that I would be nothing more than another conquest, a shipboard romance."

He smiled down at her, stepping back and sitting in the chair again. "I rather doubt the possibility of conquering you."

Sitting in her own chair, she silently questioned his supposition. In fact, she was pretty sure he could easily have conquered her in another time, another place.

It was time to bring this all to an end, and he sensed it. *Was she saying good-bye?* "Will we meet again?"

"Perhaps. Someday," she said as she stood. Andrew rose with her. Then taking the single stride that separated them, he took her hand and raised it to his lips, brushing her fingers with a kiss. He released her hand and made a gallant bow.

"So this is farewell."

She smiled in response.

He returned to the chair, leaned back, and closed his eyes.

Ann stood behind the chair and put her hands on his shoulders. "Ted?"

"Yes."

"Are you in the garden?"

"Yes."

"Let's lock the doors and be done with it."

"All of them?"

"Well, not the gate that opens into your garden."

"*Our* garden."

She smiled and waited a bit. "Is it done?"

"Yes."

"All right. I'll count backward from five, and when I reach one you'll wake feeling refreshed and relaxed."

"Five... four... three... two... one." She waited until he opened his eyes. "How do you feel?"

He sat quietly as though he hadn't heard her.

"Ted?"

"I'm thinking." After another moment he said, "Strangely enough, I feel like it's over. I'm not even sure what that means, but somehow it feels like the end." He looked at her. "Does that make sense?"

"Well, let's hope it is over."

He tried to discern her meaning. Did she mean she hoped it was over because she knew what it was doing to him, or did she mean she didn't have to see him anymore? He opted for the latter, but before he could say or do anything she asked, "Has Sara said anything to you about Andrew?"

He looked at her as though she was crazy. "Why would Sara have said anything about Andrew? I've never told her about him."

"I've been trying to figure out a way to tell you this but without much success, so I guess I'll just say it."

He waited. Finally, his question was filled with impatience. "What is it?"

"Sara told me that after Josh died, she was visited by a man she called Mr. M."

He jumped up. "What man? What do you mean, a man visited her?"

"This is why I didn't know how to tell you. I knew this is how you'd react, but you need to calm down."

Standing over her and hollering, he said, "Calm down? You just told me that some strange man visited my daughter when she was a little girl. How am I supposed to react?"

"He wasn't some strange man." She smiled "He was you. *You* are Mr. M."

He stood staring at her. How could she smile? "Me? How is that..."

"Mr. M is Andrew Mcnaughton. The name was too cumbersome for a young child, so she called him Mr. M."

"Why am I hearing this from you and not her?"

"You'll have to ask her that. I only told you because it was evident that you didn't know, and I thought you should."

He fell into the chair and buried his face in his hands. "Oh, God, what have I done?"

"You haven't done anything."

"What are you talking about? My own daughter thinks I was pretending to be someone else, and I didn't know it was happening. She must have been terrified."

"First of all, you do need to calm down. Sara wasn't afraid. You and Andrew helped her through a really rough time. She sees it as something very special the two of you shared."

He was looking directly at her, but not really. She had intended to discuss Sara's hypothesis that it was Andrew she saw kissing someone else twenty years ago, but he was in a daze. There was no way for her to broach the subject now.

Ted stood up. "I think I should go now."

"Really?"

Was it possible he heard disappointment in the single word question? It didn't matter. He needed to talk with Sara Jane. He nodded and headed for the door.

She went with him. "There's more to the story."

"I don't think I can take any more right now."

She gently caressed his face. "I'm sorry. I didn't mean to upset you."

His wan smile did nothing to change the fear she saw in his eyes.

"Bye," he said.

Ann watched from the sidelight as Ted stepped onto the sidewalk in front of her house.

Chapter Forty-Six

Ann stepped away from the door and returned to the living room. What would happen now? Would she ever see him again?

The air conditioner turned on. It must be hotter than she realized since she had the thermostat set at seventy-eight. The fireplace was cold and empty, but all she saw was the fire in her parents' fireplace. The first thing she did after moving out of the condo she shared with Ted was burn their wedding invitations along with the contracts for the caterer, photographer, florist, and venue. She'd even burned the ribbon she bought to tie on the brass rings that were to be favors for their guests at their carousel reception. She had been filled with an anger she carried for a very long time. *Had it been an unjustified anger?* All these years he knew he hadn't cheated on her, but she had never believed him.

In the deep recesses of her walk-in closet was a large antique book that she put on the bed. She went into the kitchen to pour a glass of iced tea, then went to the back door to let Gigi into the cool house; the summer heat was difficult for the white furry dog.

Sitting cross-legged on the bed with Gigi lying next to her, Ann opened the book, which wasn't a book at all but a box filled with cards and letters and photographs. Most of them were from Alex and her family. She looked through them. She and Alex had been very happy. What would their lives have been like if he hadn't died? Different than hers was now, she supposed. She set the memorabilia aside.

In the seemingly empty box, under a false bottom, were the remnants of her relationship with Ted, including the pictures she was taking the day they met. Most were the buildings for her class assignment, but he had insisted on taking a few of her, so she had taken a few of him as well. God, they were so young. There was one of the two of them at the wedding of a mutual classmate. They had only been dating a few months, but even then they looked like they were in love. At the very bottom of the box was an envelope. Inside was the only wedding invitation she saved from the flames of her anger.

Antoinette Marie Rishel and Edward Evan McConaughy
Request the honor of your presence in a celebration of
their love
at the Carousel on the Santa Monica Pier

Surrounded by the keepsakes of her life, she fell against the pile of pillows that decorated her bed and picked up the pink bear. Several months after their breakup, she had had second thoughts. She never doubted that he loved her, and she never stopped loving him. She started to believe that the meeting she saw had been more innocent than she thought or it was just his last little fling, so she tried to get in touch with him, but the phone number they'd shared was disconnected. When she asked her Uncle Jamie if he had a current number, he told her that Ted was married. She'd been devastated and then had gotten angry all over again. Obviously he *had* been cheating on her. How else could he have met someone and gotten married in less than six months? Of course, now she knew that he hadn't even met Melinda until after they broke up. It seemed as though she had everything wrong and certainly had handled it all badly. Her mother had tried to get her to calm down before doing anything rash but, of course, she knew best, and her life was never the same.

She reached over and scratched Gigi's head. "Well, cuddle bear, what's that quote? 'You can't start the next chapter if you keep rereading the last one.' I guess it's time to stop rereading." She gathered up all the memorabilia, put it in the box that looked like a book, and closed the lid on the past chapters of her life.

Ann was staring at nothing in particular, which made standing in front of the open refrigerator door silly. Snapping out of the daze, she removed leftover pasta and the ingredients for a salad and set them on the counter. She wasn't hungry yet, but if she made the salad now, all she had to do was heat the pasta, and she wouldn't have to think about dinner when it was time.

The refrigerator door held a bottle of margaritas which she poured over ice in a highball glass. Tortilla chips left over from the wake last week were in a giant bag, so she dumped some into a small basket. On the counter was a pile of mail, mostly sympathy cards. She wasn't sure how she felt about them. The thoughts behind them were very nice, but Alex had been gone so long that some of the sentiments seemed strange. In any event, they didn't belong in the kitchen, so she carried them into the office and set them on desk.

On the computer screen, a single, silver three-dimensional word tumbled on a field of black—*YOU!* Why after all this time had the word changed from *forgive* to *you*? As her eyes blurred slightly from staring at the constantly moving image, she suddenly remembered. The day of Alex's funeral she had added *who* and a question mark to the *forgive*. Was this his answer?

In the heat of the late August afternoon, Ann considered an explanation of her late husband's message, if it was a message. Why would he think she needed to forgive herself? Was it because she had loved him differently than she did Ted as Ellie said? Or was it because she had accused Ted unjustly all these years? Why would Alex care about that? Did he just want her to be happy? Was Ellie right about that too? She could think of no other explanation. Suddenly she felt blessed that he loved her so much.

She laughed out loud at the whole idea that she was communicating with her dead husband and that a past life had been responsible for the breakup of her engagement twenty years earlier. What had happened to her rational, logical world? It was as though the earthquake shook up her life as much as it did the city. In spite of all the strangeness, the only thing she really cared about was if she would ever hear from Ted again.

Ann and Gigi relaxed in the shade of the umbrella and old oak. The salty tortilla chips were the perfect complement to her margarita on the rocks on this hot summer day. She reached down and pet her dog. "Come on, Gigi. Time for dinner. Besides, we need to get you into the air-conditioning." They went through the back door near Gigi's run so Ann could feed her on the back porch. She glanced inside the office as she walked by and saw a new message tumbling on the screen—"you will."

I will what?

Ted was in no condition to return home. Like Ann said, he needed to calm down before seeing his daughter. When he reached the corner, he turned in the opposite direction of his own house. He walked, his mind reeling with all of it. Almost a block away from Ann's house and two from his, he sat down on the curb and hung his head, dread tightening his chest.

What must Sara Jane think of him? His mind was whirling with the possibilities, the least of which was that she thought he was a lunatic. How must his young daughter have felt about her father pretending to be a complete stranger? Why had she never said anything? How was he going to explain it to her when he didn't understand any of it himself?

The questions continued to flood his mind without a single answer to dam the flood. The concrete curb was hot. He rubbed his face with his hands and stood up. He had no idea what he'd say to her, but there was no point putting it off.

Sara Jane was on the couch, reading with her arm propped up on a pillow.

Forcing cheerfulness, Ted asked, "What's you reading, sweet pea?"

"*Emma.*"

"In the mood for a love story, are you?"

"Yeah, Austen really gets it. It's not all lovey-dovey or steamy romance, but it's still romantic. It's neat."

"There's a reason people have been reading her for more than two hundred years."

Sara set aside her Kindle. "So how did it go? Is Andrew all locked up?"

"I guess we won't know for a while, until it happens again or not. It feels like it's over."

"Did you find out why he kept coming back?"

"We need to talk about that."

"About what?"

"His coming back." He headed toward the kitchen. "I'm getting a Coke. Would you like something?"

"Lemonade sounds good. Do you want me to help?"

"No. You're an invalid, so just relax."

He returned a few minutes later with a can of Coke and a frosty glass of fresh lemonade. "Here you go, kiddo."

"Thanks." She looked up at him as she took a sip. "What's wrong? You look like you've seen a ghost."

"Why didn't you ever tell me about meeting Andrew?"

"Great! You guys talked about it."

"Yes, but I want to know why you've never mentioned meeting a strange man."

"He wasn't strange, Dad... he was you."

"It was me pretending to be a nineteenth-century Scottish nobleman. Didn't you think it was strange?"

"I thought it was how you grieved. The grief counselor you sent me to back then said that there was no wrong way to grieve and everyone has to do what was best for them. I just figured it was what worked for you. It certainly worked for me. Since you never mentioned it, I assumed you wanted it to be a secret. It was kind of neat having a secret just between us.

"Even when he stopped coming, I thought about him, and it always made me feel better because he made me feel better. You made me feel better."

"He did? I did?"

"Yeah. There were nights that I couldn't stop thinking about Josh, and Mr. M would come in and sit with me. It was like he knew when I needed him. He'd comfort me when I cried. And then he'd tell me the most wonderful stories."

"What kind of stories?"

Excited by the memory, she said, "They were about traveling the world on the high seas and living an almost-perfect existence on a tropical island." She sighed and cocked her head. "I've always considered that time a special bond for us. It would be awful if you don't think it too."

"Well, if it was our special bond for you, then it was a special bond for me too." He hugged her. "And you never saw him again?"

She pulled away. "I thought you said you and Ann talked about this."

"She told me that you'd seen him when you were eight, if that's what you mean."

"Well, that wasn't all of it, so I guess I need to tell you."

"Tell me what?"

"He came to the hospital the night of my surgery. I hadn't seen him since I was little. He said he came because I hurt, and he wasn't talking about the accident. I was kind of loopy, so I wasn't sure what he was talking about when he said that all would be well, but after the funeral when Ann mentioned his name, it all came together for me, and I understood what he meant."

"Honey, you're not making any sense. What came together?"

"My theory about him."

"What theory? What are you talking about?"

"I was really hoping you and Ann would sort it out."

"Sara Jane, I'm not sure how much more I can take. Just tell me what you're talking about."

Sara Jane told her father of all her meetings with Andrew when she was a child and the most recent encounter, adding, "The first night I was home from the hospital, I got up in the middle of the night and took a pain pill. The doctor suggested I take them with milk to keep from getting an upset stomach. When I went in the kitchen, I could see you in the garden. I realized then that when we thought you might be sleepwalking, it was really Mr. M. There's a difference in the way you move. Because I had just seen him the night before at the hospital, I realized it was him in the garden and not you. I almost went out to talk with him again, but it seemed like he wanted to be alone. It started me thinking, if it happened now and it happened after Josh died, then it might have happened the first time too."

"What do you mean, the first time?"

"When you were with Ann."

"I don't follow."

"I think that when her friend and Ann saw you with another girl, it was really Mr. M... Andrew. And that's why you didn't think you'd cheated and she was absolutely sure you did. But it turns out that you were both right... and wrong."

Stunned, Ted said nothing.

"So what do you think, Dad?"

He shook his head. "I don't know what to think. I thought he was only in my dreams." He thought a moment. "Did you tell Ann *all* this?"

"Yes."

"Why didn't you say anything to me?"

"I thought you knew about the visits, so the part I thought was important was about what might have happened twenty years ago. I knew if I told you, you'd never say anything to Ann because *you'd* think that *she'd* think it was just an excuse for what you did. Was that too confusing?"

"Unfortunately not." While he wanted to refute her supposition, she was probably right. He wouldn't have said anything to Ann about it. "What did she say?"

"I asked if the possibility had ever occurred to her. She said no and then suddenly said OMG and started crying and didn't stop. That was why I called you."

"She said OMG?"

Sara Jane rolled her eyes. "No, she said, 'Oh, my God!' But that was why she was crying."

"Honey, she'd just buried her husband. I doubt tremendously that she was crying about something that may or may not have happened twenty years ago."

"Dad, she wasn't crying when I got there. She didn't start crying until after I asked her about the possibility that Mr. M was who she saw."

He took a deep breath. "I guess that's what she meant when she said there was more to the story."

"What are you going to do?"

"I don't know. What are your plans for the evening?"

"Jenny, Clara, and Tanya are coming over to hang out. They'll probably sleep over."

"Then what I'm going to do is make dinner *and* breakfast for you and your friends."

"I was talking about what you're going to do about Ann."

"I know, but I need to process it all. My head is spinning."

After cleaning up the kitchen, Ted retired to his own room. The girls were in the attic doing whatever girls did these days. He smiled to himself. He suspected it wasn't a whole lot different than what his sister had done at their age. Through the ceiling, he could feel the bass from the music they were playing a bit too loud.

He kicked off his shoes and sat in the club chair he'd had reupholstered when they bought the house. He leaned his head back against the glove-soft leather, and thoughts of Ann filled his head. Assuming he accepted Sara Jane's premise about Andrew, he *had* actually cheated on her as Andrew, but it was still him, at least it was for Ann. No wonder she hated him. Thinking about the kind of man Andrew was, or at least was trying to be, she must have thought he was seducing whomever she saw him with. There was no way she could have known any differently since even he hadn't known what was happening. All these years he'd thought she'd been mistaken and had carried his own anger that she hadn't trusted him. Turned out she had no reason to trust him.

His apparent betrayal made her willingness to help him and her kindness all the more amazing. She even kissed him—him, not Andrew. Of course, she had been emotionally distraught, so it didn't really count. Still, she'd already talked with Sara Jane at that point.

What did any of it mean? She said there was more to the story. *Would the story have answered that question?* He wasn't at all sure he'd be able to sleep tonight.

Chapter Forty-Seven

Sara Jane cheerfully greeted her father when she went into the kitchen the following morning. "Good morning."

"Where are the girls? I'm making breakfast."

"They left early to go surfing. By the way, Clara and Tanya say that you're officially the coolest dad. The girls were impressed that you fire-baked the pizza on the grill."

"I'm glad everyone liked it. Shall we breakfast on the patio?"

"Absolutely."

Over scrambled eggs and ham with hash browns on the side, Sara Jane asked, "What are you going to do about Ann?"

"I'm not sure."

"You didn't really cheat on her, but she did see you with another woman. It just wasn't really you. It's kind of convoluted, but the bottom line is you love each other, and isn't that what's supposed to matter?"

He smiled at her. "Maybe the exorbitant tuition I pay for that school you go to is worth it. You've turned out to be pretty smart."

"So what's your plan?"

"At the moment, my only plan is to call her with some information I got yesterday. I guess we can talk about it then if she wants to."

"Why do you need to call her? She's a neighbor. Just go over to her house."

He gave it some thought. "Maybe I will after I clean up breakfast. What are you going to do today?"

"Read, watch TV. Nick said he might stop by later."

"Oh, good. So if it takes a while, you'll be okay?"

"Take however much time you need." Quietly, she added, "I hope it takes all day."

After putting the dishes in the dishwasher and washing the pans, Ted changed into a pair of jeans and a polo shirt because Toni—Ann once told him that she particularly liked him dressed that way. He had no idea what the discussion might be or the outcome, but he was hopeful that all was not lost. He wasn't sure why. It was just a feeling. He folded the letter he'd received in half and slipped it into his back pocket.

Sara Jane was on the couch, flipping through the channels on the television, when he got to the living room. He stood for a few minutes without saying or doing anything.

"What's up, Dad?"

"Isn't Sunday when Ann does her long rides?"

"Yeah, but she does them really early, so I'm sure she's back by now."

"Maybe I should call first."

"You're just stalling. If she's not there, come back. It's not like you have to go cross-country."

"I guess you're right." He walked over to her and kissed the top of her head.

Sara Jane stood up. "Wait a minute. I have something I'd like you to give her." She was gone only a few minutes.

When she returned, she handed him a plate of cookies. He looked down at the plate. Sitting atop the plastic wrap was a small object. He looked at her. She smiled. He slipped it into his pocket and kissed her again.

Blue sky peeked out of a light cloud cover that was raising the humidity while the temperature rose. Ann cut her ride short as the moist, warm air made her exceedingly uncomfortable.

The shower was washing away the sweat that had matted her hair under the bike helmet. She scrubbed it a bit harder than necessary, but it felt good as did the shower set on pulse. She turned her head back and forth and side to side to allow the water's massaging properties to do their thing. What was it about a shower that felt so good? She imagined a waterfall in a deep forest and raised her face to the stream of water.

The doorbell rang as Ann turned off the hair dryer. Quickly, she ran her fingers through her hair and went to the door. She opened it just as the bell rang a second time.

Surprised, all she could say was, "Ted."

"Hi," was his only response.

Flustered, she finally said, "Um, come in."

As he stepped through the door, he told her he'd made cookies for Sara Jane and her friends the evening before. "She insisted I bring these." He handed her the plate.

"They look good. Would you like coffee with them?"

"Just had breakfast, but the coffee sounds great."

"Well, I put it on before I showered, so it should be ready. Make yourself comfortable."

"Inside or out?"

"I'll leave it to you." She headed to the kitchen, unaware that he followed her.

Ann busied herself with the coffee preparations, nervous and excited. His being here certainly answered the "would she ever see him again" question. She stopped what she was doing for a moment and stared at the wall in front of her. Is this what Alex meant when the monitor screen said "you will"? She smiled and continued getting the coffee ready.

She could feel him behind her, so her hand shook slightly as she poured half-and-half into the cream pitcher. She shivered when he moved the hair off the back of her neck and pushed it over her shoulder. With a feather-soft touch, his fingertips traced the contours of her neck. He leaned down and kissed her now-bare shoulder, lightly kissing his way up to her ear. A small whimper escaped her throat. She turned toward him and slipped her arms around his neck. The long, deep, and passionate kiss weakened her knees, so she leaned against him when their lips parted.

She said with a sigh, "I've wanted you to do that for weeks."

"And I've wanted to." Gently, he stepped back, forcing her to stand up again. "I guess we have stuff to talk about."

"Yes, I guess we do."

On the patio, Ann asked, "So where do we start?"

"I believe we already started. A few of my questions were answered in the kitchen."

"Mine too."

"Really? You questioned how I felt about you?"

Almost sadly, she said, "I really did. Most of the time we judiciously avoided touching on it. I didn't know if Sara would tell you about her theory or not. And if she did, would you hate me for accusing you unjustly? My biggest fear was that you'd never want to see me again."

"I thought you wouldn't want to see me because I actually had cheated on you. I couldn't imagine you wanting anything to do with me. I kept thinking about how livid you must have been every time I denied it."

"You're right. It did make me livid because I had seen you with someone else. But the worst thing for me was until that moment I had never questioned your love, then suddenly all I had were questions. If you loved me, why were you with someone else? If you loved me, how could you hurt me like that? How could you lie to me? It seemed clear that you didn't love me."

"I'm so sorry I put you through that."

An understanding smile curved her mouth. "As it turns out, you weren't the one who did it. The"—she tried to think of a way to say it—"previous you did it."

Ted laughed.

"Why is that funny?"

"You know, the song in *On a Clear Day* about her 'previous me' and the doctor preferring that one."

"How did you remember that?"

"Sara Jane is a Streisand fan too, so we watched it the day she got home from Chicago." He waited a moment. "You liked the previous me too, didn't you?"

Ann blushed, unable to deny the enjoyment of Andrew's attentions. "I liked the man he was, not the man he was pretending to be. But I realized something this past week. It wasn't really Andrew I kissed. It was you."

"I vividly remember that it was Andrew."

"I think he was just my excuse."

"Excuse?"

"Like I said before, I've wanted you to kiss me for weeks, but I still felt a sense of betrayal, so I couldn't let myself go. But when I kissed Andrew, it was like I was giving myself permission to kiss you." She almost giggled. "Nuts, huh?"

"Nuts? Is that your professional opinion?"

She actually giggled. "I don't know what my professional opinion is, but I've felt a bit nuts during all this."

"Well, I can't say whether it's nuts or not, but I'm more than a little glad to find out that it was me and not Andrew you were kissing." He stood up. "Speaking to that..."

Ann jumped up. "You're not leaving, are you?"

"No." He reached into the back pocket of his jeans. "This came in the mail yesterday." They both sat down again. "After the slave conversation, I wanted to know if he really existed and, if he did, to find out more about him."

"Why?"

"Ostensibly because Maura said that we needed to know as much as possible about the past lives in order to banish them, but the truth is that I was jealous of him. It was obvious that you were attracted to each other, and you seemed to be susceptible to his charms."

"No, I wasn't."

He smiled. "You disliked his cavalier attitude and the fact that he kept slaves, but you liked the attention. You fought it, but you were definitely attracted to him. Anyway, I was hoping to find something worse than the slaves that would turn you off. I'm glad it didn't come until yesterday."

"Why?"

"Because you would have liked him even more." He handed her the folded letter.

She opened it. The letterhead said that it was from the Antiguan Embassy in Washington, D.C. She looked up at him with a question in her eyes.

"Go ahead. Read it."

Dear Dr. McConaughy:
    Thank you for contacting us about this matter.
I checked the censuses of the era as well as church

and court records and found that Andrew James Mcnaughton (the N was not capitalized) did, in fact, have a sugar plantation in Antigua, which he inherited in 1809 on the death of his father. In 1810, he became the first plantation owner to free his slaves.

According to church records, he married Isabel Keenan in 1806. Isabel was the widow of an indigo plantation owner. After Mr. Mcnaughton became sole owner of the sugar plantation, he bought the indigo plantation from his wife's late husband's estate. He and Isabel baptized four children—Thomas, Frederick, Ann and Elizabeth. As leaders of Island society, the Mcnaughtons can be found in many records.

One of the most unusual things I found was a court record of Andrew's last will and testament. When he died in 1842, he left the bulk of his vast holdings to the older of his two daughters rather than to his eldest son. The sons and other daughter received equal portions of land, but Ann inherited the business and most of the land. Isabel died two years later. Some of the property is still held by the Mcnaughton family.

I hope this answers all your questions, and I must say I found it quite enjoyable to see that this man is a part of our history. If you have any more questions, feel free to contact me.
Best regards,
Amy Thomas

Ted offered, "You really had a major impact on him." She snorted. "I doubt I had much to do with it."

"You must have had something to do with it. He got married the year after he met you. You and I both know that he wasn't even close to the possibility when he first appeared. Besides, he named his first daughter after you."

She laughed. "Ann was a very common name then."

"You missed the post script."

Squinting at him, she looked at the bottom of the letter."

PS: A small but interesting historic footnote, his daughter Ann's baptized name was Antoinette. As the Napoleonic Wars were still fresh in people's minds and the French Revolution was considered recent history, Antoinette was an unusual name for a subject of the British Crown to bestow upon his child.

Ann shrugged. "He must have just liked the name since I didn't tell him what Ann was short for."

"He saw it perusing your books."

"How do you know?"

His only response was a knowing smile. "Don't sell yourself short. You helped him realize that he could have a happy life even after losing someone he loved so much."

She grinned. "Well, at least we know he was real and not just a figment of your imagination." She folded the letter and handed it back to him.

He took it but laid it on the table. "Yes." He couldn't stop gazing at her.

"You've got a strange look on your face. What are you thinking about?"

"The Beach Boys."

"The Beach Boys?"

"'Good Vibrations,' the song. You remind me of the line"—he sang—"'I love the way the sunlight plays upon her hair.'" He reached out and brushed an errant curl off her cheek. "The sunlight is playing on your hair." He smiled.

Ann shook her head. "You're nuts." She stood up. "I'm getting more coffee."

She stepped away from the table. He grabbed her hand as she walked by and pulled her down to him and kissed her. She started to step away again, but he stopped her.

"How would you like to take a drive?"

"Where?"

"It's a surprise."

She smiled.

Chapter Forty-Eight

Ann knew where they were headed as soon as Ted turned on to the 10 freeway. The Santa Monica Pier was the site of their first date. She smiled at the nostalgia of the gesture. She'd forgotten just how romantic he was. As they neared the ocean, she rolled down the window in spite of the heat and breathed in the salty, moist air. Memories of that first date flooded her mind. Even though they were far from a relationship, the entire day had been more comfortable for her than any she'd experienced outside her family. She had started wondering then if he was her soul mate because being with him just felt right.

Ted parked on the street not far from the entrance to the pier, and they walked along the sidewalk that overlooked the Pacific Ocean, then turned right and went under the arch welcoming them to the hundred-year-old boardwalk.

Hand in hand, they walked the length of the pier and stopped at the end, watching the birds dart in and out of the surf. The conversation was mostly small talk, but in truth, even after all this time, conversation wasn't necessary. However, while she felt perfectly at ease with him, there seemed to be something he wasn't saying, something he was holding back. He denied it, but at the house he had been relaxed and playful. Now, suddenly, he was serious and quiet. Had the kiss in the kitchen been to determine if he still had feelings for her? Did he discover he didn't? Was he going to throw her aside, as she had him?

The butterflies in her stomach were going nuts when he suggested a ride on the carousel. She loved the carousel, but now was afraid that if he chose here to tell her they had no future together, she would hate it.

He lifted her onto the back of a black-and-white horse in the center of the merry-go-round, its saddle studded with colored gemstones. He hadn't smiled since they came in, and it made Ann even more nervous. *Why was he so serious?* The carousel started to move, and Ted took her hand.

He stood silent as her horse rose next to him. Was he being foolish to do this now? He fingered the object in his pocket. Sara Jane seemed to think it was the right time. And while he would never admit it to her, she had been right about almost everything when it came to Ann. Should he risk it? He looked up at her and took a deep breath. No pain, no gain.

"Ted, what is it? You're making me nervous."

He looked up at her but said nothing.

She was on the verge of tears when he finally spoke.

"Antoinette Marie Rishel Hart, will you marry me?" He opened his hand.

Her engagement ring sat in the palm of his hand.

She picked it up. "Yes." She took a quick breath. "Yes." She looked into his eyes. "Oh, yes." She slid off the horse and threw her arms around him. She couldn't stop the tears. "I can't believe you kept the ring all these years."

He took the ring back.

"I guess I always hoped I'd have another opportunity to give it to you," he said as he slipped the lovely piece onto her left ring finger.

"I'll keep it on forever this time." She looked from the ring to his face. "I love you so much."

Cupping her face in both of his hands, he whispered, "I never thought I'd hear you say that again." He kissed her nose. "I never stopped loving you."

The kiss was deep and passionate as the carousel came full circle.

www.ingramcontent.com/pod-product-compliance
Lightning Source LLC
Chambersburg PA
CBHW032133190626
46814CB00005BA/1669